The Legendary Fighting Fox

Paul Viscount

Mivi Books

Copyright © Paul Viscount 2000

All rights reserved. No part of this book may be reproduced by any means, nor transmitted, nor translated into a machine language, without the written permission of the publisher.

Mivi Books
37 Athelstan Road
Canterbury
Kent
CT1 3UW
01227 379385

A CIP catalogue record for this book is available from the British Library.

Co-ordinated by Prospero Books, Chichester.

Printed and bound in Great Britain.

ISBN 0 1 902320 17 4

Cover illustration by Karen Perrins from an idea by Peter D Viscount.

My thanks go to Geraldine Pamela Judith Mitchell without whom this book could not have been written. You gave me encouragement to use my imagination and many wonderful childhood years in a little town called Edenbridge. Thanks go to you and I love you dearly.
Your son Paul Viscount.

And also to Donald Mitchell, my uncle.
Thanks for being there when needed and pulling me out of many a scrape. For ever in your debt.

Chapter 1

In between a large castle that belonged to the Dragon King and a wood inhabited by stick-like creatures called treedwellers, nestled the village of Castlewood. It was a nice and peaceful place to live, well for the moment. The village was surrounded by a giant fence made of whole trees which were sunk into the ground to a depth of about five feet; above ground the fence reached twenty-five feet high and each log was as wide as a man, making it virtually impregnable to most enemies or raiders.

In the middle of the village stood a large building, the focus point and heart of the community. It was the meeting hall where all the villagers could meet and have their say or just talk and relax. The hall was about fifty feet long and twenty feet wide and the walls were covered with the shields of every warrior from Castlewood, past and present. Tables and benches filled the room. When in use the hall was full of the sounds of people laughing and talking. Even when there was a serious matter to be discussed, some comedian would stand up and say something ridiculous and have everyone rolling round in laughter. So on the whole it was a nice place, filled with peace, love and warmth even in the bad times.

All around the hall nestled the village huts, all exactly the same round shape with thatched roofs, apart from one which was square and painted red. This building belonged to the leader of the village and stood out nearly as much as the meeting hall. Then, as the people of Castlewood were horse traders, there were corrals full of horses and a large fenced area where the horses were broken ready for selling. Giant barns for storing hay and food for the animals towered above the huts. The only thing in the village taller than them was the watchtower which stood about forty feet high and was manned at all times day and night.

The leader of the village was a man named Fox. People of his time and place took their names from animals or objects such as trees, grasses, flowers and so on, just like the American Indians. It was easy to see why Fox got his name. He was now in his forties which for the time made him an old man. He had been fighting battles on and off for twenty-four years, since he was sixteen years old. He had long red hair which he wore in a pony tail and the underneath part was white and bushy like a fox's tail. He was slim and quick and pretty tricky - he had to be to come through so many battles with his life. He wore a white breastplate with a fox emblem on it. Looking at him, he appeared worn and carried many scars on his arms, chest and face. He was a loving and gentle man to his family and friends, loyal and true to the end. With Fox by his side, no man ever fought alone. But most of all he adored his five children above everything else. After his wife had walked out they became his world and he would lay down his life for them. By his side as always was his dog. Patch was brown and white and resembled a Border Collie. But he was a very special kind of dog called an energy mutator which means the dog would live as long as his master. However, the two had to bond together, which was not always so, but Fox and Patch were like a pair of gloves made for each other.

Today was the day that all the warriors of the village took out their armour. Swords, battleaxes and whatever else they happened to fight with. It was the beginning of a three-day festival, a chance for the warriors to prove their valour on the battlefield. And of course a good enough reason to eat, drink and be merry - even if the men lost, it would not end the festivities. As well as watching the warriors in combat, the women and children had the time of their lives eating and drinking and playing.

So the place was a hive of industry, with men carrying tables and benches outside the village. Because there was not room inside, the field of honour was outside the confines of Castlewood. The field was bristling with activity, with children dancing round a maypole, bobbing for apples and playing chase. There seemed to be people everywhere. The smell of cooking filled the air from a whole bullock being cooked over an open fire. There was food everywhere you looked - fruit cakes and bread and wine. Couples were dancing, laughing, having fun; everyone was having the time of their lives.

Then the sound of a trumpet brought everything to a standstill. The people gathered round the strip of field called the Field of Falls where the jousting took place and many a warrior would take a fall this day. The gates opened and two horses galloped out, passing the little white tents dotted all round the field.

The first onto the field of combat was a man called Eagle Eyes. He sat astride a white horse. His armour was made of tiny pieces of metal cut in the shape of feathers which gave the impression that you were fighting a giant bird. His helmet had a beak-like visor. The armour on his legs went down like birds' legs, ridges all the way down to his boots which were just like a pair of talons. His shield was star-shaped. He was about twenty years old, with ginger hair, black eyes and a baby face. He was very broad and short and he thought he was the best fighter in the village.

Now he had to back up his boastfulness on the field of honour.

Then his challenger took the field. It was a woman named Pacer. She was on a white dapple horse. She had long blonde hair, beautiful dark blue eyes, a slim figure and was gentle and kind. She wore just chainmail and carried an old round wooden shield. It turns out they belonged to her father who had died in the battle that they commemorated every year. Pacer had been only a year old when her father had been lost in battle. Bandits had been raiding villages around Castlewood. Some women and children had been killed and the bandits were now heading towards Castlewood, but this time they had bitten off more than they could chew. Even though there were over a hundred bandits, the villagers were ready for them and put an end to their rampage of death and destruction. They lost a lot of good warriors that day. Unfortunately Pacer's father was one of them.

Wild applause filled the air as the two warriors met in the middle of the battlefield. A trumpet sounded, then a man walked towards the pair and shouted: 'Choose your weapons.' Eagle Eyes picked a chain and mace and galloped to one end of the field. Pacer chose a battleaxe and rode to the opposite end of the field. Then the trumpet sounded for the second time and each of the riders charged towards the other at a furious pace. Eagle Eyes hit Pacer's shield, knocking her backwards. But she managed to stay on her horse. When she reached the other end they were both still moving very fast. As they turned, the horses slipped, spraying clods over the crowd. Then the two warriors rode off again in a cloud of dust, hurtling down the field towards each other. Eagle Eyes swung his chain and mace round his head and made a connection. It wrapped itself round Pacer's arm and no matter how hard she struggled she could not free herself from this vice-like grip. Eagle Eyes saw the look of panic and frustration on her face.

'I've got you this time,' Eagle Eyes laughed.

'That's what you think,' snarled Pacer.

She then began to lash out with her battleaxe. Again and again her blows battered at his shield, crash bang. But she could not seem to penetrate his defences till finally Eagle Eyes' shield could no longer stand the pressure. As she brought her battleaxe round for the last time it sliced straight through his shield cutting his arm to the bone. As luck would have it, to add insult to injury, both horses reared up.

He was taken aback that she had got the better of him. When he thought he had it all sewn up he lost his concentration, then his balance and ultimately the battle. Then with an almighty crash of armour hitting the ground, it was all over for Eagle Eyes.

The crowd roared with approval. Pacer was a favourite with them, and a lot of people wanted Eagle Eyes taken down a peg or two because he was such a bighead. Eagle Eyes just sat where he had landed, blood pouring from his wound. He was so shocked he just kept saying over and over again: 'I had her. I had her. What went wrong? I can't believe it.' Two of the stewards had to remove him from the field. He was so shocked and dazed he couldn't move. They finally got him off the field and he just sat nodding his head in disbelief.

Fox was next up. He was facing a man named Crusher. Fox was soon to discover why. The trumpet sounded once again. The two of them charged down the field. Fox swung his sword catching Crusher's shield. He in return swung his battleaxe round hitting Fox's shoulder. Luckily as the blade hit it turned side-on, so it didn't cut him. Then they turned for another encounter. They raced up to the centre of the field and the horses clashed together. Crusher brought his battleaxe down towards his opponent's head but Fox managed to bring his shield up in time to block what possibly could have been a fatal blow. Fox thought to himself: 'This nutter is serious. Perhaps he quite likes the idea of being Leader of Castlewood which he will be if he kills me in combat. I think it's time to stop playing.'

So Fox hit Crusher round the head with the side of his sword, knocking him senseless. Then, bending down, Fox cut the strap holding his opponent's saddle on. Crusher began to fall but to Fox's surprise Crusher grabbed hold of him, pulling him off his horse and pulling over his own horse too. Both men landed with a crash on the ground. Crusher's helmet fell off and rolled across the field. Fox lay there with the wind knocked out of him. Crusher took full advantage of the situation. He picked Fox up, grabbed him by the waist and showed Fox why his name was Crusher. Fox just hung like a rag doll. His body was in an S shape, his head and shoulders leaning back, his arms limp at his sides with his sword still in his hand. His feet were just touching the ground by the toes of his boots.

Then Pacer shouted: 'Come on, Fox, snap out of it,' and the crowd started to chant 'Come on, Fox; come on, Fox.'

Fox came round. 'This man is trying to kill me,' he thought. He summoned all his strength, pulled his arms above his head and smashed the man in the face. Crusher's nose just seemed to explode and blood poured down his face. He released his grip on Fox and fell to the ground, but quickly got up and kicked his opponent in between the legs. Fox screamed in pain. Fox had had enough and despatched the man without delay. He hit him over the head as hard as he could with his shield and Crusher fell to the floor in a crumpled heap. Fox rolled the man over, put his sword to his throat and said: 'Surrender or as the gods are my witness I will run you through here and now.'

'I give,' shouted the man.

Fox walked off the field towards the crowds, and to rapturous applause walked over to his sister Elk who was standing in the crowd. She was tall and thin with jet black hair and blue eyes. As she saw Fox her face lit with a big smile. In her arms she had her son Mole. All round her stood Fox's children. 'Hello my little ones,' said Fox. His children all ran towards him at once, clamouring for his attention. 'Hold on, I've only got two arms.' The girls cuddled their father from the front and the boys jumped on his back. 'You won, Dad,' said the boys.

'Yes, only just. This is the last year I'm entering before I end up making a total fool of myself.'

'That will never happen, Fox,' said Elk.

'I'm getting too old for this game. Come on, children, I'll buy you some sweets.' So Fox wandered off with five little people in tow. The six of them set off for food and fun. They had strawberries and cream, home-made biscuits and cakes, and they played and ran off all their energy. Then Fox's name was shouted, so he took his tired but full children back to Elk.

Fox fought and won his next battle. The contestants kept taking to the field and slowly they were whittled down to four warriors. Pacer was one. She had fought hard for her place in the finals and hopefully at the end of the day she would be the victor. But first she had to beat a man called Growler. He was nearly twice her weight which gave him some advantage but that didn't overly concern her. Fox was matched against a man called Puma.

Pacer took the field and once again chose a battleaxe. Her opponent had his own weapon. It was lethal-looking. It had a handle with a blade coming out of the middle and three metal heads with spikes on chains. The sight of this evil-looking device sent shivers down her spine. It was time to begin. Pacer sat astride her horse, placed her hands together and whispered: 'Father, help me win and prove my valour again.' The trumpet sounded and her heart raced as she galloped down the field. Growler came in hard and fast. He wasted no time in attacking. She was given no quarter by her attacker. He swung his chain and mace around catching Pacer on the back and winding her. Then the blows rained down on her time and again, hitting her legs, arms and chest. She struggled to get her shield up to protect her head. From the crowd came 'Oh's' and 'Ah's' as the strikes kept hitting home. With each blow she swayed from one side to the other.

Pacer and everybody else thought she was going to fall until Growler hit her father's shield so hard it just disintegrated into hundreds of pieces. Bits flew everywhere and the crowds were showered with splinters of wood.

'That was enough, you stupid thickheaded fat lump. Now you've asked for it.' Pacer brought her battleaxe round, striking Growler's chest. This knocked him off balance. Pacer became like a woman possessed. She struck again and again and her blows were so strong that Growler was knocked clear off his horse. As he landed on the ground,

Pacer jumped off her horse straight onto him. Then started a frenzied attack. First she kept hitting him about the head. Fox and others ran across and took the battleaxe away from her. So she just kept punching him in the face. It took six men to get her off her poor unfortunate victim. When they had dragged her to the side of the field Fox threw a bucket of water over her. She screamed, then shook, then burst into tears. Fox knelt down and cuddled her. 'Are you all right now, sweetheart?'

'Yes, I'm fine. Hold me, please.' Fox squeezed her tightly.

Pacer said: 'Thank you. I feel safe in your arms.'

'That's all right. You don't have to go on with the tournament if you don't want to. No-one will think any the less of you,' said Fox.

'Oh no, you don't get out of it that easily. I'm going to fight you for the title of best warrior of Castlewood.'

'How do you know I'm going to win against Puma?' asked Fox.

'Because ever since I was a little girl you've won every year easily,' said Pacer.

'Well, we all have to lose eventually - perhaps this is the year. I must go and get ready. See you later.'

Fox mounted up and rode to the Field of Honour, possibly for the last time. Puma was about the same build as Fox but fifteen years younger.

'Well,' Fox thought, 'this will be hard work.'

The trumpet sounded. Puma charged down the field at a hell of a pace but just to confuse his challenger Fox's horse just slowly trotted down the field. Puma raced past Fox and swung his mace at him. Fox ducked and it missed; he then sat up and hit Puma across the back. Puma rode off looking very bewildered by the whole situation, then he turned. Fox was still standing in the middle of the field. He seemed to be waiting for him so Puma charged again, hit Fox on the shield, but Fox just sat there motionless. He seemed to be in some sort of a trance. Puma spun round very sharply to attack again. Once more he struck Fox on the shield. Then Fox suddenly retaliated, swinging up with his sword and knocking Puma's shield from his hand. Then he struck out again, smashing Puma across the arm, slicing the strap that held the armour covering his arm which left a clear shoot for Fox to aim at. But instead of cutting him, Fox jolted forward, smashing Puma in the face with his shield, knocking him out of his saddle and sending him head over heels off the back of his horse. As he hit the ground Puma's own horse kicked out catching him a glancing blow to the side of the head which left him rather dazed to say the least.

Fox jumped off his horse and took out his dagger. He put it to Puma's throat and said: 'Do you yield?'

'Yes, I yield,' said Puma.

By now the sweat was running down Fox's face. He wiped it off and swept his hair back into his long red ponytail before replacing his white helmet with its red plumes. He dusted down his white breast plate, pulling bits of grass out of the red fox emblem. Then he mounted his red chestnut mare for the final challenge to his title of unbeaten warrior of Castlewood.

This last battle was to be fought with lances. The two riders rode to opposite ends of the field. Both were ready and eager to start. The trumpet sounded for the final time. Fox charged down the field towards Pacer. There was a crash as the lances came into contact with the riders' shields. Fox was knocked backwards but managed to stay on his mount. Pacer was smiling; she thought she had beaten Fox, but as they turned at the end Pacer was very surprised to see that Fox was still very much in the saddle. So both set off down the field again. This time Fox placed his lance straight into Pacer's right shoulder. The blow took her clean off her horse and she landed with a thud on the ground.

Fox stood victorious, then he rode over to Pacer. 'You shouldn't have borrowed a loser's shield - it's bad luck. Well done, you fought well.'

'Thanks a lot. Now you tell me. I knew you would win,' said Pacer.

Fox limped off the field. His neck was bleeding from where the lance had slipped up when it hit.

'I'm going to tend to my wound,' he shouted to Elk.

'Want a hand?' she called back.

'No thanks, I can manage,' replied Fox and he wandered off with five children running alongside his horse.

After the dust had settled, Pacer saw Fox's sister walking towards the refreshment tent. Pacer shouted: 'Elk, wait for me, I want to talk to you.'

'All right, come and have a drink with me and we will have a chat.' So the two of them sat down.

'You know, I thought you had my brother for a moment.'

'So did I,' replied Pacer. 'So tell me, why is your brother named Fox?'

Elk set about explaining the whole story. 'Firstly because of his long dark red hair. And, if you look closely underneath, it's quite white and bushy, just like a fox's tail. It's been that way since he was a child and never changed. Although he has a slim build, his upper body has the strength of two men his own size. And he has the skill and craftiness to outwit most folks around here including me, his own sister. No-one will ever know how his mind works, not even his own family. Even as children Fox was the only one of the six of us who could outwit our parents. He also ran rings round Old Grey Bear his older brother and Wolf his younger brother.

'My father taught two of my brothers many things but gave up on Fox as he could teach him very little. Fox only had to see something done once and he could then do it for himself, and his mind and wit was much quicker and sharper than any of us. So what more can I tell you? Except that he is a loving man if you can get close enough, which isn't easy, as he does not trust anyone well unless he thinks you're all right. When he first meets you he likes to think he's a good judge of character, so if you see a sparkle in his eyes when he talks to you or if he can't do enough for you, then you know he thinks you're all right.

'But never, never cross him because he has a lust for revenge. And running will do you no good because he can run in a chase for many miles and cannot be shaken off. He sticks on your trail like hounds after their quarry,' Elk concluded.

'High praise indeed,' said Pacer.

'No, I speak only the truth,' replied Elk.

'Well, thank you for filling me in,' Pacer said.

'You would not happen to be interested in him, would you?' asked Elk.

'I might be. Why do you ask?' replied Pacer.

'He has had nothing to do with women since his wife broke his heart and walked out on him, leaving him with the five children. That was many years ago. He has not been able to bring himself to love anyone else. He has not laid eyes on her from that day to this. If she and her new man were to turn up, there would be hell to pay.' Elk finally finished speaking.

Pacer said: 'I must go now,' and walked away. She went to find Fox. As she walked through the crowds she saw Fox surrounded by his children. Sunny his eldest daughter was unbuckling his breast plate. Her long blonde hair hung over her father's shoulder and her big blue eyes were filled with tears which made her normally pretty, happy face look very sad and down. She was tall and thin, a proper little lady, whereas her sister Badger, who was undoing the straps on the opposite side of the breast plate, was the complete reverse. She was a tomboy already wearing armour and battling with her brothers and anyone else daft enough to start a fight. Her mousey brown hair reached down to the small of her back and her blue eyes sparkled with a zest for life. When she smiled, the whole of her pretty, round face lit up.

By this time, Fox's boys had got the armour off his legs. Jage the eldest boy jumped to his feet. 'I'm going to take Dad's shield back home.' He was very slight of build with mousey brown hair and black eyes which were a throwback from Fox's father. Wildcat shouted: 'I'm going to carry the sword, then.' He was the second eldest and although he was the smallest he was not one to be picked on as he was the bravest and strongest of the three boys. Even Badger thought twice about starting on Wildcat. He had red hair like his father, blue eyes and was very broad and muscular.

Then there was Sky - blonde hair, slim build but strong with it. He was very placid. 'What can I take, Dad?' The boy was very upset.

'You take my bow and arrow back home, there's a good boy.' With this Sky cheered up and trotted off after his brothers.

Fox took his knife and stuck it in the fire. Beside him, Sunny looked at her father. The blood was running down his shirt.

'Dad, why is it bleeding so badly?'

'It must have cut a main artery. Don't worry, it will seal once the blade is hot enough. You go and look after your brothers. Badger will stay with me.'

Pacer had been watching and listening intently. 'You'll never close that with the blade. If you've cut an artery, let me stitch it.'

Fox by now was too weak from loss of blood to argue, so he sat back and let Pacer do the job.

'I'm sorry, I didn't mean to hurt you. Please forgive me,' said Pacer.

'Nothing to forgive. You enter, you take your chances. Just luck of the draw.'

'Perhaps I'll beat you next year without killing you,' Pacer laughed.

'I won't be entering next year. I'm getting too old and slow to take to the field of honour,' said Fox.

'Rubbish, you could whip anyone,' said Pacer. She finished stitching, took Fox's hot knife from the fire and said: 'Brace yourself, this is going to be painful.' She placed the hot blade on the wound, then sizzle and the air was filled with the smell of burning flesh. Fox clenched his fists tightly, grimaced and arched his back. Then it was all over.

'Well, at least when you were sewing me up I was drowsy.'

'When I cauterized the wound I thought you were going to pass out, Fox, but you managed to hang on.'

'Badger, let me lean on you till we get home.'

'I'll help,' said Pacer. 'After all, I'm responsible for your being in this situation.'

So Badger and Pacer took Fox to his house. They put him in his bed. The other children came running to his side.

'Are you all right, Dad?'

'Yes, I'm fine. All I need is rest.'

Pacer told the children to leave their father to sleep and said she would return later to make sure he was all right.

Chapter 2

The next morning Fox woke up feeling very rough. There wasn't a part of his body that didn't ache. His legs hurt when he moved, so he hobbled out of bed and went outside his house and sat down. 'That's enough exercise for today.' Fox sat and watched the villagers. He had never looked at the village from this point of view before. There was a hustle and bustle of everyday life going on all around him. His children were playing happily. It was a sunny, peaceful day. It seemed the whole world was content. But that was not quite so.

Castlewood people were peaceful and as a rule avoided trouble if at all possible. Unfortunately they were too proud and fearless on the battlefield and would not walk away when threatened. The village was steeped in folklore of defeated invaders, triumphs on the battlefield, whole armies being wiped out and not a single defeat. Three things Castlewood was famous for - the bravery of its warriors and tactical leaders, and its horses. And Fox's generation had lived up to their ancestors' reputation: no village would cross swords with them or even try to cheat them. But they hadn't the faintest idea that someone would risk all for what he considered the greatest treasure of all time, or in his case a necessity. So, unknown to Fox, his village was about to be invaded by dragons.

'Why?' I hear you ask. That's a simple question to answer. The dragons had discovered a large deposit of rare stone called cadadite which the dragons needed because as everybody knows dragons have pilot lights that are situated in the roof of their mouths and as the creatures expel gases from their stomachs the pilot automatically ignites the gases and turns the dragons into walking flame throwers. The flames have a reach of about twenty feet which gives them a hell of an advantage because they don't have to get too close to their enemies to disarm them. They make the gases inside by fermenting certain plants that they eat in vast quantities such as death weed, sleep rash and burning nettles which are extremely toxic to most living things. Example: if a full-grown horse were to eat a spoonful of death weed it would be dead in under a minute. However, dragons get round this problem due to the fact that they have two stomachs so the poisonous mixture never gets into the creatures' bloodstream.

The dragons stand about eight feet tall and they walk upright not on all fours like many other breeds of dragon. They are mainly green with big red blotches, looking almost as if they have caught some dreadful disease. Their stomachs look as if they have swallowed a beer barrel which means they store enough gases for two to three days' worth of fighting. The other unique feature is that you can smell dragons a long time before you see them. They are continuously wet and slimy and covered in all sorts of bacteria so just by touching them you could become violently ill. They have tiny eyes, a massive single horn on their noses and small rounded ears.

The cadadite was found by a race called burrowers. It was common knowledge that under everyone's feet these giant mole-like creatures lived and played, coming to the surface only to trade with what they had found in their tunnels. When standing on their hind legs they were about five feet tall. They had long snouts, very small eyes with limited vision, thick black fur and whiskers about two feet long to enable them to find their way through the dark tunnels. They were fairly comfortable around other races but were still very cautious. Unfortunately for Castlewood, they informed the Dragon King of the large deposits of cadadite under their village. The burrowers were hoping that he would ask them to get at the precious stones in exchange for goods, but it was not to be. There was bad blood between Fox and the Dragon King. He was not in favour of the easy way out, of course. The Dragon King couldn't ask the people of Castlewood to move because if they refused and he threatened them, they would be alerted and on their guard, which could have involved other villages joining forces and given rise to a mass battle with massive losses on both sides. Their lives without pride would not be worth living. There was no chance of his getting his own way without someone getting hurt, or even worse, defeated which meant he would have to relinquish his reign of death and destruction.

So the Dragon King decided to mount a surprise attack. He would flatten the village, murder all the men and take the women and children for two reasons: firstly as slaves and secondly as protection, just in case anyone was intending to attack, when he could use them as a bargaining chip.

In the Courtyard the dragon army was beginning to assemble. There were one hundred and fifty foot soldiers and fifty flying dragons. The courtyard was now full of dragons. All stood and faced the west tower to listen to their King giving them their orders. The King stepped forward to the window, a loud cheer went out and there was a lot of roaring and banging of shields and chants for a speech from their leader.

'Well, men, this is a most important day for us. We must take Castlewood or we will lose the cadadite which we need so badly. I'm sure you are going to make me very proud. When I look out of the west tower tomorrow, I don't want to see Castlewood anywhere or a single trace of it. And remember, there must be no males left alive or women warriors. They also must be eliminated. To victory!' said the King. Then all the men shouted 'To victory! Hooray, hooray!'

Then the officer in charge shouted: 'Squad, squad, 'shun.' The soldiers all came to attention. 'Squad, right turn. Then by the right quick march.' As the first soldiers passed the west tower the officer shouted: 'Eyes right' and they gave a salute. Then the two hundred strong marched out through the castle gate on a rampage of death and destruction.

Meanwhile, Castlewood and its inhabitants were sleeping peacefully, and why not? They had no idea that there was an army of dragons heading their way bent on destroying them. Everyone felt the whole village was surrounded by massive tree trunks sunk into the ground four feet deep so no worries of anyone or any thing pulling them out of the ground.

The sun began to rise and everything seemed to come alive all at once as if someone had flipped a switch on. The cockerels started to crow and the animals started to get restless looking for food.

The man Eagle Eyes was on guard duty in the tower high above the village, even though it was a peaceful time. Fox insisted there be a guard every night. Most of the people thought it was a waste of time, but Fox said: 'It's better to be safe than sorry,' and was most insistent about this rule. He would not back down no matter what anyone said. Thank goodness he did. Eagle Eyes shouted down: 'I can see columns of dust heading this way.'

Fox shouted up: 'What is it?'

'I don't know yet,' came the reply.

'Could it be a herd of wild horses?' asked Fox.

'Possibly,' said Eagle Eyes, 'hang on.' He continued: 'No, it can't be. There's something flying over them - it's too big for any bird.'

'Then what in hell's name is it?' asked Fox.

'Well,' said Eagle Eyes, 'they are storm-makers.'

Now a storm-maker is a cross between an elephant and a rhinoceros. It has two horns on its forehead, a trunk, four tusks, big ears, no tail and worst of all is twice the size of an African elephant and weighs about ten tons.

'What do you mean, storm-makers? The only storm-makers around here belong to the dragons,' said Fox.

'Yes, but that explains the things flying around in the air above them,' said Eagle Eyes.

'Well, what are they doing coming this way?' asked Fox.

'Hang on a minute. The only time they take them anywhere is when they are going to attack a village. Are you sure they are heading this way?'

'Yes, no doubt about it,' answered Eagle Eyes.

'Quick, sound the alarm,' commanded Fox. So Eagle Eyes took the hunting horn from the side of the tower and blew for all he was worth. The villagers all ran out of their huts. One woman yelled at Fox: 'I hope this is not one of your little jokes, because if so it is not one of your better ones.'

'No, it is not. Grab your weapons and defend yourselves.'

The dragons heard the alarm and started to bear down on the village. The officer sent in the flying dragons ahead to keep the people busy, but they were armed when the fifty flying dragons arrived overhead. Firstly they swooped on the tower. One attacked Eagle Eyes and he stabbed a spear at it. The creature backed away but not for long. One caught his attention by blowing flame at him, then a second one lunged at him, grabbed him by the shoulders and flew upwards still hanging on to him. The two worked as a team; while one held him fast the other blew flames at him. By now Eagle Eyes was screaming in pain. The archers below took aim and fired a volley of arrows bringing both dragons down along with Eagle Eyes. He smashed through the roof of a hut automatically setting fire to it. A child and her mother came out screaming. The mother was on fire and a man named Puma threw water over her to put out the flames.

Then a man named Horse Breaker rushed into the burning hut and pulled Eagle Eyes out. His clothes were still smouldering and his face was unrecognizable even as a human being. Horse Breaker was bending over Eagle Eyes trying to comfort him and ease his pain when from behind him came a snorting sound. He spun round, looked up and there was a dragon. It lunged forward. With his pike Horse Breaker picked up an old table. The pike got stuck in it. He grabbed a heavy saucepan and smashed the dragon round the face, breaking the creature's jaw. It fell to the ground frothing at the mouth a mixture of green blood and saliva. The creature rolled around on the floor in agony until Horse Breaker said: 'Sod it, how can I concentrate with this noise going on?' So he picked up the dragon's pike and stuck it straight through the creature's throat, silencing it immediately. 'There, that's better. Now I can hear myself think.' He went back to tending Eagle Eyes' wounds, then thud, Horse Breaker fell to his knees, his mouth opened but no sound came out, just blood. It poured all over Eagle Eyes. He was trying to breathe but choking on Horse Breaker's blood. Then he heard the most awful cracking and tearing. It was the dragon pulling his pike out of Horse Breaker. As he did, it was breaking the bone and ripping the muscle. Eagle Eyes looked up and could see straight through Horse Breaker's chest where the creature had hit so hard. Eagle Eyes could see the dragon and unfortunately the dragon saw that Eagle Eyes was still alive. The pike finally slipped out with a squelch and Horse Breaker's body fell forward crashing on top of Eagle Eyes. He let out a blood-curdling scream. The pain was so unbearable he began to lose consciousness. He heard the dragon say: 'Don't worry, little man, I won't leave you suffering. I'm not that evil, despite our reputation.' Then the creature raised his pike above his head and rammed his weapon straight through Horse Breaker's limp and lifeless form into Eagle Eyes' body. He gasped as he looked into the dragon's eye and said: 'Thank you.' The creature wandered off.

The whole village was full of fighting men and dragons' blood and carnage everywhere. The flying dragons were swooping on the men. Fox slashed at one of the creatures, snuffing it out with one blow. The other men were attacking with great ferocity, wielding axes and swords, slicing and hacking at the dragons. By this time they had halved the number of flying dragons. Suddenly they withdrew as quickly as they had attached. 'Hooray, they're defeated and running away!' the men shouted. Everything became quiet and still. The villagers sighed with relief and wiped the sweat from their faces. But the peace was not to last long. The silence was broken by an almighty crash and the outer walls shook.

Fox shouted: 'Step back from the walls,' but his warning came too late for some. The walls came crashing down on top of the warriors crushing them and smashing their bodies like egg shells. As the defences fell the storm-makers charged through and those who were not killed instantly let out screams of agony. But they were soon to be silenced for ever as the storm-makers tramped across the logs which were once the barricades to keep intruders out.

The air was filled with the sound of breaking logs and the crushing of bodies snuffing the life out of the warriors that were still alive. All the villagers rushed to defend the outer perimeter. Of course it was hopeless: the storm-makers just kept moving forward, stamping on anyone who got in the way, impaling the warriors on their horns and picking them up with their trunks and launching them into the air to send them flying across the village.

Then the foot soldiers moved in, slicing and killing the brave fighters. There were skirmishes all over the village. It seemed as if one dragon was killed only for three more to take its place. The warriors were despatching dragons right, left and centre all to no avail - they seemed almost to have multiplied every time they turned round.

The girl Pacer was fighting with two dragons. One attacked. He thrust a spear towards her. She hit it so hard that the end snapped off. The sword carried on round and sliced his arm. He made the mistake of taking his eyes off her to look at his wound. She grasped the opportunity with both hands and brought her sword up, taking the creature's head clean off. Then the second dragon charged towards her with steam pouring out of his nose. She stuck her foot out, tripping him up, and thumped him over the head with her shield. Then she followed home by pushing her sword in between his shoulder blades and right through and out of his chest.

Just as she thought it was over a flying dragon swooped down, snatched her up into the air to about sixty feet and just let her fall to the ground, leaving gravity to do the damage, which it did. She came down on the logs that used to be the wall going round Castlewood. As she hit, her feet slipped away from under her, then her back came into contact with such a force that it just broke in two. Fox heard her bones snap from a few hundred yards away. As her life force was crushed from her body by the force of the impact Fox shouted to the archers: 'Shoot that evil sod down.' They fired and down it came, crashing to the ground. It gave Fox a feeling of satisfaction, as he was fond of Pacer in his own way. Fox stopped fighting and ran towards where she was lying. He scooped her smashed and broken body up into his strong arms. She lay as limp as a ragdoll. He looked into her eyes.

'I'm finished, aren't I?' she asked.

He looked at her face. It was such a waste of a life. He felt a tear roll down his face. He knew he could not lie to her however much he wanted to. She had the right of honour to speak her dying words knowing that they were the last she would ever utter. Pacer gasped for breath and coughed. Then blood poured from her mouth down her chin, onto her neck and down to her breast.

Pacer looked at Fox. 'I did well, did I not?'

'Yes, very well. You were the best and most formidable warrior on the battlefield,' Fox told her.

'Thanks, that means a lot coming from you.' Pacer then asked Fox: 'Am I allowed a last request?'

'Of course. It's your right as a warrior. What is it?'

'I have spent so much time being a warrior that I haven't had time to be a woman. I have never been kissed and no man has ever told me he loved me. Will you wipe my face and kiss me and tell me you love me? It would make me very happy and dying wouldn't be so bad. I wouldn't feel alone and unloved. You know of course I've always had a crush on you.'

'No, I did not know,' replied Fox. So he did as he was asked and wiped her face. Then he took her in his arms and held her tightly. He looked into her eyes and said: 'I love you more than life itself.' Then he kissed her long and passionately.

Pacer looked at him, smiled and said: 'I've always loved you with a burning passion.' A tear came into the girl's eye. 'I just wish I had had the courage to tell you before today.' She was only eighteen years old. Fox did not like telling lies to anyone, but it made Pacer happy. What else could he do under those circumstances? Besides, he was genuinely fond of her. She looked up and said: 'Hold me tight one more time - I'm feeling cold.' She shivered, then passed away in his arms. Fox gently laid her body down on the ground, covered her up with a cloak and went back to the matter in hand. As he walked away, he said: 'See you on the next battlefield, my battling beauty.'

Sword in hand, he went back to the fray. He ran to what had become the front line. It was now a case of turn the battle their way or face defeat. Fox tried to rally his army by shouting: 'Let's push them back and put a stop to this invasion. Kill - kill them!' The people were fighting hard and just about holding their own. Fox was standing next to a man called Crusher. They had just despatched a dragon apiece and Fox turned to say: 'A nice one' when Crusher suddenly jolted backwards. There was Crusher nailed to a hut door by a dragon's pike. It went straight through his stomach. He screamed: 'Help me, Fox.' The man looked down at his insides hanging out. He placed his hands on the wound with an amazed look on his face. 'Fox, look at me, I'm nailed to this door like a picture on a wall.'

'Do you want me to get you down?' Fox asked.

'No. I have something to say. Getting me off this door will probably kill me. I'm sorry I got so nasty on the field of honour. I wanted to prove my valour and if I had beaten you there would be no doubt in anyone's mind that I was worthy to call myself a warrior of Castlewood like you. I have not proved what I'm made of on the battlefield - I'm sorry.'

Fox looked at the young man hanging on the door. 'You've nothing to apologise for. I would have done the same if I were in the same situation.'

'Thanks.' Then Crusher twitched and the top half of his body slumped forward. Fox took hold of the pike and pulled it out of Crusher's body. He fell forward. Fox just managed to catch him. The body was limp and floppy. He laid it on the ground. 'See you on the next great battlefield.'

Then Fox gave the order to fall back and they took up new defensive positions. Flying dragons swooped in for the attack on the watch tower again, setting light to it. The man in the tower jumped for his life and landed on the roof of a hut, smashing through it. The door swung open and chickens and a woman with her children ran out. Surprisingly enough, the man who had just jumped from a forty foot high watch tower did not have even a scratch on him. His luck didn't last long, though. As he came out of the hut, a smile on his face, a battleaxe flew through the air hitting him in the chest and knocking him straight back into the hut, dead on arrival.

Flying dragons began to dive at the people, swooping time and again, tearing at their flesh. Men were bleeding from arm and chest wounds. One man was swinging an axe at the creatures. Suddenly one dived and grabbed the axe, taking bits of flesh with it. The man in question looked up and shouted: 'You miserable overgrown housefly!' While he was looking up, another dragon swooped down and ripped his throat out. The man placed his hands on his throat, fell to his knees then flat on his face in the mixture of blood and mud.

Fox had seen enough. He watched as time and again his men were lifted into the air and simply released, so that they fell to the ground. So Fox commanded the archers: 'Light your arrows and aim for the left-hand side of the stomach.' So they did and to their amazement the creatures exploded into hundreds of pieces, raining flames down on the people and on the huts, unfortunately setting them on fire. Now it seemed like the whole world was on fire.

'Keep hitting the left-hand side of the stomach - it's where they store the gases,' shouted Fox. More arrows went up; more creatures exploded. The sky was filled with burning flesh falling to the ground. It was like a giant firework party. As before, the flying dragons withdrew and once again the foot soldiers moved in, pikes down, making an impenetrable fence as they marched forward. The razor-sharp points were cutting into the villagers' flesh. Fox stopped one by knocking it down and thrashing upwards with his sword, slicing the dragon's face. Then Fox slipped. The line just continued to move over him. A dragon spotted him on the ground. Fox pushed his sword upwards catching the creature in the stomach, then scrambled backwards to his own lines.

Warriors were being pushed back into burning huts screaming in pain but their own people could do nothing to help. The poor souls were like lambs to the slaughter. Not being able to see, they ran straight onto the dragons' lines, impaling themselves on the creatures' pikes. The final blow came when they moved the storm-makers back in and used them to trample the warriors into the dust under their mighty feet. One by one the men of Castlewood fell to the overwhelming odds. The village was being smashed right in front of Fox's eyes and he could not stop the carnage. The warriors were now in a corner and surrounded. There were only a dozen or so left. The situation was impossible.

But still they continued to fight to the last man or woman. In front of Fox stood two men. Then a dragon lopped off both of their heads as simply as picking heads off flowers and showed as much emotion. The blood sprayed all over the men standing directly behind them. It had turned into a wholesale bloodbath. The crashing of swords and the crushing of bones filled the village, along with screams of women and children crying as their husbands and fathers were cut down and killed in front of their very eyes. Smoke now filled the air - there were burning huts everywhere. The smell of burning bodies and the stench of death lingered through the village.

Finally the remaining warriors were overrun by the overwhelming odds. Even though they faced certain death not one man could bring himself to surrender. The humiliation would be more than they could bear. Fox was struck on the back of the neck and fell to the ground. In the same instant his dog Patch fell to the ground.

Now the crashing of swords and the yells of warriors and the sound of men in pain was no more. Silence fell over the village. The only sounds were fires burning, women weeping and dragons snorting as they scuttled past Fox's five children gathered around him. His daughter Sunny held her father's head in her lap, kissed him on the forehead and said: 'Please don't leave us. We love you and need you.'

'Yes,' the boys chipped in, 'we love you. Please don't give up the fight. You've never run away from a fight before. If you live, I promise I will never ask you for anything again.'

Badger just stood watching the blood slowly pumping from her father's head and chest. She looked at her sister and asked: 'Is he going to survive?'

'I don't know. I hope so,' Sunny replied. 'Dad, speak to me,' Sunny said, but Fox only murmured something they couldn't understand.

Then one of the dragons came up and kicked Fox's body, knocking it off Sunny's lap. Fox's body lay face down in the mud. His sons jumped up. 'You will pay for that, you evil green lump.' Then Jage picked up a battle axe. The soldier just laughed and slapped the boy round the side of the head with his giant hand, knocking him onto his father's body. Sky and Wildcat jumped the guard by his leg. He laughed again until both boys sunk their teeth deep into his leg. He let out a yell of pain. Another dragon came to his rescue. He hit the boys so hard they went flying head over heels. The boys were then manhandled to one of the carts and unceremoniously thrown in the back, followed very closely by their sisters.

There on the cart was their aunty Elk. She was holding her son Mole. He was bleeding from a chest wound. He had been cut by a flying dragon whose claws are highly infectious. If claw wounds are not treated immediately they will give rise to a high temperature and eventually death.

'Where's your father?' asked their aunty.

'He's dead.' Sunny burst into tears.

'I don't believe it, not Fox. That means we are stuck - no rescue. I can't bring myself to face it. Dead - Fox - no way.'

'It's true, aunty. All true, I promise. We saw him,' said the children together.

Fox's youngest daughter found all the talk of death too much to handle. Badger then jumped onto a dragon's back and bit his ear. But the creature just grabbed the girl from his back and threw her straight back into the cart.

Jage asked: 'Why did the dragons explode when the men shot them with burning arrows?'

'Well, you see, dragons store gases in their stomachs and when the archers hit the left-hand sides they split the stomachs and the gas all escaped at once and the flame from the arrow ignited it, which caused it to explode,' said their aunty.

The children watched in horror as the dragons collected war trophies, cutting off fingers, ears, noses and even scalps. One dragon even took a man's head. Then the officer in charge walked over to Fox's body.

'Can we at least bury Dad?' the children asked their aunt.

'No, they won't let you.'

The commander started to unstrap Fox's armour. 'Please, aunty, stop him. Please, please,' the children pleaded.

'I can only try.' So she got down from the cart. The dragon guarding them said: 'Where in hell's name do you think you're going?'

'Please let me talk to that officer,' said Elk as she pointed to the dragon standing by Fox's body.

So he shouted: 'Sir, this woman wants to talk to you.'

'Send her over.'

So Elk walked over to the commander. 'Well, what do you want? I haven't got all day, you know,' snapped the dragons' commander.

'Well,' started Elk, 'please don't take my brother's armour. Leave him in death with some dignity. Please, please. On my knees, I beg you, leave his armour. You have his life and many other trophies.'

'Why worry? He's dead,' said the officer.

'I know that, but in life he saved me many times and helped me when he could. At least I can try to help him in death. It would mean a lot. Please show some compassion. I will gladly give anything I own.' By now Elk was in tears.

'All right, I will leave him some dignity. Men, leave this body. I have given my word. If anyone touches this warrior I will run them through personally. Is that clear?' shouted the commander.

'Yes, sir,' all his troops replied.

'Oh thank you, thank you very much,' said Elk.

As the people were horse traders there were horses everywhere. The dragons rounded them up and strung them together. 'This little lot will fetch a nice price, a nice bounty for us.' Dragons were checking huts for valuables. Then they went on to check dead bodies, going through pockets, taking boots off, picking up undamaged clothes and throwing them all into a wagon which like everything else they had commandeered. Then they started to collect weapons that were scattered all round the village. Swords, battleaxes, chains and maces, daggers, shields, all sorts of weapons were picked up and placed in yet another wagon. Jage saw his father's sword and shield on the ground by one of the huts. He was just about to jump out of the cart when Sunny said: 'No, don't go. Stay here with me.'

'No, they're not getting my dad's shield and sword.'

He took no notice of Sunny, jumped off the cart and scuttled to where his father's shield and sword were lying. He picked them up and ran to his home. Under the floor was a secret compartment. Jage lifted the lid and placed the precious items inside for safe keeping. Then he shut the lid down and ran back to his brothers and sisters, jumped onto the cart and sat down.

'Well?' Badger asked. 'Did you get them?'

'Of course. One day I'll return and get them and revenge dad's death, no matter how long it takes.'

Sunny piped up: 'Leave it, Jage. Dad's dead. It's over - finished.'

'It might be for you, but not for me,' said Jage.

'Nor us,' said Wildcat and Sky together.

'That goes for me double,' said Badger.

The dragons were tearing everything apart. They were emptying the storehouse of the sacks of grain and barley and loading them on wagons. Then they set fire to all the buildings - huts, storehouses, meeting hall - and the crops left in the fields. The trees that had surrounded Castlewood were thrown into a big pile and burnt. The village had virtually disappeared under a veil of smoke. Everybody was coughing and spluttering. You couldn't even see your hand in front of your face. The children kept low in the carts. 'I hope we are leaving soon - this smoke is horrible,' they said.

Then the commanding officer shouted: 'Gather up your spoils of war, and let's move out.' So the dragons hastily gathered together anything of value they could lay their hands on and formed ranks. They were loaded down with goodies. By the time they had finished, some of them could hardly move, they were carrying so many trophies. The storm-makers moved out first, crushing things as they went - it was easy to see why they got their name. Dust flew everywhere and the sound of their feet crashing on the ground sounded just like thunder. Next the foot soldiers moved out, then a massive string of horses. They would sell well at market. Then the captives all tied together by the neck, warriors that had not been killed, their bodies cut and bleeding. They would be lucky if they made it to their destination. Women, old men, all were forced into slavery. A bleak future lay ahead of them.

A column of carts was assembled. The first cart passed what used to be the village gates. It was filled with weapons; something else the dragons didn't need but could sell. Next the one filled with clothes and boots - more money when sold. Third was jewels, money and gold. It looked like the Dragon King was going to make a tidy profit out of this little escapade. Then, fourth, barley; fifth, oats; then last but not least the sixth and final cart containing Fox's children and many others including their aunty and cousin. Fox's children sat right at the back waving goodbye to their village. And a last farewell to a loving father they had left behind in the village of death. Because that's all it now contained. There was no sign of life anywhere; even the birds had become silent as if out of respect for the dead. There was just the sound of crackling wood as the village burned.

The children's eyes were full of tears. They felt as if their hearts were going to break. The boys stood up and Jage shouted: 'We will see you on the next great battlefield, Fox! Your sons love you more than life itself and this much I promise you on my life and honour: we your sons will revenge your death some day, no matter how long it takes. Bye, Father dear.'

The column moved off further and further from Castlewood till nothing could be seen but a small cloud of dust. The warriors in the line were finding it hard going. Many were still bleeding badly. The line of slaves came to an abrupt halt as three of the warriors dropped to the ground from sheer exhaustion. The children watched as the men on the ground were cut from the bondages that bound them to the others.

'Look, aunty, they're setting them free,' Badger said.

'No, my dear, I don't think so somehow.' Just as she finished speaking, the guards looked towards their commanding officer. He drew his thumb across his throat, then the guards swung their battleaxes down across the warriors' backs with a thud. The children winced and looked away. The column then moved on again. The carts just ran over the bodies. Jage looked down. The men's backs had been split open to expose the backbone. 'Oh, my God,' said Jage, 'I feel sick.'

'You shouldn't have looked, sweetheart. Haven't you seen enough blood today?' asked his aunty.

'Why but why did they have to kill them? Why not just leave them?' asked Jage.

'I'm not sure, but I think it's that they don't want any warriors from Castlewood wandering around causing trouble for the dragons.'

'I'm glad in one way Dad died in the village. I would hate to see him being treated like these warriors. Don't get me wrong, I love Dad and wish he was still alive, as long as he didn't have to be a slave - it would be too degrading for him to lose his honour in this way,' said Sunny.

All the children turned to the front. 'Look, there's our destination - the Dragon King's castle.' It was scary even from a distance. As they moved closer they began to see more detail.

Surrounding the castle was a great moat but instead of water it was filled with sharp spikes and an evil-smelling green slime that covered half the stakes. As they got within feet of the castle the drawbridge came down, across the moat. The column came to a standstill. The children looked in amazement at the giant walls. They were wet with a gooey substance trickling down similar to the disgusting mess in the moat. It was still light but the castle looked so dark. The Gatehouse was built to resemble a giant dragon's head. The two towers on either side of the portcullis were enormous arms with claws hanging over the tops of the towers. The head sat in the middle complete with ears, horns and evil red eyes. The portcullis itself so terrified the children that they screamed and hid their faces in their hands. Even some of the adults screamed with fear.

The bottom jaw was another bridge with the front teeth missing so carts and storm-makers could go through. As the commander went in, the top jaw came down slotting together like a real jaw. The teeth on top had no gaps and were painted red. Wildcat thought to himself: 'I hope that is paint and not blood. I would hate to get caught in that.' If he didn't know better he would have said the castle had eaten the storm-makers. Then the gates opened up again and guards came out and beckoned the column to move forward into the castle.

Inside it was more horrific than the outside. There were men chained to walls being flogged. They were screaming in pain. One man's back was just a mass of red lines. There were men from Waterdown, some hillanders and even some men they knew from Castlewood. Also there were skeletons hanging on the walls. By the time they had finished whipping the flesh off the men's backs, the walls were covered in blood. It's not a sight anyone should have to witness, let alone children. The reason the children knew which villages the men belonged to was down to their father. He had taught them all about coats of arms. They had just looked at the pile of shields in a corner. Then came the sound of chains rattling and wood creaking as the portcullis came down behind them with a crash. Then another bang and the children gathered the drawbridge had also been shut. Looking forward once more they saw the Dragon King's lair, the Castle Keep - the heart of the castle where the throne room was located. More horrors were to come once they stepped through the twenty-foot doors.

The children huddled together in fear of the unknown yet to come. The carts were driven into the keep. The King had a big smile on his face. 'Oh, you have done well, my brave warriors. What a lovely haul you have brought back for me and of course you will have your share of the booty.'

'What's going to happen to us, Aunty Elk?' asked the children.

'I don't know - I wish I did. I also wish Oak or your father were here,' she replied.

The King was for the moment distracted looking at the gold and jewels. Then he looked into the wagon full of weapons. 'These will fetch a nice price at market.' Next clothes and boots. He looked disappointed. 'My lord,' the general said quickly, 'they are of the finest quality. These humans will always need clothing to protect them from the elements. It will make a tidy profit, I promise you.'

'Well, perhaps you're right.' Then to the fourth, barley: 'Good, no trouble selling this. And grain, good, good. Ah - my slaves.' The line of slaves was then brought in. 'Kneel to your King.'

'He's not our King!' shouted one man. The guard whipped the man in question then the others repeatedly until they gave in and were on their knees. Blood was pouring from the mouth of the man who had questioned an order. The King turned to the guard. 'This one's a trouble-maker. Put him to death.' So he was run through with a sword. The children watched as the man slumped to the floor. 'Quick, guards, the thing is bleeding over my nice marble floor. Remove the carcass now.

'Now we could use them to dig up their own village to get at all that lovely cadadite. Wouldn't that be ironic? Or we could just get the burrowers to mine under the village without even disturbing the ground. Ha, ha!' laughed the Dragon King. As he did, the whole court laughed as well.

'Look at them - pathetic. So these are the so-called warriors of Castlewood. I thought they were supposed to be fearless. What kind of honour do you call this, cringing on the floor like frightened little rabbits? Is there anybody here related to the so-called great leader of Castlewood?'

'Yes, my lord.'

Then Fox's children were unceremoniously thrown from the back of the cart and sent sliding across the floor to the King's feet. The King grabbed one of the boys by the ear and pulled him to his feet. 'So who are you, little man?'

'I'm Jage, Fox's eldest son.'

The King then put his giant wet slimy hand round the boy's face. He squeezed the little face so hard that it became distorted. 'So, little boy, where's your brave father now?' taunted the King. He watched the boy's face and took great pleasure in seeing the pain on it at these contemptuous remarks about his father's honour. Jage just could not stand it any longer and burst into tears and shouted: 'You had him killed, as well you know. But at least my dad was there and died fighting, unlike you. My dad's no coward.' This remark from a little boy infuriated the King. He squeezed the boy's face so hard that the others thought his eyes were going to pop out of his head.

'Leave our brother alone, you're hurting him. Haven't you done enough by killing our father and making us into slaves? Don't you think you've hurt us enough? You're just a big coward, picking on little boys and not having the courage to face my father,' said Badger.

'Yeah,' said Jage, and then spat at the King.

'You little animal!' Then he launched Jage across the hall. On landing Jage slid across the shiny floor, finally coming to a stop when his head hit the pillar supporting the roof. The boy lay still, completely motionless, not even a twitch. Sunny screamed and ran over to where her brother lay.

'Jage, please don't die! Wake up, please!' She held his limp little body in her arms and rocked backwards and forwards, weeping.

'To answer your question, no I haven't done nearly enough to your father. He and your people drove me out,' replied the Dragon King.

'Yes, because you're evil and have to destroy everything you touch. You enjoy hurting people for no reason - you get some perverted thrill. You're twisted and hateful and you make others feel the same way. You're just a disease that needs destroying.'

'Oh, is that so? And who in hell's name are you?' demanded the King.

'I'm Elk, Fox's sister, you evil green lump of slime. I know why you killed my brother. It's because you're scared of him.'

The Dragon King snorted and swung his arm round, catching Elk across the side of the face, knocking her to the floor. She raised her head and spat a mouthful of blood on the dragon's foot.

'I'm not going to beg you for my life. You don't scare me. I'm not a child. I'm prepared for death.'

So he turned his attention to Elk's son Mole. 'So who does this belong to?' he asked with an evil grin on his face.

'You damn well know he's mine,' said Elk.

The King started to squeeze the baby's arm. It let out a squeal then burst into tears.

'You sadistic bully. That's it, pick on a child.'

'I should be very careful what you say to me, and it would be a good idea if your attitude towards me changed as well,' said the Dragon King.

'So what do you want of me - to humble myself before you on my knees?'

'That will do for starters,' laughed the King.

Elk's tone changed immediately. 'Please don't hurt him,' she begged. 'I will do anything you ask of me, but don't injure him.'

'Anything?' said the King, as the smile returned to his face.

'Yes, what do you require of me?' she replied.

'Take my dagger and kill the little blonde boy,' said the King.

'No, you can't kill Sky. He loves you and trusts you. Please don't,' Sunny begged her aunty.

Sky meanwhile stood there absolutely oblivious to everything going on around him. He was still in shock from seeing his father die.

'I can't kill him, he's my brother's son - family. I love him. You ask too much. I just can't. I could not live with myself,' said Elk.

'Is your son not your own flesh? Does he not mean more than Fox's children?' said the King.

'You will have to kill me instead, because I just can't do what you ask of me.'

'Then go, you have sealed your fate. You will die in my dungeons or in my slave gangs. Now go. Take these so-called proud people out of my sight. I don't want to see their sad pathetic faces before me again.'

So all the prisoners were taken away. Sunny picked Jage up. He had still not regained consciousness. They were marched off to the depths of the castle. Then they were pushed into the dungeons and the door slammed shut after them.

'Well, children, this is a fine mess to be in,' said Elk. 'No chance of reprieve or escape from this situation and, to make it worse, no help from the outside. Well, sit down, make yourselves at home because this is it from now on.'

Then Jage came round. 'Where am I? Oh yes, I remember now. I was hoping it was all a bad dream but I'm awake and it's not a dream. Oh, rats.'

'Plenty of them, my dear,' said their aunty.

Then another crash and the bolt slammed across the door. The children huddled together to stave off the coldness of the cell.

Meanwhile, back in the great hall an officer was giving a glowing report of how the dragons had smashed any and all resistance to the onslaught. The King could be heard laughing all over the castle as he was told of the total annihilation of Castlewood and its people. The King was full of praise for his brave and fearless soldiers. Then he turned to his general and asked: 'Are all the men of Castlewood dead?'

'Yes, my lord.'

'Does that include female warriors?' enquired the King.

'Yes, everything and every one in the village are dead. The only ones still alive are in your dungeons below our feet now. You have my word on it,' said the general.

'I'll have your word or your life, that's a guaranteed certainty.'

'But why should it worry my lord so much if one of these insignificant warriors has survived our attack? They are nothing, just bugs under my lord's feet to be squashed, as simple as that. You know no fear. So why in the name of the gods do you bother to worry about something so trivial?' The general finished talking.

'Because, you idiotic gormless lump, one man won't make any difference, but it won't stay at one man. He could persuade others to join. There's nothing gets this lot of ignorant peasants going quicker than the thought of an injustice done and they will absolutely see what happened this morning as a revenge attack. And of course they will be right, won't they? That's why it's so important. I don't need anyone to start a revolt and bring my rule finally to an abrupt ending.'

'Yes, my lord, I see.'

Chapter 3

Meanwhile, back at Castlewood, Fox regained consciousness. He could not move. 'Oh, no, the rotten sods have crippled me and left me to starve to death.' Then he realised it was some weight holding him down and not that his body had packed up. Fox put his hand behind and felt flesh. It wasn't a something but a someone. He stayed still. His breathing became very shallow and slow. He could see nothing due to the mud in his eyes. He had never been so terrified in his life as he was at that moment. After staying motionless for what seemed to be hours he decided to take his life in his hands. He wiggled his legs; the body on top of him made no movement or sound. Fox managed to grab a stake. He pulled with all his might and got his chest and shoulders clear. As he stopped pulling, the body on top of him slipped down, trapping his waist. He tried desperately to push it off, but his hands would not grip in the mixture of blood and mud. So once again he pulled at the stake, slowly heaving himself free from the weight that held him down. As his feet were released he crawled away to regain his strength. He lay face down, panting, trying to catch his breath. He sat up, wiped the mud from his eyes, then coughed and mud fell from his mouth. He cleared his throat and spat the contents onto the ground. 'It's everywhere - in my ears, up my nose, all over my face.' He looked around - the body that had been on top of him was a dragon. 'No wonder I couldn't move with that fat lump lying on top of me. It's a foot soldier. Those things weigh a ton. It's badly cut up - at least that's one that didn't survive.'

Fox looked around. There were bodies everywhere. Men stuck to doors by pikes. Warriors with arms missing, legs hacked off. One man had been cut completely in two. The top half of his body was by a hut, the legs and waist were about twenty feet away as if someone had pulled him apart and discarded him like some broken toy. There were bodies squashed so badly they were unrecognizable as people. It was like hell on earth. Blood, bodies, limbs, fires everywhere Fox looked. The ground was red with blood. As it had been a hot day the village smelled of rotting bodies.

Fox heard warriors moaning in pain. He went to one man stuck to a door. He lifted his head. 'Hullo Fox, my leader. Please grant me one last request.'

'Of course I will,' said Fox.

'Kill me - I can't take the pain any more - and make it quick.'

So Fox walked up to the man, put his hands on either side of his face, then twisted his head sharply to the left. His bones cracked and his suffering was over. He pulled the pike from the body and it dropped to the ground.

Fox just sat there amazed at all the carnage that surrounded him. He could not believe his eyes - so much death and destruction in one place. Fox sat there thinking, trying to get his mind back to the reality of what had gone on. He head just kept on spinning round and round. He was feeling very old and lonely. Everything was sore - his legs, his arms, his back, his chest. He felt like death warmed up. Which was not a bad description considering how close to death he had come that day. Then he put his hand down by his side and felt for his sword. The fact that it wasn't there was enough to jolt his mind back to its full function.

'What have they done? What's it all in aid of, and where the hell are my children?'

He jumped to his feet and ran towards his home. His legs felt like lead. It was painful, every step he took. When he reached his house, it was burnt. Just the timber frame stood and the door. He pushed the door open and it fell off its hinges. I'll have to fix that later, he thought. He walked in and pulled the lid off the secret hiding place beneath the floor. 'They are here, my sword and shield. This means my children were alive at the end of the battle. There's a good possibility they're still alive now. Maybe they've hidden themselves in the village.' So Fox started searching, frantically rushing into burnt-out huts looking under beds, in cupboards, behind doors. Then he checked what was left of the stables, went on to the meeting hall, but that had been completely destroyed by the fire. His last hope was the storehouses. He pulled the massive doors. 'Children, come out, it's your father Fox! Sunny, Badger, Jage, Wildcat, Sky, please come out!' Still no reply. He fell to his knees and sobbed for his children. Then he thought they could be lying under some of the dead.

So he started to move bodies, but still no luck. 'They must have been taken back to the castle,' he thought to himself. His mind was still in a muddle. He got ready to leave, taking nothing, until he heard a whimpering coming from under one of the bodies. Fox moved it, and there was Patch. The dog crawled out, looked up at his master's face and wagged his tail. Then Fox patted his shoulders and the dog leapt up, placed his front paws on his master's shoulders and stood there quite contented. He then set about cleaning his master's face, licking him excitedly. 'Well, at least I'm not totally alone. Apart from the children, I couldn't think of anyone I'd rather see right now.'

Then, just to add insult to injury, the sky opened up and the rain poured down. The whole village seemed to disappear beneath a cloud of steam. Rain was hitting the hot ashes, and Fox could hear it hissing and bubbling as the fires began to die. Fox sat awhile and watched as the rain hit the burning pieces of wood - they seemed to disintegrate and turn to dust. Fox had never felt so empty and in pain. It was worse than any injury or pain he had ever had before. He wanted to cry one moment and kill someone the next. Afraid and hurt, confused, in such pain, with no chance of relief, no magic pain-killers, it had become an unbearable situation. Fox started to bang his head against what was left of one of the huts and kept saying: 'I must get my head together.'

By now he was wet, fed up and hungry. 'Right, I must stop feeling sorry for myself and get on and do something about this disastrous and intolerable situation.' So he got up and started to put some things together. Surprisingly enough, he found two rabbits hanging on what was left of one of the huts. The dragons had not eaten them. 'Lucky for me,' he said to the dog. 'I just haven't got the strength to hunt today. Which means, my friend' - looking at the dog beside him - 'we wouldn't have eaten.' He stood up: 'Look at the state of me.' He had cuts and bruises all over his body from top to toe. He started searching for useful items. First he found a rucksack. 'This will do nicely.' Then he found some rope, always useful, and firestones from which, when banged together, flames would shoot out as long as you had the right combination, one red and one green. It was the friction between the stones being opposites, like fire and water just don't mix, which sets them off. Then he found his bow and arrows and put them on his back. 'Ah yes, I mustn't forget water,' he thought as he picked up two water bottles. 'Now, what else? Oh, I remember - must take salt tablets, as I don't know when I will come across another village. They might have befallen the same fate as Castlewood.' So he packed everything in his rucksack. 'Now, what else? Dagger - got it; sword - yes; shield, bow - yes, I seem to have everything.'

By now Fox was in an extreme amount of pain but that was the least of his worries. The heartbreak of the whole situation was too much to bear. He had lost his children, home, honour, friends, livelihood, all in one fell swoop. He felt ashamed, alone, if only he hadn't survived. But, there again, if he had died who would rescue the children? 'Good point,' he told himself. This thought lifted his spirits a little. It was chucking down with rain on top of everything else - what more could possibly go wrong? He spoke too soon. Between banging his head and the rain washing the mud from the wound on his forehead, it opened up. When he had been hit on the back of the neck, he had fallen forward and cut his brow near the hairline. The blood started pouring down his face, mixing with rain, making it very difficult to see anything.

'Oh, sod it, I'm going to have to do something about this. I can't see to walk, let alone defend myself if I have to.' So he started to search again, this time for a needle and cotton, which was not an easy task. Every time he bent down, the blood ran faster, obscuring his vision. He pulled out a white sheet to try and stem the flow of blood but ended up just mopping it away. After looking through three huts he had not found what he was after. He went to yet another. In the burnt-out shell of the building sat a half-burnt rocking chair. Fox sat down. 'I've got to stop this bleeding, otherwise I'm going to bleed to death.' By now the once-white sheet was completely red.

He sat looking at all the devastation that surrounded him. Something caught his eye. In the corner was a child's doll - half its leg had been burnt away. He picked it up and sat holding it in his hand. He started to think how terrified the children must have been. After all, he was full-grown and had been in many battles, and it still scared him sometimes, all the yelling, the blood and pain and death and destruction. So it must have been sheer hell for them, something children shouldn't see, let alone be in the middle of. Then something else caught his attention - a woman's sewing kit. He opened it up: there was a rounded needle and white thread. He shut the lid down. He knew herbs were stored in that metal box in the meeting hall - the fire shouldn't have burned them. So with his sewing kit in hand he ran off to get the pain-relieving herbs. Yes, it's still there - he opened the box - a bit singed but still usable. Now something I can use to see what I'm stitching up. He looked round the village, then he saw it: a full-length mirror smashed into two halves, outside a hut. He placed one piece of the mirror on top of a box, then sat down on a barrel. There, perfect. He took a handful of the herbs and waited for them to take effect. The top of his head became tingly and then completely numb. So he started to sew up the wound on his head. As he pushed the needle through the skin, it didn't hurt. This is amazing. As the stitches closed the wound he wondered: how did the herbs know where to numb the skin? No wonder they call them magic herbs. I might as well do my chest while I'm at it. So he took another handful and the same thing happened with his chest. It took twelve stitches to close the gaping wound in Fox's head. Lucky that was only a glancing blow, otherwise my head would have been in two.

All the time Fox was repairing himself the dog was sitting watching. He looked puzzled, twisting his head and whimpering. 'It's all right, it doesn't hurt - you must know that already.'

He had already put the things away. Then he noticed Patch had a large gash on his shoulder.

'Come on, there's a good boy - it won't hurt, I promise.' The dog walked over to his master and sat down. Fox took a handful of magic herbs and said: 'Come on, eat these - they will make you feel better.' The dog took the herbs. Fox gave them a couple of minutes to take effect, then started to tear up rags and carefully cleaned Patch's wounds prior to sewing them up. It took quite some time because as Fox pushed the needle through, the dog whined and moved away.

'Come back here, you baby. If you keep still, it won't take long. Stop fidgeting.' Fox turned round to cut the thread and the dog walked off with the needle still in him.

'Come back here.' Patch ran. Fox chased him but couldn't catch him, which is not surprising as Patch could run at fifty miles an hour. So Fox fell to the floor and started to moan as if in agony. The dog stopped in his tracks, turned round, then ran towards Fox. As Patch got close, Fox grabbed him by the scruff of the neck and pulled him to the floor.

'I didn't think you would fall for that - you would have felt it. Look, once I've cut this thread then it's finished and we can go and get into more trouble. But this time we will pick the time and place. And this time the results will be completely different, I promise you that much. So let's go and find ourselves an army and bloody the Dragon King's nose. I swear this on my life and honour: the Dragon King will die. In fact, the Dragon King must die if anyone else is to survive.'

So Fox and Patch walked to where the gates used to stand at the entrance and took one last look at the burning village with a heavy heart. Fox turned away, then he thought he heard a child's voice shouting 'daddy'. He glanced back and could have sworn he saw his children standing at the gates waving. The village was full of happy, laughing people, horses everywhere. He closed his eyes and hoped it wasn't his imagination playing tricks on him. When he opened them again all he could see was smoke and death and the pitiful remains of what was once a happy thriving village. Both of them set off to find the evil invaders who stole their family.

They headed towards the land of the treedwellers. They came to the edge of the wood and peered in. It was dark even during daylight, let alone when the sun was going down. The trees were only two to three feet apart. There was one main track running straight through the middle of the wood and you could see a big circle of welcoming light at the other end of the wood. There was only one problem and that was to make it through the wood without getting yourself killed. As a rule Fox would give this place a wide berth but due to the fact that he either had suicidal tendencies and just didn't care or the fact that it was shorter - he didn't know or care which - he decided to cut through the wood. There were lots of little tracks running off the main track, but nobody in their right mind would leave the main track if they ever wanted to be seen again.

As the light flickered through the trees Fox could see platforms bound to branches and objects that looked like giant nests. Fox not being in his right mind could not resist investigating further. He left the main track and walked towards one of the structures. It was about fifty feet up. In one tree was a giant nest of sorts. It was round and by the way the rain ran off it appeared to be waterproof. The entrance was underneath. Fox started to climb up the tree for a closer look. Patch sat on the main path squeaking. Then Fox found out what the platforms were for: they were defensive positions. The air was filled with tiny arrows. One hit his hand which was holding on to a branch. Fox let out a scream and let go of the tree. He landed in a big bush, flat on his back, temporarily winded. He just lay in the bush trying to get his breath back. It felt like his chest was caving in. He finally caught his breath and somehow managed to scramble out of the bush and ran back to the main track. Now Patch was very jumpy and you could almost smell the fear coming from Fox and Patch.

'That was a really dumb move - I don't believe I did that.'

The arrow was still stuck in Fox's hand. He could not pull it out the way it went in because the barbs kept catching on his flesh. So he had to push it straight through, flights and all. Fox placed his arm over a log, then hit the shaft of the arrow with the hilt of the sword. Rip, it came out followed by a fair amount of blood. 'That really hurt. Let's not hang around here.' So they started to move cautiously down the track. The woods smelled musky, almost a deathly smell of things decaying, and the further down the track they went the more claustrophobic they became. The trees seemed to move even closer with every step they took.

The total silence made everything seem worse and unnerving. Fox patted Patch.

'It's all right, boy, we'll make it I hope.' The dog seemed to take comfort from his master's words.

As they progressed down the track it seemed to get darker. Then, as they looked from one side to the other and back again, the light seemed to flicker as if small creatures were darting around. There was a snap of twigs. Fox froze in his tracks. The dog had also spotted something. Fox looked in between the trees, and there were hundreds of pairs of tiny piercing eyes. Before he knew what was happening they were surrounded.

Hundreds of pairs of eyes all stared at Fox and Patch. The dog started to bark. 'Oh, my god, now we're for it,' said Fox. He took out his bow. His hands were shaking with fear and apprehension and the sweat was running down his forehead. He took aim at the eyes in the darkness and fired two arrows off in rapid succession. Two treedwellers fell to the ground. Fox fired again and more treedwellers hit the ground. He had taken six or seven out when suddenly the air was filled with hundreds of tiny arrows. Fox called Patch to him. The dog got underneath Fox. He pulled his shield down for protection and the arrows hit it with clangs as they ricocheted off.

Then the noise stopped. Fox looked out from under the shield: he was surrounded by treedwellers. He put his bow down and drew his sword. As he did, two of them lunged forward with spears. With one swipe Fox cut off the ends of the spears, then he slashed one creature across the chest and took the other one's arm off. With a high-pitched scream, they retreated to the safety of the trees. Fox shouted: 'Go get 'em, boy!' Patch jumped into action, grabbed one of the treedwellers by the throat and shook the creature until it stopped moving. Then he released his grip and charged at another. Meanwhile two treedwellers swung out of the trees. As the first one came into range, Fox hit it square in the face. It just dropped splat on the ground. Another one swung in: Fox sidestepped it and as it went past Fox cut the vine it was gripping. It landed on the ground with a thud. He then stamped on its head, breaking its neck.

Then a third swung in: Fox punched it in the face with the hilt of his sword, knocking it off the vine. Then yet another: Fox took his sword, catching the creature in the stomach with such force that he nearly cleaved it in two. From behind him came a loud crack. He turned round but there was nothing there. As he turned back, a whole tree suspended on two vines hit him full in the chest, knocking him backwards. As he went down, six treedwellers jumped him at once. He grabbed one by the antlers, put his feet in the creature's groin and threw him. He sailed through the air and landed in a bush in a crumpled heap. Fox headbutted another, then managed to kick one more off.

'Now only two left,' Fox thought, then lo and behold six more took the place of the four he had defeated. 'I must get to my feet.' He had just got up when one of them hit him on the back of the knees, bringing him down. Then a spear caught him a glancing blow on the cheek. Fox brought his hand up to the wound and the end of a spear thumped him on the back of the neck. He started to go down. 'I'm finished.' He looked over to his side and saw his faithful dog still fighting. Now on his knees Fox shouted to the dog: 'Run, for god's sake run!' but Patch would not leave. He stood whimpering. One of the treedwellers was just going to run Fox through with his own sword when Patch attacked, grabbing the creature by the arm and shaking it violently until it released its grip on the weapon. The creature shrieked with pain. Patch swung it round and then let go, sending it flying into the darkness from whence it came.

Patch kept attacking, hoping to give Fox enough time to recover and get to his feet, but every time he moved one out of the way as before it was replaced by more. It was a hopeless situation. By this time they had overcome Fox's resistance and had tied his hands and feet behind his back. He was as helpless as a new-born baby. Six treedwellers jumped on Patch. He was lying on his side looking at his master.

'Well, my boy, this looks like the end of the pair of us.' The dog just lay quite still panting and occasionally squeaking. He didn't struggle. He accepted what Fox had said was true and there was no point in prolonging the inevitable outcome, death. They had tried their best and lost.

'You should have gone, but I don't suppose, when you think about it, that it would have done you much good.' Fox watched as the treedwellers raised their spears above Patch. They were just bringing them down to finish him off when a loud roar came from the beginning of the track. Then an unknown creature banged his mighty battleaxe against his shield. It sounded like thunder and sparks flew from the shield like strikes of lightning. The treedwellers just stood there in shock and amazement. Patch jumped up, ran over to Fox and started to gnaw through the vines that bound him so tightly. The creatures were mesmerized by the large intruder. He was yelling and swinging his battleaxe from side to side, chopping trees of two feet thick in half with one blow as he walked.

Then into the clearing where Fox lay came a giant of a man six foot six and nearly as wide. The man just stood there. In his right hand was a double headed battleaxe. On his chest he wore a gleaming red breast plate. On his head was a helmet with two enormous horns cut at an angle so they went straight up. They were at least eighteen inches long and very deadly as the treedwellers were to find out to their cost. The horns had once belonged to dragons, but were now the stranger's pride and joy. Fox knew the man very well and was extremely glad to see him. The treedwellers just stood there in total amazement. They had never seen anyone so big. The man took full advantage of the situation. He bent down and jammed the horns on his helmet into one of the treedwellers. As he stood up, the creature's blood ran down the horns. He shook his head and flipped the treedweller off.

The night air had become very cold by now. This, combined with the fact that it was still pouring down with rain, seemed to make Bull take on a new appearance. As he bent down to charge again, he started to exhale through his nose. As his hot breath hit the cold night air it looked as though steam was pouring out. Fox could clearly see another reason how Bull got his name. By now Bull was completely surrounded by a cloud of steam. Suddenly he charged six of the treedwellers all standing in a row. They didn't even see him coming. Their attention was still firmly fixed on the cloud of steam. The next thing they knew was Bull knocking the six of them over like a line of skittles.

Then the treedwellers attacked like a pack of wolves. Two or three jumped on Bull's back; he swung round and caught four sneaking up behind him. He put his head down, caught two of them with his horns. With the others on either shoulder he just kept going until he hit a tree. Their backs snapped like twigs and they fell to the ground. He then spun round and jammed his back against the tree. The creatures let out high-pitched squeals and released their grip. Two more attacked; Bull smacked them in the face with the side of his battleaxe and they fell backwards into the undergrowth. He then grabbed two more and banged their heads together. As they fell to the ground, he picked both of them up by their ankles and chucked them clear back to the treeline.

Fox watched as they attacked again and again. All that could be seen were treedwellers flying all over the place. They were hanging in trees, upside down in bushes, bodies lying all over the place. After seeing so many of their band thrown around like ragdolls, they decided enough was enough and beat a hasty retreat to the safety of the trees.

'Thank god you turned up, Bull. It's always nice to see family and I can't think of a time I've been more glad to see you, my dear cousin,' said Fox. He sat there with a big smile. Bull had changed a lot over the years since Fox had seen him last. His baby face was scarred and he had a couple of days' growth on his chin. His long blonde hair hung over his shoulders and needed washing.

'Looks like you've been travelling quite a long time,' said Fox.

'About a week,' Bull replied. He knelt down. His big muscular forearms were scratched and bleeding slightly. He held out his hand to Fox and pulled him up. 'It's good to see you, Fox, and I'm glad I could return the favour at long last. Every time you're in trouble I'm never around.

It's really great to see you.' He pulled Fox towards him, wrapped his arms around him and gave him a big hug. Now Fox's feet were off the ground; he heard his back cracking.

'Okay, Bull, you're happy to see me, but put me down - you're crushing me, you big lump,' said Fox.

'Oh, I'm sorry. Sometimes I forget how strong I am. I suppose you're still an old rebel. I could never understand why you lot call yourselves rebels,' added Bull.

'Well, actually, we didn't. We were called rebels by a nasty bit of homework called Badlock. He was our first ever fight. After that, any tinpot rulers called us that because we would not bow down to their authority and would always overthrow them. So it stuck. I suppose I was only sixteen when we faced Badlock - a long time ago.' Fox finished talking.

'So this is a treedweller. I always wondered what they looked like. I've never seen one before,' said Bull.

'Not many people have and lived to describe what they've seen,' replied Fox. Then both of them just stood looking at the creatures.

They were about four feet tall. On their heads were horns resembling a deer's antlers which, like everything else about them, were very woody. Their arms were very thin and branch-like. The fingers were very small and twiggy. The feet and legs were similar. The creature's face was very flat with the nose sunk into the skull - just a triangular hole, no flesh. The ears were just about visible, tiny holes set high on the head. The eyes were set deep into the head and as black as death itself. There was no emotion over the death of their comrades. They just walked away as if they didn't care at all. The wood seemed to have got darker now, if that was possible. Fox and Bull took one last look at the dead treedwellers.

'Now let's leave and quickly,' said Fox, and then asked: 'Where were you off to?'

'I was coming to see my favourite family member and to see Castlewood again,' replied Bull.

'Don't bother - there's nothing left. The dragons flattened the village completely and have taken the women and children away,' answered Fox.

'So what in hell's name are you doing here then?' Bull asked, looking puzzled.

'I'm looking for Oak the chippy so we can get our families back,' snapped Fox. Then he went on to ask why Bull was not in the north.

'Well, that's simple. It seemed the battle was over before it had begun. So I was at a loose end. But it looks like I've found myself another fight,' laughed Bull.

'I have no pay or goods to trade. Everything I owned went up with the village. I have nothing to give for your help.'

'I ask for nothing except the privilege of fighting by your side and paying the many debts I owe you,' Bull said with a smile on his face.

'Thanks, Bull, that means a lot to me. How's Patch?'

'He's fine,' replied Bull.

Fox called the dog to his side and patted him. 'There's a good boy. You fought well today. Right, let's go and find Oak and sort out these over-sized lizards.'

'I'll second that,' Bull chipped in.

The next village on the way was Waterdown but they wouldn't make it there tonight. It was far too late and dark;

besides the two were so tired. They came to a clearing at the end of the woods and just collapsed in a heap.

'I'm really hungry,' Bull said.

'It's a good job I found these earlier,' said Fox, pulling the two rabbits out of his bag. 'I'll get a fire going - you skin them.' A few minutes later Bull said: 'Done them - I'll put them on to cook now.' Fox watched Bull over the fire and noticed a large scar down his cheek.

'Where did you get that from?'

Bull put his hand to his face. 'Oh, that. I was in a brawl with six of the meanest-looking scumbags. Two of them held me and one cracked me in the face with a bullwhip. They thought it was quite funny, considering my name, but I tell you the laughing didn't last long. My three brothers came in and not one of them walked out after us.'

'So what started this fight?' asked Fox.

'Well, they were locals - they knew my family - so because I was on my own they started taking the mick. I sat and drank three or four pints and took the insults. Then they turned round and said my whole family were cowards and had no honour, especially that jumped-up so-called hero Fox who is just a little mummy's boy. By this time I was well drunk. I just stood up, picked up the chair I had been sitting on and smashed two of the men in the face. Then all hell broke loose. Two men jumped on the tables, then on my back. The two men I had hit got up and started to punch me in the stomach. I got my hands round the heads of the men on my back and slung them forward, landing them on the ones in front of me. Another dived at me from the bar. I caught him mid-air above my head and sent him crashing into some beer barrels, his weight breaking them open. He lay in the corner of the room in a crumpled heap with beer running down his face. The sixth man then ran at me, his head down, and hit me in the stomach. Of course I didn't even flinch. He looked up in amazement and fear. I grabbed him by the scruff of his shirt and punched him in the face, sending him sailing across the room to land on top of his mate in the beer barrels. I remember thinking to myself: 'That's over and done with,' when suddenly someone hit me on the back of the neck with a beer flagon, knocking me senseless, and the rest you know or can figure out.' Bull finished his story. 'So how come you've still got Patch? You've had him since you were a child, which means he's ancient,' laughed Bull.

'You cheeky sod, don't you remember Patch is a special breed? He will live as long as I do but as soon as I go, half an hour later tops, he's gone as well.' As Fox told the tale, Bull suddenly jumped to his feet.

'Dinner's ready - let's eat.'

'What a good idea.'

So they sat back and ate the rabbits. Fox shared his with Patch.

'I'm sore all over - I must get some sleep,' said Fox.

So they banked up the fire and settled down to some well-deserved rest. The rain was not coming down very hard now, just drizzle. It made no difference because they were so worn out. They all slept soundly knowing that no animals would come near the fire. Even Patch had a good night's sleep.

Chapter 4

The next morning when the sun had risen it was still misty and damp. Fox was woken by the dawn chorus of birds.

'Well, my friend, let's find Oak,' said Fox.

'What about breakfast?' moaned Bull.

'We'll get Hawk to cook us a big breakfast,' Fox replied.

So they set off towards Waterdown chatting and laughing on the way.

'So why are we going to Waterdown?' asked Bull.

'You mean, apart from filling your face with Hawk's breakfast? I know Oak was selling there and had some carpentry to do there too. Besides, Hawk lives there, as you already know.'

Then they spotted the village surrounded by mist. It looked so beautiful - a great expanse of water. In the middle was the village itself. The huts were on stilts so if the water rose the houses would be safe and the inhabitants would not get wet feet at least.

There were fishing nets hanging from the houses drying out. Through the mist they could see boats on the lake, with people fishing from the sides. Then Fox spotted Hawk and her son Colt. He waved at the pair of them. They looked puzzled - they didn't recognise him from that distance. So Fox and Bull started to walk towards the village, closely followed by Patch. Then they stepped onto the mighty drawbridge which in times of trouble was pulled across to a small island halfway between the shore and the village. Even if anyone got there it was still a long swim for a would-be invader, let alone a whole army in full armour. It would also be very easy to pick soldiers off as they swam nearer the island.

But Waterdown was a fishing village, as you may have already figured out for yourself. It had no great riches and was not a military stronghold - just a beautiful and peaceful village where everyone who lived there was content with life just as it was.

Into the village the three of them marched. Hawk then recognised Fox and Bull and ran towards them.

'Fox, my dear brother, it's great to see you,' she cried as she threw herself into his arms and hugged him.

'Be careful, sweetheart, I ache all over.'

'Who's looking after the children?' Hawk asked.

'As it happens, the dragons are,' replied Fox.

'What do you mean?' said Hawk, and her voice and body seemed to strain with anger.

'So how about some breakfast?' asked Bull.

'Still thinking of your stomach first, I see, Bull,' Hawk laughed. 'I'll make breakfast and you can tell me what's going on.'

'Sounds like a good idea to me,' said Bull.

'Before you do, is there anywhere I can have a wash? I smell of death and BO,' said Fox.

So Hawk led them to a natural waterfall in the middle of the village. Fox pushed his head into the cool clear water as it bubbled up from the rocks. He took his shirt off.

'Oh, my god, Fox, you've taken one hell of a beating.' His back was covered in cuts and bruises. Hawk placed her hand on his back and he flinched.

'I'm sorry - turn round.' His chest and stomach were in the same condition. What happened to your neck?'

'Nothing - just a glancing blow from a battleaxe.' Fox sat down at the edge of the waterfall and Hawk tore up some rag and cleaned his wounds. Fox watched the stream in between his legs turn red as Hawk rinsed the rag out.

'You need someone to look after you,' Hawk said.

'Got anyone in mind?' asked Fox.

'I'm sure I could find plenty of candidates.'

'I haven't time to think of that at this moment. I've got to get the children back. If I'm still here when we've succeeded, we will talk again.'

'I still can't believe that evil sod the Dragon King has stolen your babies.' Hawk was now nearly in tears.

'Believe it, it's true.'

Hawk made breakfast and all four of them sat down. Fox told of the battle at Castlewood. The other two listened intently to the story.

'Patch looks well, so I must assume you are fit, apart from your battle scars.'

'Yes, health-wise I'm fine, Hawk, thanks,' said Fox.

'So how does she work out that you're well because the dog looks fine?' asked Bull.

'Well, remember what I told you about Patch living as long as I do?'

'Yes,' said Bull.

'Well, you see, he can live so long because he draws his life energy from me. So when I'm ill, so is he. That's why he needs plenty of physical contact - to draw off the energy he needs. I don't know, but I suppose he could draw it off other people as well,' explained Fox.

Hawk walked off to do something in the house and left Fox and Bull to chat amongst themselves. Fox started to talk about Hawk.

'When it comes to a fight, Hawk could match anyone I know, including you. She's a nasty little bitch when provoked. She beat me a couple of times but mostly she wins by the tongue-lashing she gives her opponents.'

Hawk came back. 'Talking about me, were we?'

'Only the good things about you, flower. So where's Oak hiding himself?'

'He's not here.'

'What do you mean, he's not here? Where's he gone now?'

'He's gone back home - he forgot his tools,' said Hawk.

'The dozy little wood gnome. How come we missed him?'

'He went out the back way by boat. Someone told him a big hardwood tree had come down. He went to look at it. You know what he's like,' said Hawk.

'Yes, unfortunately I do. Look, I hate to eat and run, but we must catch up with him,' said Fox.

'Wait for me - I'll come with you.'

'What about Cat and Colt?'

'Don't worry, Cat's not here. And Colt can go to Mum's,' said Hawk.

'I don't want you along. It's going to be very bloody and a lot of people won't come back,' said Fox.

'That's not fair - I've never let you down. I'm as good as you or anyone else you can scrounge up. Besides, you're going to need everybody you can lay your hands on. Please, Fox, they're my blood too. And I do love them so, as if they were my own. I want to see their faces when we save them. Hang on, why the hell am I pleading with you? I'm coming with you or I will just follow,' Hawk concluded.

'Now that sounds more like the Hawk we all know and love. I'm just glad you're so confident,' said Fox.

So Hawk went to her mother's to see if the old lady would look after Colt.

'Of course I will. It's always nice to look after him. He's company for me.' Then she spotted Fox standing behind Hawk. 'Oh, Fox, my son, come here. Give your mum a cuddle. Where are your children?'

'It's a long story and I haven't the time. Hawk will tell you.' So Fox went to see what Bull was up to while Hawk explained about the children.

Colt saw Bull's battleaxe. 'Can I pick it up, please?' the boy asked.

'If you can,' Bull said with a smile, knowing full well the boy wouldn't be able to. Colt took hold of the handle and strained but could not move it. So he sat and looked at the black handle which was five foot long, covered in leather and had studs all the way up. Both the blades gleamed in the sunlight. The boy just looked in amazement at the lethal weapon and then asked: 'Do you really fight with this, Bull?'

'Of course.'

'So what weapons do you use, Uncle Fox?'

'I have three weapons: my bow and arrows, my sword and my dog,' Fox replied.

'Can I see your sword, Uncle?'

'Yes, but don't push the fox's head on the hilt,' Fox told him - but too late. The boy had pushed the button and a blade sprang from the hilt narrowly missing his throat.

'So who are you going to fight this time, Uncle?' Colt enquired.

'Well, this time it's the Dragon King.'

'What's he like?' the boy asked.

'Well, the king is about ten feet tall and stands upright like you and me. He is the most evil and mean creature living and he eats little boys like you for breakfast. His foot soldiers are about eight feet tall, green with red blotches all over them, one great big horn and they smell awful. All of them are fire-breathers and have quite a long range. Then there are the flying dragons. They are the worst to fight, although they are smaller at six feet. They work as a team: one distracts you while the other attacks - a pretty lethal combination.' Just as Fox finished talking, Hawk reappeared. She was wearing bright orange armour and a round shield hung over her arm. Her brown hair was cut short. Her big brown eyes sparked with a sense of excitement. She looked as though she could handle herself, which was very true.

'Well,' said Bull, 'they couldn't miss you.'

'Well, if you've got it, why not flaunt it?' Hawk picked up her weapons and added: 'Well, are you coming or not?'

'Yes, of course.'

'Then pick up your gear and let's get going.'

So Fox picked up his bow and put it on his back. Then his white shield which had a bright red fox painted on it. He pushed the blade back into the hilt of his sword. By this time Bull had his battleaxe in his hand and his shield on his arm and was ready to go.

Colt said: 'You will be back, won't you, Mum?'

Fox reassured him. 'I promise she will be, and I never break a promise.'

'Thank you, Uncle,' Colt said.

Then from behind came Fox's mother. 'Fox, my son, come back safe with the children. And, boy, keep your little sister safe and return her to me.'

'Yes, Mother, I promise either to bring her back or send her, one or the other. How can you call me 'boy'? I'm in my forties, for God's sake,' said Fox.

'Because you'll always be my little boy.'

Bull started to laugh. 'Mummy's little boy.'

'I don't know what you're laughing about. Come here and give your aunty a kiss.'

'That brought you down a peg or two, you smart arse,' said Fox.

'You're not going to attempt a rescue with just you three and Oak, are you?' asked Hen.

'No, of course not. What kind of a fool do you take me for? Don't answer that,' said Fox. 'You can see how Mum got her name - always fussing over children like a mother hen. Look, we must go. We haven't got time to mess about any more. Say your goodbyes and let's get going.'

So Hawk kissed her son goodbye and caught up with the others. Colt shouted: 'Remember your promise, Uncle Fox!'

'I will, boy, I will.'

Now they were on their way at last. 'Let's move it and catch Oak.' As they walked along, Patch started to growl.

'What in hell's name is that?'

In a clearing stood a jet black unicorn and on his back sat a little man. He had long black hair which was flecked with grey. His long black beard hung down to his waist. In his hand he held a staff. It had a unicorn's head on top. The horn of the living creature looked quite a lethal weapon, as well as being magical.

As they drew closer the man jumped down from his mount. The suddenness of his movements made the rebels jump back in surprise. Bull shouted: 'What's your problem?'

'I have no problem, unlike you,' said the man.

Hawk retorted: 'And what's our problem, then?'

'You are going the wrong way,' said the man.

'You don't even know where we are going. So how do you know we are going the wrong way? And, for your information, we are not,' replied Hawk.

'Are you not going to Castlewood?'

'Yes, that's right,' answered Fox.

'I know everything about this area,' the man said.

'Is that so? Then which way is Castlewood?' Hawk snapped harshly.

'Well, well - um.' The man was stumped.

'You see, you don't know everything, do you,' said Hawk.

'Maybe not, but this I do know: that path leads to nothing but trouble.'

'And what path is that, pray tell,' said Fox.

'The path of revenge brings nothing but death and destruction and many of your party will be slain on the battlefield,' said the man.

'What's it got to do with you? Go stuff it in your ear,' said Bull.

So he jumped back onto his mount, then the pair of them disappeared.

'I wonder if he does that often - I bet it makes his eyes water,' laughed Bull.

Meanwhile, back in the dungeon in the dragons' castle, the prisoners were not finding life to their liking. Badger as she was known because she kept badgering everybody, was Fox's youngest daughter and she had been making trouble. She had bitten one of the dragons because when he brought the bread in he had said that the so-called leader of Castlewood had run away and hidden himself which

Badger knew was not true because she and her brothers had seen their father fall in battle. She told him so and added: 'At least my father was there, unlike your cowardly King.' The other prisoners clapped and cheered, but the cheering didn't last long.

Just as she had finished speaking the dragon punched her in the face blacking one of her eyes and breaking her front teeth. Unfortunately her sister Sunny had also been punished for Badger's rebellious behaviour. Sunny was sitting in the corner of the cell weeping and nursing two broken ribs. It was damp and cold. It was difficult to find a place to sit without getting drops of water falling on you. What straw there was on the floor was wet and smelly. The bread was rock hard and stale; the water tasted disgusting. Everybody was miserable which was not surprising considering their surroundings.

Elk was cuddling her son Mole, who by now was very ill. The first part of the infection had set in and he had a very high fever. The next step was death. Elk shouted: 'Guard, guard!' The guard opened the door.

'What do you want?'

'My son is going to die if he does not get help soon,' cried Elk.

'So let him. Just one less to feed. You're all scum anyway.' Then he slammed the door shut again.

Suddenly Sunny burst into floods of tears. 'Why did they kill our dad and all the other men?'

'I don't know, sweetheart, no-one here does,' replied Elk.

'Do you think they got Uncle Oak?'

'I don't think so,' Elk answered.

'If they didn't, do you think he will be able to get us out of here?' asked Badger.

'I do hope so. I don't know how long Mole can hang on,' their aunty answered.

'Uncle Oak will really give that Dragon King a good beating when he gets hold of him, won't he?' said Wildcat.

'Yes, of course he will, you know Uncle Oak,' Elk replied.

'Do you think our dad is really dead?' asked the children.

'Yes, I'm afraid so,' Elk told them.

'Will we ever get out of here?' Sunny asked.

'I'm sure we will,' said Elk.

'We will when we've finished our tunnel.'

'Yes, boys,' said their aunty, wishing it were that simple. The boys started to talk amongst themselves.

'Hey, Jage, what are you going to do when we get out of here?' said Wildcat.

'The first thing I'm going to do is go back to Castlewood and get Dad's armour, sword and shield and keep our promise to him.'

'Me too,' said the youngest boy, Sky.

'I want Dad's sword,' said Wildcat.

'No, I said first,' Jage shouted at his brother.

'I'd just like Dad back,' said Sky, beginning to cry.

'Don't cry,' Badger said, cuddling her brother.

'Why don't you dig your hole?' said Elk.

'We can't,' said the boys.

'Why not?' Elk enquired.

'Because the rats are in it.'

'Oh, I'll get them out,' said Badger, and she threw them out.

'Thank you,' said the boys.

'Let's get on with it and get out of here,' said Wildcat.

'The sooner the better,' said Jage.

Sunny said: 'It's horrible here - I hope we get out soon.'

'So do I,' said Elk.

Fox and the others got to the edge of the wood and saw a short stocky figure. He had long hair and straight down the middle of his head was a blonde streak. On his back was a tool chest. In his right hand he held a staff. On his left arm he had a tattoo of a tree.

'Where did he get his tattoo from?' asked Bull.

'It's a birth mark - all the people of his tribe are born with the mark of the tree.' His face was that of a young man, not a man of his years. 'That's another trait - they don't age very quickly. So, enough about his background - let's catch up with him.'

Oak had just about reached the middle of the woods. The others watched him strolling along without a care in the world, then from nowhere hordes of the treedwellers jumped out at him.

'Oh, so you want to play, do you?' Oak raised his staff and just to confuse the poor creatures totally he sang a little ditty: 'Wood, wood, do these creatures good.' Then, without another word, he cracked one under the chin, then swept the legs of another away and it crashed to the ground with a bump. One of the creatures pushed a trident at Oak, slicing his arm.

'You little sod!' he shouted, then smacked it round the back of the head. 'That's three down and far too many to go.' So he raised his staff to eye level and said: 'Look - my impression of a windmill.' Then he spun his staff round in front of him. The creatures were again hypnotised. He suddenly brought the staff up fast and caught two of them under the chin.

The treedwellers decided that they had had enough of Oak's games. Three of them grabbed the staff from behind his back and hung on for dear life. Oak didn't have enough strength to pull them over. Then one, unfortunately for Oak, grabbed his leg, overbalancing him, then crash all of them fell in a big heap of arms and legs. The others just stood there and laughed.

'Don't you think we should help him?' asked Bull.

'No, let's wait and see what happens next,' replied Hawk. So Fox took an arrow from his quiver and placed it in the bow, just in case it became necessary to use it. A treedweller pinned one of Oak's arms down with a trident, then the other arm and finally his legs. He was as helpless as a newborn baby.

It was now the creatures' turn to have fun with Oak, prodding him with their tridents and making him jump and squirm like mad.

'Let me up, you little hobgoblins!' The creatures seemed to understand what Oak was saying, which puzzled him because he could not make head or tail of their squeaks and whistles and a sort of rasping sound. They seemed very put out by what Oak was saying.

Just then, one of the creatures raised his trident above Oak's neck. He was just about to strike when Fox said: 'It's time.'

'For what?' asked Hawk.

Pulling back on his bow, Fox released the arrow. It flew straight and true, hitting the creature so hard that it knocked the treedweller sideways and killed him instantly.

'For that. Oak's had enough,' said Fox. 'Now we go and get Oak out of his problem. Bull and I will start with that lot.'

Then the creatures charged towards Bull and Fox. Fox dropped his bow and took his sword out. Two went for Fox. They rammed their tridents towards him. He knocked one trident aside with his shield. Then he cut the top off the other one. He said to the creature: 'You're unarmed - now sling your hook before I have to hurt you.' The treedweller looked surprised. He ran at Fox who just blocked him with his shield. The creature bounced off and Fox kicked him up the backside; then it ran off.

Two of the treedwellers charged Bull. He stopped them in their tracks by taking hold of their tridents and lifting them straight into the air. He just stood there smiling at the creatures dangling on the end of their own weapons, just like a pair of fish on a hook. Bull then put them back on the ground. The creatures started to pull backwards with all their might. Bull shouted to Fox: 'Look at this!' As Fox looked over, a trident sliced his ear. 'Thanks, Bull.'

'Sorry, mate.' Fox raised his sword above the tridents and Bull nodded his head and shouted 'Now!' Fox brought his sword down slicing the heads of the tridents off. The treedwellers fell backwards.

Suddenly, from the trees, creatures fell like rain straight on top of Bull and Fox. Even Bull could not take all that weight on him. His legs buckled and he hit the ground with a thud. Patch bounced over and jumped on the creatures, pulling at their legs.

Bull said: 'I don't think this peaceful approach is working.'

'No, I don't think it is,' replied Fox. 'So let's get tough.'

Just then Hawk came up and stuck her tomahawk into the back of one of the treedwellers. Then Oak smashed one round the back of the head with his staff. Bull managed to get to his feet, then just started to pick up treedwellers and throw them one after the other. Fox dropped his sword and started to push them and hit them with his shield. Then he told Patch not to kill, just to wound. Hawk started to hit them with the side of her tomahawk.

The creatures got fed up with going backwards and forwards like a yo-yo, so they withdrew and disappeared back to the safety of the trees. The rebels straightened up and dusted themselves down.

'So what took you three so long?' said Oak.

'Nothing, we've been here for ages,' said Hawk.

'You mean to tell me you watched me struggle and get myself humiliated and did not lift a finger to help?' shouted Oak.

'We thought you were enjoying yourself. Anyway, we were,' said Fox.

'Ha bloody ha. I don't think it's very funny,' replied Oak.

'You didn't see yourself like we did - stranded like a turtle upside down,' laughed Bull. 'Now for the bad news.'

'What's that, then?' asked Oak.

Hawk continued: 'Well, Castlewood has been flattened and Elk and Mole have been taken prisoner.'

'And how do you know this?' asked Oak.

'Fox was there.'

'Is that right? Then why didn't you protect your sister, for God's sake?'

'Now look here, I've lost my children. All the people that were not taken prisoner were killed. They took everything - the horses, weapons, clothes, food - everything,' said Fox.

'Then how come you're still alive - did you run away and hide?' said Oak.

'Now just take a look at my head - does that look like I cut myself shaving? There are twelve stitches in there - I know, I put them in myself. If you had been at the village, you would be dead too,' added Fox.

'Yes, of course I would,' said Oak.

'That's enough - you know Fox better than that,' said Hawk.

'Oh, do I?' said Oak.

'No, let him get it off his chest,' said Fox. 'I'm only here because after I was hit I became unconscious and they didn't check on whether I was dead or alive. Look, the Dragon King's got our families, so let's do something about it.'

Suddenly Oak smashed his staff onto Fox's head.

'I'm going to kill you.' Bull went to strike Oak.

'No, let him finish me off,' said Fox. 'Here, Oak, use my sword - but if you do you can say goodbye to my children and your family. No-one will help you when they find out you killed me for being the only survivor of a massacre which was none of my doing.'

Oak raised Fox's sword and was just about to strike when he saw the blood running down Fox's face: his head wound had opened up from Oak's blow. Then suddenly the blood just poured down Fox's face. Bull could no longer stand and watch Fox being humiliated in this way. He rugby-tackled Oak to the floor, then punched him on the nose. Sitting on Oak's legs, Bull pulled him up and punched him repeatedly. By now Oak's face was a mess with blood everywhere. Bull pulled his head back then lurched forward, head-butting Oak on the bridge of the nose, at the same time releasing his grip on Oak's body. Oak flopped to the ground, his body lifeless, just twitching. Bull then stuck his fingers behind Oak's windpipe and started to squeeze. Oak's face started to turn blue.

'Leave him, Bull,' Fox shouted.

'What do you mean, leave him - the ungrateful fat sod. You owe Fox your life and an apology,' said Bull. 'You have no honour, so it's not worth you going on with life.'

Bull then lost his temper completely and was shaking Oak, still hanging on to his windpipe, and slapping him round the face.

'You're scum - dirt - and I'm going to kill you,' Bull said.

Fox could do nothing to help because he could not see, as blood was continuously running into his eyes. 'For God's sake, stop him. He's going to kill Oak,' said Fox.

'Hawk said: 'What can I do?'

'Are you a warrior or not?'

'Yes.'

'Well, don't you know how to stop someone without killing them?' said Fox.

'Of course I do. What kind of a fool do you take me for?' replied Hawk.

'Well then, do it and quickly, before he kills Oak,' said Fox.

So Hawk walked calmly up to Bull and, without any emotion at all, kicked him straight in the mouth. As he went back, she kicked him in between the legs. He then fell forwards. As he did so Hawk held her shield in front of his head and pushed his head at the same time, bang his head hit with such force that he was dazed. Then she put one knee into the small of his back, grabbed his long blonde hair and pulled him backwards. She took out her dagger and put it to his throat.

'Calm down,' she said, 'or I'll slit your throat. I mean it, Bull - listen to me. We need Oak - he lost his rag in the heat of the moment, that's all. We can't afford to lose either of you now.'

'Bull, keep still or she will do it,' said Fox.

After about five minutes Bull calmed down.

Oak was not with it. Bull had given him a hiding. He had blood all over his face.

'Well, have you had enough?' asked Bull.

'Yes, I don't think I want any more - my body couldn't take it. Thanks, Hawk - if you had not stopped him he would have killed me,' said Oak.

'Don't thank me. I would have been quite happy to see Bull kill you for what you said and did to Fox. I did as my big brother told me to. It must be for the first time,' said Hawk. Then she looked round at Bull. 'Are you all right?'

'Yes, I've got my breath back now, thanks,' Bull replied. They turned to look at Fox. The blood was still pouring out. He had slipped into unconsciousness.

Hawk said: 'He's lost a hell of a lot of blood. He can't move but we can't stay. If the treedwellers attack again, we can't fight them off and protect Fox. They will kill him where he sits, an easy target.' Patch was sitting next to his master, looking worried.

'But Patch would fight to the death before he'd let anyone hurt Fox,' said Bull.

'Yes, but that's not the point: if they came back, they'd take Patch, no trouble.'

'Look, we have to get out of these woods.'

'Yes. Bull, take some of the smaller trees down. Oak, you're responsible for this whole mess. You can make a stretcher for Fox and if he dies you'd better leave the whole of this land, because there will be nowhere to hide from me or my family. I swear this on my son's life and on my honour.'

'I just saw red. I didn't mean to hurt him. I didn't know he had a wound,' said Oak.

'You're lucky he has a heart of gold. Otherwise he would have killed you dead,' said Hawk. 'He saved your life twice today and this is what he gets for his trouble,' she continued.

'The stretcher's done. Bull, can you manage to pull Fox and his gear on your own?'

'Of course I can,' said Bull. 'Oak, help me put Fox on the stretcher.' So Hawk and Oak placed Fox on the stretcher. It pulled Bull backwards slightly. Then they put his weapons on and of course he was still in full armour. Then to their surprise Patch jumped onto the stretcher and cuddled up to his master.

'Is he all right on there, or do you want me to get him off?' asked Hawk.

'No, if it makes him more comfortable and at ease, then let him stay. Perhaps he will give Fox the strength to carry on,' said Bull.

'Right, let's get going. Oak, you get out front and take any flak that's coming our way,' said Hawk.

So they slowly and cautiously moved up the main track.

'Can we walk a little faster? The sooner we are out of here, the better I'll like it. When we get to the end we can rest,' said Hawk.

Halfway along the track the light at the end of the trees was getting closer, but not fast enough for Hawk's liking. By now Bull was getting very weary. He was beginning to feel every bump in the track and every little jolt seemed to pull him back. Fox's body seemed to have doubled in weight.

'Please, Fox, hang on. I won't let you down. I would pull you all round this land if that's what it takes. So don't you dare let me down. I haven't dragged you all this way for you to die on me.'

The end of the trees was getting nearer and nearer with every step, but to Bull it seemed like miles away. The sweat was pouring off his head and his hair was soaking wet. Hawk was now on edge, seeing things that were not there and jumping at snapping twigs or the slightest sound.

Oak was way ahead of the others, thinking 'If only I had not hit Fox, we could have been out of here ages ago. What's going to happen if Fox dies? How will I ever live with myself after all Fox and his family have done for me over the years?' Even if he got his family back he could no longer live in Castlewood - he would be an outcast. He didn't even know whether Elk would want him after killing her brother. And, if she did, she and Mole would have no home, no tribe or family. Hawk would hound him to the ends of the earth and kill him if she could. He knew this was true because she had sworn so on her son's life and her honour. She could not go back on this for she would no longer be able to call herself a warrior with honour. Without that you are nothing, thought Oak, and this is what he would be - nothing - which means no self-respecting person would talk to him or have anything to do with him. He would be destined to wander this beautiful land forever, never being able to settle anywhere, just continually on the move. There would be no great battlefield when he died, only men with honour may spend eternity there. He was to spend it as he had spent his life, forever wandering.

At last they came to the end of the wood. They took the stretcher from Bull's back, sat down and breathed a sigh of relief. They were only two feet away from the woods but it was enough: the treedwellers did not consider it their territory, because it was not surrounded by trees.

Just as they had relaxed fully, Hawk looked at Fox. 'If Fox pulls through, it's going to take quite a few days. But by the looks of him he is done for.'

Just then, in a puff of smoke, the strange little man appeared again. Oak was just about to hit him on the head when Hawk shouted: ' Don't - he's harmless.'

'Thank you, milady. You do know of course you will never defeat the Dragon King,' said the little man.

'And, just out of interest, how do you know?' said Bull.

'Because I know all you know,' he answered.

'Oh, is that right?' snapped Hawk. 'Why don't you go away and hinder someone else?'

Just before going, he saw Fox slumped against a tree.

'He's hurt,' the man said.

'So what's it to you?' said Bull.

The little man went up to Fox, put his hand on the wound and whispered something. Then in a puff of smoke he disappeared again.

Suddenly Fox opened his eyes and said: 'What's going on here?'

'He's awake! Where's his wound gone? There's no more blood.' Hawk was amazed.

'How in hell's name did he do that? I didn't know Fox was magical,' said Bull.

'He's not, as far as I know,' said Hawk. 'It must have been the little man.'

'Well, are we going to get our families back now?' asked Oak.

'We can't,' said Fox.

'Have you lost your bottle?' queried Oak.

'Look, don't start that again, or this time I'm going to hurt you,' said Fox. 'We must get some more warriors and I know just where to get them,' he continued.

'He is right, Oak,' said Bull. 'If we go now they will just cut us down like dogs. It would be a futile gesture and would not get your families back. Look, let's get out of here and make camp where Castlewood used to stand, then get off in the morning.'

'Sounds good to me,' Fox agreed.

'Who was the little man?' asked Oak.

'I don't know, but I do know he will be back just when we don't want him,' said Hawk.

So they started off towards Castlewood. It did not take them long to get there.

'Oh, my God, it is in a state, isn't it? Look at the outer walls - what did that?' asked Bull.

'Storm-makers. They as good as just walked through them as if they were made of cardboard. We lost a hell of a lot of men from that coming down on top of them, crushing them to death,' said Fox. 'So, less chat - let's make camp. I'm starving.'

Oak collected firewood together, took out his fire stones and lit the fire.

'So what have we get to eat, then?' asked Oak.

'There's some roast chicken, bread and mixed veggies in the bag, and some wine.'

Then Hawk said: 'We can't leave these bodies here.

'It's going to take forever to dig graves for all these men,' said Bull.

'We will burn them,' said Fox.

'We can't - the dragons will see the smoke,' Bull pointed out.

'It does not matter,' Fox replied. 'The village has been burning since yesterday. If more smoke and flames go up they will just think that something else has started to burn. And, if they don't, they will realise they've got trouble coming their way. Either way I don't care. But you leave the dragon to the birds. Don't bother to move any of those evil green lumps.'

So they started to collect the bodies and pile them up on the funeral fire.

'There's some oil in barrels round behind the meeting hall,' said Fox. Bull came back with the oil. 'Come on, pour it over the bodies. Let's get it done.'

So Bull, Hawk and Fox poured the oil on the funeral fire.

'Now set it alight.'

The flames shot up in the air lighting the sky with a blood-red glow. The air was filled with the smell of burning flesh. The three just stood and watched as the bodies burned.

'How did it happen?' asked Bull. 'The village had such a good reputation for being unbeatable.'

'Well, it's like this. The whole village was asleep, for starters. We had no idea there was any trouble between us and the dragons, not even a cross word. The watch saw columns of dust and could not at first identify them. We were not sure whether it was that herd of wild horses or not. By the time we found out it was not, it was too late - they were on us. The first wave was made up of flying dragons; then, as we started to push them back, the second wave - the storm-makers - just smashed the walls down and we lost half our men in one fell swoop. Then the foot soldiers finished us.'

While the others were talking and clearing up the mess, Oak was sitting by the fire thinking of how he could make up for what he had said and done to Fox and how he could get his family back. Suddenly he heard a spine-chilling howling noise coming from the darkness all around. Then he thought he could hear the sound of bushes rustling and twigs snapping. He turned but could see nothing.

'Oh, very funny, you three. All right, come out - the game's up.' But there was no reply. Then there was a crack and a rustle; Oak turned round and a horrified look came onto his face. There standing in front of him was a giant hound whose favourite meal was anything that vaguely resembled a human being. Then it purred, which was not a good sign at all, its back went up and it prepared to pounce. Oak turned to get his staff but was not quick enough. The creature sunk its teeth into his arm.

The houndcat never killed its victims outright, it just tore pieces off, in case it never got to finish its meal. Then at least it would have had a snack. Oak didn't stand much chance: it stood as tall as a small horse and had teeth like a sabre-toothed tiger. It was called a houndcat because, although it was a cat-like creature, its kind ran in packs like fox hounds.

The creature had got a really good grip on Oak and was ripping flesh from his arm. Blood was spraying into Oak's face as he screamed in agony. The houndcat just ignored the screams. Oak could do nothing to protect himself. Then another howl went out: the rest of the pack was coming.

'This is it,' thought Oak.

Then from the clearing came Fox. 'Oh, my god,' he said. Hawk ran over, jumped on the creature's back and started to hack at it with her tomahawk. The creature hissed and squawked but would not let go. Bull swung his battleaxe round striking the houndcat on the back. It released its grip and Fox pulled Oak clear of the creature's jaws. Bull brought his battleaxe up, catching it in the throat and killing it outright.

Then Fox picked up his bow and fired arrows into the darkness, hitting houndcats until they gave up and left the area.

'What were they doing coming so close to the fire? It's not like them,' said Bull.

'They probably could not resist the smell of death,' Fox replied. 'Sometimes that smell makes them braver than normal.'

'Look at Oak - he's got no flesh left from his shoulder down to his wrist. And look at the blood,' said Hawk. 'It's everywhere - he can't have much left in his body.'

Then the other two looked at Fox. 'You know what's got to be done,' they said.

So Fox knelt down in the puddles of blood.

'Well, Oak, you've had it. You know I can't lie to you. What are your last words?'

'Tell Elk I did try to free her and I love her and Mole.'

Then there was a big bang and smoke filled the air around them.

'Stop! Let me help you,' said the little man.

'And what can you do?' snapped Hawk.

'I can sort that out, no problem,' he replied.

'There's nothing you can do,' said Bull.

'Let me try. What have you got to lose?' said the man.

'Nothing, I suppose,' admitted Fox.

Then the little man went over to Oak and placed his hands over Oak's arm.

'What are you doing?' asked Bull.

'Just wait and see, oh giant one.' Then he chanted: 'Back, back, flesh grow back, take this healing from Tac, make this limb strong and right and ready for the next fight.'

Then there was a flash and a bang and to everybody's amazement the flesh started to grow back as Tac moved his hands down the limb.

Oak came round. 'What's going on? My arm's back in one piece. Who's responsible for this miracle?'

'I am,' said the little man.

'And who exactly are you?' queried Oak.

'I, Sir, am Tac, Keeper of the Unicorns.'

'So how can I ever repay you for your service?' asked Oak.

'Well, Sirs, I would be honoured to help defeat the Dragon King.'

'If that's all, then let it be done,' said Oak.

'So sit down and join us round the fire. Have something to eat and drink and tell us about yourself,' said Hawk.

'What would you like to know, milady?'

'Well, for starters, why would you want to fight the dragons?' said Fox.

'It's a long story, Sir,' said Tac.

'Then begin now,' said Fox.

'Well, it started about ten years ago. I was the Keeper of the Unicorns then. It was a large herd and I was responsible for protecting them from harm and evil doers, which I did for many years. I also had a wife and children. The unicorn is a very magical beast and in the wrong hands can be dangerous. The unicorns lived on the Great Plains and my family used to have a home in the foothills. The animals would come up to me and feed from my hands. They had no fear of me. When they were injured they would come and I would heal them with this - it's magical.'

He held up a long, thin, whitish cone.

'What is it?' asked Bull.

'It's a unicorn's horn. That's how I healed your friends' wounds. Going back to what I was saying,' said Tac, 'one day while I was sitting watching the herd of unicorns I turned round to see smoke coming from my settlement. So I jumped onto the back of one of the creatures and rode towards the smoke. The Dragon King was standing there with my wife and children. As I dismounted one of the dragons attacked me from behind. So I made my staff disappear, so they could not get their hands on it. Then the most horrible sound I have ever heard filled the air - the sound of the unicorns screaming as the dragons slaughtered them. Then the sky went dark, lightning flashed and rain began to fall. All you could hear were the creatures screaming and the crash of thunder. The Dragon King said: 'Tell me the secret of the Horn.' 'No, I can't,' I replied. 'Then I shall kill your children first, then your wife, then you,' said the King. 'Don't tell them, Tac,' my wife said. 'If you do, our world will come to an end as we know it. Let them kill us. You must not betray the trust the unicorns have in you.'

'So I went to the great herd of unicorns and shouted: 'Go, my friends - scatter yourselves to the four corners of the earth. You must leave this place: it is no longer safe for you. Never again can you gather in such numbers in one place.' Then I returned to my settlement to find my wife dead and my children with their throats slit. It was too late for them. I had chosen to keep my word to my beautiful unicorns, but in the process I lost my lovely family and my wonderful herd of unicorns. Never again would I see them playing together, but at least they were safe and would live on in peace.

'I returned to the Great Plains. There in the dust lay nearly a hundred unicorns, dead and dying. I did what I could for some and stopped the hearts of the ones that I couldn't help. It left me with nothing in my heart but hate and the thought of revenge. I cannot live or die until I have settled with the Dragon King,' concluded Tac.

'It's a sad tale, and no mistake,' said Hawk.

'You have every right to join us and we would be most grateful for your help,' said Fox. 'So, Bull, how come you're here?' he added.

Oak put more wood on the fire and settled down to hear Bull's story.

'I was fighting the Sand People in the North,' began Bull.

'The Sand People are a peaceful people,' said Fox.

'They were until some greedy traders stole the statue of their god. Then they stopped traders crossing the desert which meant that it would take them two weeks to get from one market to another,' explained Bull.

'You attacked them for that? It was their territory - they have the right,' Fox said.

'No. That was not the reason. First they took the village called The Dunes, then they went on to The Palms. They killed everyone and every thing. They had to be stopped. So the army moved into the desert for the showdown. Then from the top of the dunes appeared the Sand People, weapons raised, ready to kill. We formed a line, then the Sand People charged down the hill onto our lines. The battle had begun. Swords drawn, we began slashing and slicing. The Sand People were getting bloodied and so were we.

'Then from the hills a shower of spears came raining down on us. After that, from the side, came a rider holding a white flag. Behind him he had another horse and two prisoners were being dragged behind the horse. They looked badly beaten. The rider announced: 'A present for you, the Sand People.' The fighting suddenly stopped. The leader of the Sand People said: 'And what's that?' 'It's the two no-good scumbags who started this war. Here is your idol and the two responsible for taking it,' said the rider. 'Thank you, we accept your gifts with many thanks,' said the leader of the Sand People. 'You can't hand us over to them - they will kill us,' protested the two men. 'Tough - you should have thought of that before you stole their god and before all these people had been killed,' said the rider.

'The two men dropped to their knees. 'Please don't leave us with them.' The rider turned round to move away, then looked back at the leader of the Sand People. 'I assume there is no further need for these men to be here?' 'No,' said the leader. 'And the desert will be a safe place from now on?' asked the rider. 'You have my word on that,' said the leader of the Sand People.

'Both armies turned and marched away, the prisoners screaming as they were dragged behind the Sand People.

Then it was all over, so I came to find out what you were up to - and here I am,' Bull finished.

'Well, I think that's enough story-telling for one night,' said Fox. 'Let's get some sleep.'

So they settled down to sleep. It was quiet now, the only sound was the funeral fires crackling as they continued to burn.

Chapter 5

Morning came round all too quickly. They ate and then left the remains of Castlewood. Now they were five rebels. Their aim was to find more fighters for their quest to save their families. So they headed away from the dragons' castle and went to find more rebels at Scrapford.

'Come on, let's run,' said Hawk.

'You have got to be joking,' replied Bull.

'No, come on,' said Fox. So they set off at a jog.

Scrapford was as it sounds: somewhere where people take broken and old things to be turned into something else, mainly metal, but almost anything would be accepted. The village had many steel forges and its inhabitants were master weapon makers. The whole village was fenced in by piles of scrap metal. Fox's and Hawk's big brother was chief, and his name was Old Grey Bear. He lived there with his wife and four children. It was three miles from where Castlewood used to stand.

Soon they saw the gates of Scrapford.

'It's a long time since I've been here,' said Hawk.

'Me too,' said Fox.

'Hullo, little brother, how are you?' greeted Old Grey Bear.

'Not so good,' replied Fox.

'What's going on here? Haven't you got homes to go to?' said Old Grey Bear.

'No, as a matter of fact we haven't,' snapped Fox.

'What you are going on about now,' asked Old Grey Bear.

'The dragons attacked and destroyed everything and everyone except me,' Fox explained.

'Oh, my! Talk about putting my foot in it.'
'We are looking for fighters. Are you in?'
'I would if I could, but I have a family.'
'So did I,' taunted Fox.

Hawk added: 'He's your brother, his children are slaves to the dragons and you are not prepared to lift a finger to help your own family. You should be ashamed of yourself! You're not safe, the dragons are on the march. No-one will be safe from their greed for power and riches. If you don't help now, you might not get the chance later. Still, stick your head in the sand if you want to. It won't do you any good,' Hawk concluded scathingly.

Fox then turned to his younger brother, Wolf, who was the same as himself - slim, fast and fearless. He had blonde hair and his arms were as hard as rock from many years of fighting battles. He had many scars on his body and he could tell you where he got each one. He had not shaved and he looked very gaunt: you could see he had not had an easy life. However, he had a good sense of humour and always seemed to be smiling. His most noticeable mark was a scar down the right side of his face which he had received saving someone from a flying dragon. He was just two years younger than Fox and very similar in looks and attitude towards life. Unlike Old Grey Bear, he had not let himself go to seed. Old Grey Bear had become fat through too much easy living in the peace that Scrapford had enjoyed, and he had not fought with his brothers for many years.

'Too much like hard work,' Old Grey Bear had told them.

'Well, Wolf, what say you, little brother? Will you fight?' asked Fox.

'Of course,' replied Wolf. 'You should know there's no need even to ask. I've nothing to lose.'

'Thanks,' said Fox, and they put their arms around each other and laughed.

Just then Old Grey Bear shouted: 'Quick - a spy bird!' Before anyone had time to think, Wolf had launched a knife from his side. A screech went out and the bird was dead before it hit the ground. Then Tac (who was not a local) asked: 'What was that?'

'A spy bird,' replied Wolf. 'It listens to conversations then flies back to its master and repeats what it has heard word for word. We must watch out for them.'

'Thank you,' said Fox.

'We'd better have a scout around and make sure that was the only one,' instructed Wolf. A couple of minutes later they came back.

'All clear,' said Wolf.

'Who else is around, then? Black Knight, or perhaps Opium?' asked Fox.

'Yes, in the stables, or they were,' said Old Grey Bear.

'Let's see if they're as good as they say they are,' said Bull.

So Bull took out his battleaxe and crept round the back of the stables. He peered through the half-open doors. There was Opium, grooming his horse. Bull slowly opened the doors and went in very slowly and carefully. Then he placed his axe in the small of Opium's back. To Bull's surprise, Opium started to sing: 'Another man's about to fall, for he's taken Opium for a fool.'

Bull laughed. 'See, Fox, I knew you were over-doing the praise.' As Bull finished speaking, something jumped from the hay and Bull felt a blade on his neck. Then a voice said:

'If you want to leave this place with a head on your shoulders, I suggest you drop the axe,' and Bull did pretty sharpish too.

Fox explained: 'It's a big mistake to touch Opium, the song is a code and means the Black Knight is around. Many men have died over that song.'

Bull looked at the two men, then turned to Fox. 'You told me they were brothers.'

'And so they are,' answered Fox.

'But, look, Opium is tall and thin and has curly hair. He must be at least six feet tall.' Opium stood there listening intently to what Bull had to say. He was by now dressed in his armour. It sparkled in the sunlight. He had a bright blue breastplate and a heart-shaped shield. His helmet was full-faced, which was very handy for keeping your identity secret, because if you didn't know his armour by sight, you could be fighting anyone.

Bull continued: 'And look at Black Knight: he's five foot five, stockily built and has long black hair. They look like complete strangers. And then there's their personalities: Opium's calm, cool and placid, and wouldn't hurt a fly, while Black Knight enjoys inflicting pain, is hot-tempered and could bite your hand off for just saying hullo.'

'Yes, but they do even each other out and create a sort of balance,' said Fox. 'Each of them keeps the other in check.'

By now Black Knight was in his armour. The whole thing was jet black. He helmet was round with one long spike in the middle. The only protection for his face was a small strip of metal over his nose. At the back he had material covering his neck so as not to get burned when in the desert, where of course he comes from. On top of that was chainmail. He looked quite evil.

'Well, my dear cousin, are they as good as I said?'

'I'm sorry I doubted you, Fox, it's true,' Bull admitted.

'Well, my friends, long time no see,' said Fox. The friends shook hands and embraced.

Then they all went to the inn where they drank and talked about old times. Suddenly Fox stood on the table and raised his voice.

'Well, my old friends, do we fight together or do I leave you with my brother Old Grey Bear?'

'No! We fight with you, as always,' replied Opium and Black Knight together.

'So! The toast is: to the end!'

Hawk joined Fox on the table, and the cheers and clashing of weapons could be heard all around Scrapford.

Presently the noise died down. 'So where's Ibex?' asked Hawk.

'He's gone home to his beloved village,' Old Grey Bear informed them.

'That's right, he's a hillander.'

'Isn't that about six miles from here?' asked Bull.

'Correct,' Oak replied.

'So, Old Grey Bear, have you got six horses we can have, at least?' asked Fox.

'Of course, it's the least I can do. Take whatever you need,' responded Old Grey Bear.

So they picked the best horses from Old Grey Bear's stables and took plenty of food and drink. Then they said their good byes to Old Grey Bear and the other villagers.

Old Grey Bear said: 'Don't forget, be careful - the hillanders are dangerous when unknown people wander through their territory. And don't forget - you must not fight back, you want them on your side. Well, good bye and good luck.'

'Are you sure you won't join us?' said Fox. 'It would be great to have you fight at our side again.'

'I'm sorry, but no, Old Grey Bear is not for this one.'

So they mounted up and left.

As they set off for hillanders territory, Bull asked: 'Why has your brother always been called Old Grey Bear?'

'Well, that's easy. When we were all children we went to play by the Great Swamp which was then inhabited by creatures called mudlinks, somewhat like a cross between a snake and a man. It used to stand upright on two legs like a man, but had a snake's head and spat a deadly venom. Well, as I say, we were all playing chase by the Swamp when I ran straight into one. As Old Grey Bear was the eldest he pushed me out of the way, but just as he did the creature spat and got him in the face. He was lucky only to go grey - he should have died. The gods must have been with us that day.'

As Wolf finished speaking, Fox said: 'No more talking, we are getting close. Look - the foothills. Now we have to take it very carefully.'

Wolf shouted: 'Stop!'

'What's wrong?' asked Fox.

'That bush moved,' Wolf replied.

'I'll have a look,' said Bull. So he got off his horse and looked into the bush.

Hawk shouted: 'Don't!' but it was too late. Suddenly Bull was pulled into the bush and all you could hear was somebody being punched. Before anyone could move, rocks started falling from directly above. The horses began to rear up.

'Let's move back,' said Fox. But, before they could do so, they were taken off their horses. First Wolf went, followed in quick succession by Black Knight, Opium, Oak, Hawk, Tac and last but not least Fox. Everywhere they looked there were hillanders. Black Knight was being kicked and punched by a horde of hillanders. Opium was on the ground being kicked and stamped on. Wolf had two men holding him and another punching him in the stomach. Oak was lucky, one smack round the head and he was out for the count. Fox stood up and was headbutted in the nose, then pushed to the ground. Hawk and Tac were face down in the dirt with swords at the back of their necks, keeping them very still and quiet. The others were by now pretty badly beaten up and could not resist even if they had wanted to.

The hillanders finally stopped kicking and punching the rebels.

'Well, thank god that's over,' said Wolf.

'Don't thank them until Ibex turns up - it might not be over,' Fox advised.

'I hear the hillanders do some pretty awful things to trespassers,' said Black Knight.

'And so we do, son,' said one of the hillanders. 'So what are you doing here?' he continued.

'We are here to see your leader, Chief Hillmond of the hillanders.'

'So! How do you know our leader?' asked one of the men.

'My father saved his life and we've been friends ever since,' Fox explained.

'So what's your name?' the man asked.

'Fox,' he replied.

'Oh! I've heard of you,' the man said.

'I hope someone caught the horses,' Fox remarked hopefully.

'Where's your good friend Ibex when you need him, dear brother?' asked Wolf.

Then from nowhere a slim, wiry man appeared. He was well armed. Across his chest he wore a belt that was completely covered in throwing knives. Around his waist were yet more weapons including a bullwhip which consisted of a thick leather handle with a whip. On the end were pieces of razor-sharp metal. He had a scar under his right eye which was the legacy of a battle. His body seemed to be covered in battle scars. His beard hid a lot of his face but you could see that he had had many fights.

'Right then, gentlemen - oh - and ladies,' said Ibex.

'And what took you so long?' snapped Fox.

'I see you met my people,' he continued. 'Let them go,' he said to his men, then added: 'Well, my friends, you look worn out.'

'So would you if you had been jumped on like that,' answered Tac.

Suddenly there was a muffled noise coming from the bush. Ibex moved in the direction of the sound and there in the bush was Bull.

Ibex said: 'Come here, Fox, does this belong to you?'

'Well, yes, sort of,' laughed Fox.

The others followed Fox over, looked in and saw Bull there. He was tied up like a bird ready for the oven, arms and legs behind him and an apple rammed into his mouth. Three hillanders were sitting on top of him.

'Sorry, chief,' said one of them. 'He would not keep still or shut up. It's the only thing I had at hand.'

'Cut his bonds and let him up,' said Ibex.

So they cut the ropes and stepped back quickly. Bull got to his feet and spat the apple out of his mouth in disgust. He then announced: 'It's lucky for you Fox told us not to hurt you.'

'I'm sorry, old son, we did not know who you were or what you wanted. We have to be so careful. We make a living from these hills, always have,' said the man.

'Well, I think we should be able to prove ourselves later on with the hillanders' favourite test,' said Fox.

'What's that?' asked Bull.

'It's called the pole walk,' said Ibex.

'I'm none the wiser for the name. What does it consist of?' Bull asked again.

'Well, it's a long pole, well two actually, with blades set at different intervals.'

'So how do you play?' queried Bull.

'Well, the poles are turned round, you stand on one and your opponent stands on the other. You take your staffs and try to knock each other off without hitting the blades and without landing on your backs.'

'My men are quite good at it, but then they've had a lot of practice,' said Ibex. 'So before the games let's have something to eat and drink.'

'That sounds like a good idea, I could eat a horse,' said Bull.

'You'd better not pick mine, I need him for more important things than to fill your stomach,' said Fox.

'You might as well stay the night,' said Ibex.

'Well, as long as we get an early start in the morning,' Fox replied. 'We have a battlefield to find and a war to win.'

'Agreed,' said Ibex. 'So who are you fighting this time, my dear friend?'

'The dragons,' Fox told him.

'Why?' asked Ibex.

'Because my village was destroyed in an unprovoked attack,' replied Fox.

'So you want revenge?' Ibex suggested.

'No, I want justice and my children and my people back,' Fox answered.

So they sat down to eat and drink and warmed themselves by the fire and chatted. Then Ibex jumped to his feet. 'Well, gentlemen, let the games begin.'

'Well, Bull, you reckon you're capable of restoring our pride, so you can go first,' said Fox.

'No problem,' Bull replied.

So he stepped onto the pole. The men at either end started to turn the poles.

'So where's my opponent then?'

'We are giving you a chance to get used to the pole first. We don't want too much of an advantage,' said Ibex.

'I don't need a chance. I'll sort you lot out, no trouble,' snarled Bull.

'We will see,' said Fox.

Then a hillander stepped onto the pole opposite. 'They call me Ropeman. Good evening. It will be good night for you soon.'

'You reckon, you short twit,' replied Bull.

So it began. The logs were turned and the blades seemed to move up and down the poles. Ropeman jumped and struck at Bull again and again. There seemed to be no defence. Bull was a good all-round fighter, but all his efforts seemed to be useless.

Finally, the man cracked him round the back of the head, knocked him off balance and finished him by sweeping his legs away. Bull fell, catching his leg on one of the blades, then went straight into the water. The water turned red with blood.

'Quick,' Hawk said, 'he's cut a main artery. Get him out of there.'

The hillanders jumped in. It took four of them to lift Bull out.

'I'm so sorry - I didn't mean to hurt you,' said Ropeman.

'Don't worry. You certainly took me down a peg or two,' Bull replied.

'Come on, Tac, do your stuff,' said Hawk.

So Tac walked up to Bull, placed his hands over the gash and said: 'Seal, seal, let this wound heal.' Then he took his staff and waved it over the cut. A puff of smoke went up and the wound was gone.

'Thanks, Tac,' said Bull.

'Now, who's next?' asked Ibex.

'Black, see what you can do,' said Fox.

'I'll give it a go,' the Black Knight said.

So he got into position to fight for the rebels' honour. The poles started to turn. Once again Ropeman advanced avoiding the blades and hitting out at his opponent. Then Black Knight struck at Ropeman catching him on the neck and Ropeman lost his balance. The Black Knight turned to the other rebels and bowed in what he thought was a firm victory. Then Bull shouted: 'Look out, he hasn't gone down, Black,' but it was too late. Ropeman came back and smacked the Black Knight on the back of the head. It was the end. Black Knight fell forward into the water. But he did not get cut because he still had full armour on.

'Any more takers? Well, Opium?'

'No, if he can best my brother, I don't want to get wet - I hate baths.'

'Wolf, what about you?'

'Yes, I'll have a go.'

'Ah, the chief's brother is going to take a dip.'

'Don't be so sure, mate,' said Fox.

So again the two opponents took their positions on the poles. By now Ropeman had got a bit too cocky and rushed at Wolf, who knocked his staff aside. Then he struck a second blow, knocking Ropeman well clear of the poles.

'Well done, Wolf,' shouted Black and Bull.

'So now it's my turn,' said Ibex.

'I'll stand against you, Ibex,' said Wolf.

'You can try,' he replied.

'Watch him, Wolf, he's a tricky sod,' advised Fox.

'Is that right?' asked Wolf.

So they took up positions. The poles once again began to turn. Ibex was tricky and fast. Wolf struck and was blocked by his opponent. The staffs clashed time and again and the sweat was running from both men. They were getting tired. Then with one final burst of energy Ibex struck Wolf the finishing blow taking him down clear of the poles.

'I warned you to watch out for him,' said Fox. Wolf stood up soaking wet.

'Well, your rebels have had quite a washday today, Fox. Are you ready to quit, then?' laughed Ibex.

'No, not yet,' replied Fox. 'One more to go, that's me.'

'Come on, then, let's be having you. Let's see if you're still as good as you used to be,' said Ibex.

So the two of them took positions ready for the last challenge of the day. It began at a furious rate. Fox was swinging his staff, smashing it against Ibex' staff, up and down, side to side.

'If there's much more friction between those staffs they'll burst into flames,' said Bull.

Just then the two men came to a stop, their staffs locked. Now it was down to who could overbalance who. You could see the tension on both men's faces and in their arms as their muscles strained to push the other off the poles. Then Ibex' staff slipped, sending both men falling backwards into the water with a mighty splash. Both of them came up gasping for breath and laughing at the same time.

'Well done, Fox, you are still as good as ever, I see,' said Ibex.

'And you, my friend,' replied Fox.

'Well, Fox, I think we have restored our pride, wouldn't you say so?' said Bull.

'Yes, I think so,' said Fox.

'So how come your men have such good balance, Ibex?' asked Wolf.

'Well, you see, my men jump from ledge to ledge, so they have to be good at judging distances and landing correctly. If they hadn't got good balance they would not live very long,' Ibex explained.

'Well, my old friend, I don't suppose you would be interested in fighting with us?' asked Fox.

'Of course I would. It would make me proud to be one of your rebels again, as long as you promise one thing,' said Ibex.

'And what's that?' asked Fox.

'Bull doesn't eat my horse either,' said Ibex.

'Ha bloody ha, very funny, I don't think,' retorted Bull.

So once again they settled down by the camp fires to get warm. Then one by one the rebels fell asleep until there were only Fox and Hawk still awake.

'What's up, Fox?' Hawk enquired.

'I was just thinking about my children - how much I love them and miss them,' he answered.

'Don't worry, we will get them back, I promise,' Hawk assured him.

'It's not that. Between you and me, I don't think I'm going to make it through this one,' said Fox.

'Don't be silly, of course you will,' said Hawk.

'No. I've got a gut feeling it's my last time out, but don't say a word to the others, will you?' Fox looked at his sister with sadness and death in his eyes.

'No, I won't, I promise,' said Hawk. 'Now let's get some sleep - we've got a long day tomorrow.'

Then Hawk drifted off to sleep. Fox just sat there gazing into the fire. As the flames flickered he saw pictures of times gone by. Patch snuggled up to his master as if to try to comfort him.

'There's my good boy - you've always been there when needed, haven't you?' He patted the dog and gave him some meat off his plate, then got up to give the dog some water to drink. Patch lapped the water and afterwards settled down by the fire. Fox took his sword from its sheath and started to clean it.

'You, my friend, will be doing a lot of work in the next few days. Oh, my god, I'm even talking to my sword now. I'm going out of my head. That's it - I'm going to sleep before you start answering me.' Then Fox lay down by the fire to get what he thought was much-needed sleep. Patch moved closer and went to sleep too.

They were awoken by the cockerel crowing. Hawk was up first and started building up the fires ready to make breakfast. Then she made her rounds kicking the other rebels. Bull was the first to get it. She kicked him in the back.

'Hey, what's your game?' he asked.

'It's called cooking breakfast. If you don't want any, just stay there,' replied Hawk.

'Breakfast - why didn't you say so?' Bull said and jumped up. 'Come on, you lazy lot, get up.'

With lots of moans and groans the rebels got up and had breakfast, then washed.

'I would have thought you lot would have had enough of baths around here,' said Ropeman as he walked through the camp. And then he wished he had kept quiet. Bull said: 'So you think you are a comedian?' and he and the Black Knight took hold of Ropeman by his arms and legs and threw him into the pit of water. Then they stood there laughing. A moment later Opium shouted: 'Look out, Black!'

Two hillanders ran up. One jumped on Black's back. Black just grabbed him by the head and pulled him forward over his own head by leaning forward. Then splash he was in the water as well. The other one ran at Bull and he simply turned round, caught him with his arm round the back of the man's neck and continued to move round, shoving him straight into the water with his comrades.

'Okay, boys, fun time's over. Come on, let's saddle up and get going. Where's my horse? Bull, you haven't, have you?' said Fox.

'No, I have not eaten it, you cheeky sod,' answered Bull.

So they all mounted up and the sound of clanking armour filled the air. The nine rebels rode away from the village of the hillanders. A short time afterwards they came to the edge of hillander territory.

'It's not too late for you to turn back, Ibex,' said Fox.

'Why should I turn back?'

'Because you might not come back, my old mate,' Fox replied.

'Life is full of uncertainties. I could die in bed - can't think of anything worse, can you?' said Ibex.

'No, can't say I can,' said Fox.

So they carried on towards the land of the treedwellers. Presently Wolf shouted: 'Stop! Can you see that?'

'What?' asked Bull.

'Smoke coming from Scrapford,' said Wolf. Everyone came to a stop.

'So why are we standing here? Let's move it,' said Fox.

'Let's work up a sweat on these horses,' said Ibex.

They kicked their horses and set off at a hell of a pace. Riding their mounts hard, they made good time.

Wolf was first to dismount, before his horse had even stopped. What he saw sickened him to his stomach: children's bodies mutilated, cut from head to toe; women's bodies lying all round the village; even animals senselessly slaughtered. Not a living thing had survived the onslaught.

By the time the others got to the village their horses were covered in sweat. It was dripping down their bodies, even the riders' legs were wet from the horses. Fox and the others got off their mounts and tied them to a post.

'It's the same here as it was at Castlewood. No need to ask who's responsible for this mess,' said Fox.

They started to look round. There was the stench of death in the air, and the village was filled with smoke - you could hardly see your hand in front of your face. The dragons had left nothing in one piece. Fox and Hawk climbed the watch tower to see if they could spot Wolf. Hawk looked out over the remains of Scrapford. 'If it's possible, I would say it's worse than Castlewood.'

Then Fox saw Wolf through the smoke. He was pulling a woman off a door. She had her own dagger rammed through her throat and sticking her to the door.

'Oh, my god, it's Wolf's woman Running Bear,' said Hawk. 'Let's get down and help him.' Hawk started to climb down. Fox was still shocked. He just stood looking out over the scene of death and carnage with bodies spread all round the village. Even knowing how evil the dragons could be, he could not understand how anyone could be so callous and sadistic as to kill little children and apparently enjoy it so much.

Fox left the tower and ran to where Hawk and Wolf were. Wolf was holding the woman in his arms and sobbing.

'Why? Why her? She never harmed anyone. She wasn't even a warrior. I loved her. Why do this awful thing to her and the children? Old Grey Bear would not commit the village. It does not make sense.'

Wolf laid the woman's body gently on the ground. Then he went absolutely beserk, stamping his feet and kicking dust. After that he started punching doors and headbutting them. Finally he started screaming with frustration. Fox grabbed him to try to calm him down but was slung into a burning hut, smashing through the now charred supports and bringing the roof down about his head. Then Black

Knight, Bull, Ibex and Oak jumped Wolf all at the same time, got him onto the ground and held him there. Hawk slapped him really hard round the face. Wolf stopped screaming and went quiet.

'I'm sorry, Wolf, I had to do it. You were hysterical - you were going to hurt yourself.'

'Where's Fox?'

'I think he's in what's left of that hut.'

They pulled the wreckage away and there in a heap was Fox.

'Get me out of here - something's on fire and I think it's me.' They all stood there and laughed. 'Help me out of here.'

They pulled him out and Fox ran straight for the horse trough and jumped in. The others were rolling around in fits of laughter but it didn't last long. Opium shouted: 'Come quickly - I've found Old Grey Bear and he's still alive.'

So the others ran over to where Opium was standing. There on the ground was Old Grey Bear covered in blood and lying on a pile of burning embers.

'Tac, get here quick,' said Wolf. So he came over and had a look at Old Grey Bear.

'I can't help him. He's lost too much blood and most importantly the will to live. Without that he is finished - without that I can't help him. I'm sorry,' concluded Tac.

'You can't go, Old Grey Bear, you must help us avenge your family,' said Fox.

'I can't,' replied Old Grey Bear. 'I let you down. I have no honour and as you well know a warrior can't go into battle without it. I would die first battle we got involved in and one of you could die trying to save me.' Then he looked down at his stomach as the blood slowly pumped out.

'Tac, can you keep him alive so we can talk to him?' asked Fox.

'I can try,' Tac answered. So he waved his staff and a strange glow surrounded Old Grey Bear. It seemed to relax him.

'So, my brother, was it the dragons?' asked Wolf.

'Yes - we didn't stand a chance. It was a massacre. We were slaughtered like cattle,' said Old Grey Bear.

'So we see. It looks like they didn't need any more slaves,' said Fox.

'My wife and children - are they dead?' said Old Grey Bear.

'Yes, they are, I'm sorry to say,' replied Hawk.

'You are going to join them. Have you any last words?' asked Fox.

Then Wolf punched Fox. 'What's the matter with you?'

'Look, it's his right to say his last words and to know they will be his last words. You know that as well as I do,' said Fox. 'And if you punch me again I'm going to smash your teeth down your throat.'

'Oh yeah, you and whose army?' said Wolf.

'I don't need an army to sort you out, little brother.'

Fox was still talking when Old Grey Bear interrupted.

'Wolf, shut up. Fox is right. Don't you think I don't know I'm going to die? Thanks for being honest, Fox. I should have taken the threat of the dragons more seriously. I should have thrown in my lot with you. At least I would still have my honour and I would have been able to take my revenge. There are so many things I could have done. Such as putting the village on full alert or moving everybody out. I've failed as a brother, leader and warrior. I have nothing left.'

'No, you haven't. You just made a mistake. We all do that sometimes. I did at Castlewood,' said Fox.

'I want to be with my family when I go, promise me that. My back's hot,' he added. So Wolf rolled him over and they saw that his back was burned. They threw water over him.

'That's better,' he said. 'Remember your promise.'

'I will make sure it's done,' said Hawk.

'My brothers, take revenge for my family,' said Old Grey Bear. 'Make them pay for the senseless murder of my people. I did not tell them where you had gone even though they tortured me - I would not give in. They could not hurt me any more than watching them kill my wife and children. I hope to see you on the next great battlefield.'

'You will, my brother,' said Wolf.

Then the glow around Old Grey Bear's body started to fade and a pained expression came over his face. He coughed and a trickle of blood appeared from the corner of his mouth. His back arched, and then he was still.

'He has gone,' said Tac.

Wolf held his brother tight. 'Don't go, don't go.'

'Let go, Wolf, he's gone,' said Hawk. 'Save your energy for the revenge we are going to take. We shall pay the King back many times over for what he has done.'

'So, my fine rebels, just one more good reason to destroy the Dragon King and his army,' said Fox. 'Now dig the graves. Don't forget an extra large one for Old Grey Bear and his wife and children.'

So this they did, then put up headstones with the names of the dead. On Old Grey Bear's headstone they wrote:

'Here lies Old Grey Bear and his whole family. Gone yet not forgotten. A fighter till the end. No man had more honour. No brother greater missed. Till the next great battlefield.'

'Now we stop them or die trying,' said Wolf. 'Well, what are we waiting for? Let's go and get them.'

So once again the nine rebels set off to free their families and friends. It was not going to be an easy task but it was one of those things that could not be avoided. It was a case of do or die and the next couple of days would see plenty of deaths on both sides. But, if they had known that, it would not have made any difference.

Four days of sheer hell had passed in the dungeons of the Dragon King. Sunny was still a bit sore but her wounds were on the mend. She had spent most of her time crying and feeling hungry, which was nothing unusual, because wherever Sunny was she always felt hungry. Now she turned to her aunt and said: 'Now that Dad's dead, I find I have so many things I wanted to ask, so many questions will go unanswered.'

'Well, my little one, ask me,' said her Aunty Elk. 'Perhaps I can answer them for you.'

'Well, you know our village and many others take their names from nature,' said Sunny.

'Yes.'

'Why did my dad call me Sunny?'

'That's easy. When your mother was carrying you your father wanted to be there. But the night you were due to be born he was called to rescue a horse and rider. He was out all night. As he was coming back through the village gates, he heard your first cries. He turned round and saw the sun rising. It was the most beautiful sunrise he had ever seen and then when he saw you his heart felt so full it was as if the sun had risen in his chest. He felt so warm inside and was so proud. When he told your mother the story she said that it was a good omen and so they both agreed to call you Sunny. And until the day he died you always brought a little bit of sunshine into his life,' her aunty Elk concluded.

Sunny had tears in her eyes. 'Is that a true story?' she asked.

'As God is my witness, it's all true,' said Elk.

By now Sunny had burst into tears.

'What's the matter, sweetheart?' asked her aunty.

'It's so sad - I didn't get to tell Dad how much I cared and what I really thought of him. I did love him very much,' said Sunny.

'Your Dad knew that, I'm sure,' said Elk.

As usual Badger had spent most of her time baiting the guards and generally causing as much trouble as was humanly possible. The three boys had by now dug quite a large hole, so big in fact that Wildcat had fallen in and all anyone could see of him was a pair of feet wriggling around in the air. Sky and Jage pulled him out by his feet, with dirt all over except around his eyes because, when he fell in, he had shut his eyes tight, so it now looked as if he was wearing a mask. Everyone laughed for the first time since their imprisonment in the smelly rat-infested hole. It was so cold and depressing and Elk kept the children busy, encouraging them to play to keep their minds off their father's death and the situation they were in. Mole was still very ill and Elk was nursing him, trying to comfort him. She was hoping something would happen and very soon or she was not sure Mole would be able to hang onto life for much longer.

She sat and prayed that someone would help and soon, before it was too late.

Then the boys shouted: 'Aunty Elk, we are hungry, can we eat now?'

'I'm afraid you can't,' she replied. 'You have had your ration of bread for today.'

'But we are still hungry,' said the boys.

'I will get you some,' said Badger. She stood up, walked to the door and kicked it hard.

'Come on, you overgrown lizard,' said Badger.

'You're going to get hurt again,' warned Sunny.

'Oh, shut up, you wimp. My brothers are hungry. I care even if you don't. I don't care about getting hurt,' said Badger.

Then the door opened.

'What, you again, you must like pain,' said the guard.

'Look, just give my brothers some food, you ugly fat slime,' said Badger.

The dragon slapped her in the face, knocking her to the floor. She sat up. There was blood running down her face.

'You've got a nosebleed. I told you you would get hurt,' said Sunny.

Then Badger flicked blood at Sunny and said: 'Shut up or I will do the same to you, Fathead.'

'Children, come over here and I will tell you how you got your names. Sunny, you take Mole.' By now his fever had got so bad he didn't even notice that he was being moved.

'He is all wet, aunty,' said Sunny.

'I know. There is nothing I can do. Badger, come and sit on my lap and I'll tell you first.' So Badger snuggled up to hear the tale.

'Well, you were given your name because when your mum was expecting you she had a really hard time. Then, when you were born, you kept badgering your parents all the time. They never got any sleep. In fact, in a roundabout way, you broke your dad's arm. He was so tired because you wouldn't let him sleep that while herding some horses he fell asleep in the saddle, fell off and was trampled by a dozen or so horses. The very next day he was holding you even with his broken arm. He always loved you dearly and was very proud of the way you always helped him and enjoyed being with him.'

'What about me, aunty?' asked Jage.

'Well, when you were born you came out blotched and you were so sweet like a little cat that your dad wanted to call you Jaguar. But your mum said that was too harsh a name for a baby so they called you Jage instead. You were his first son and he was thrilled to bits. He thought you would make a good leader of Castlewood and he loved you.

'Wildcat got his name because when he was being carried inside his mother he jumped about as if he was fighting. Coming out, he flung his arms around and kicked. He looked so funny and wild. That's how he got his name.

'And last but not least, Sky. Your mother and father were on the way back from a horse sale. You were not due for another month so they thought it would be safe to travel but at the crack of dawn your mother had to give birth in the back of an open hay wagon. All she could see was the bright morning sky, and that's how you came to be Sky of Castlewood.'

Elk looked round and Sky was just falling asleep. She laid Badger down next to Jage and Wildcat and then took

Mole out of Sunny's arms. Sunny curled up and went to sleep with the others.

'Good night, my little ones,' said Elk softly.

Chapter 6

Little did the prisoners know that help was just six miles away. The rebels knew they had to divide to conquer, which meant they had to draw the dragons out in small numbers, because there was no way they could defeat the four hundred strong army of the dragons all at once. At least they would stand a chance if they could make the Dragon King send out small raiding parties to sort out the rebels. The plan was set: Tac would appear at the dragon king's court and sell the king some information on the whereabouts and strength of the rebels.

So Tac set off for the Dragon King's castle. It did not take him long to reach it because he could appear and disappear as he wished. He therefore appeared half a mile away from the castle, then walked to the gatehouse and banged on the door.

'Let me in - I want to see your master,' he shouted.

'What for?' said the guard.

'I have some information for him,' said Tac.

So the guard went off to see if the king would receive the visitor to his court. A couple of minutes passed, then the guard returned.

'Come in, the king will see you,' he said. So Tac went through the great gates and into a massive hall. There at the end of the room stood a giant throne encrusted with fabulous jewels. In it sat the Dragon King in all his splendour and larger than life.

'So, little man, what have you to offer and what do you want for this information?'

'Well, first I can tell you where a gang of rebels are - survivors of Castlewood,' said Tac.

'What!' said the king. 'Do you mean there are men of Castlewood still alive?'

'Yes, that's right,' said Tac.

'So name one of these men,' said the Dagon King.

'Fox of Castlewood,' replied Tac.

'Send for the commander of the raiding party,' said the king. So one of the guards hurried off to get the officer in charge. In due course the officer in question came into the hall.

'So everybody in Castlewood is dead, are they?' said the king.

'Yes, my lord, that's right.'

'You liar. Fox of Castlewood is still alive,' said the king.

'Impossible! I saw him dead with my own eyes,' said the officer.

'Well, your eyes deceived you, you stupid incompetent fool. The one man you should have made sure was dead is still alive and what makes it worse he has raised a rebel army against us. It's all your fault,' said the Dragon King.

'No, please, it's not my fault,' said the officer.

The king shouted: 'Guards, take this fool from my sight. Place him in the dungeons to await his execution.'

Then the poor officer was marched away to await his gruesome fate.

'So, my little man, what do you want for the information that you are going to give me?' said the Dragon King.

'Well, I hear that you have captives from Castlewood,' said Tac.

'That's right - what of it?' replied the Dragon King.

'I have just inherited a mine up north from an uncle who recently passed away. I don't really want to pay wages if I can get slaves. Death can be so profitable.'

'I just had some luck like that myself. Fox died and left me Castlewood, ha ha.' The king thought this was most amusing.

'So is it a trade?' asked Tac.

'What exactly do you want?' said the king.

'I want every single slave you have. I can find work for all of them, plus carts to transport them, clothes and food enough to get them to their destination. I think it's a fair trade - slaves for information,' answered Tac.

'Yes, that sounds fair to me. I don't really want them. I just didn't want them wandering around causing trouble for me. This way I don't have to feed them or take care of the leeches.'

'So may I inspect my property before we close the deal?' asked Tac.

'Of course, be my guest. Guard, take this man to the dungeons to see the slaves from Castlewood and do whatever he tells you. Do you understand?' said the king.

'Yes, my lord,' the guard replied.

'Thank you,' said Tac. He followed the guard out of the hall and down to the kitchens where they came to a great oak door.

'Is this the only way in, and why put them below the kitchens?' asked Tac.

'No, there's another door in the courtyard. The reason they are here is so the prisoners can smell the food cooking. It's pure hell when you're hungry,' laughed the guard.

Then the door was opened. Tac peered in. The stone steps seemed to go down for ever. On the walls were torches flickering as they showed the way. Down and down they went. All Tac could hear was the sound of his own footsteps echoing behind him. The walls were wet and cold.

'How much further is it?' asked Tac. 'If we keep going much longer we will fall through the end of the land.'

The guard laughed. 'It may be deep - which makes it impossible to dig your way out - but it's not that deep. Anyway, we're on the last steps now.'

They reached the bottom and turned a corner. There in front of them stretched a long dark corridor with many doors. At the end stood the officer who had just been sentenced to death. The guards pushed him through a doorway and slammed the door shut behind him. One of the guards shouted: 'Not so high and mighty now, are you? Where's all your power now?' Both the guards roared with laughter.

'Look, aunty,' said one of the children. 'That's the dragon who left Dad with his armour. I wonder why he is here.'

The dragon turned round and snapped: 'I'm here because I didn't check that your father really was dead. Now it appears he's alive and I must die for my mistake.' He went and sat in the corner of the cell.

Then the door opened once again and Tac walked in. 'Leave us,' he said to the guard.

'I don't know about that.'

'Remember what the king said,' Tac reminded him.

'Of course, I'm going,' said the guard.

So Tac looked round and saw Elk with all the children sitting around her. He walked over and asked: 'Do you know Fox?'

'Yes, he's my brother. Is it true that he's alive?'

'Yes - how do you know?'

'That dragon told us he is the reason Fox is alive.'

'Wait here a moment - I'll be back.' Tac walked over to the dragon and said: 'Is it true that you - a dragon - saved Fox?'

'Yes, to my misfortune I did. I listened to the pleadings of these miserable wretches and I am to die for my kindness,' said the dragon.

'Let me tell you something - you will not die. I shall cast a spell on you which will protect you from death. They may cut your head off but I promise you on my honour you will live with your head intact. But if you try to utter a word to the king or any other dragon, you will choke on your own words and die in minutes. And the spell will only protect you from dragons, so you can't use the power to take what you want from anyone else. You are only invincible to dragons. You can be killed by others - remember that,' warned Tac.

'Thank you,' replied the officer.

Tac returned to talk to Elk. 'Now listen to me carefully,' said Tac. 'I can't talk for long. Help is on its way.'

'What made you pick me out to talk to?' asked Elk.

'Because you had all those children around you and they look very much like Fox. Is there anything you need?' asked Tac.

'Yes, some food and some fresh water,' said Elk.

'Guard, guard,' shouted Tac.

'Yes, sir?'

'Go and fetch food and fresh water from the kitchen,' said Tac.

'But - but,' stammered the guard.

'Don't 'but' me or I'll have your head,' said Tac.

'I'm going.'

'And make it quick. What's wrong with your child?' enquired Tac.

'It's an infection,' Elk replied. 'I'm worried he's going to die.'

'No, he won't - I will sort him out.' So, again, as he had done many times before, Tac took his staff, waved it over the child's arm and said: 'Make this child free from harm, so his mother may be calm.' Then there was a puff of smoke and the wound was gone.

'Thank you, whoever you are. If you see Oak, tell him I love him and am safe and well,' said Elk.

Tac looked towards the officer and pointed his staff at him. 'Do you want the bargain? If you don't, you will die anyway. Whatever you tell the king he will not let you live. You know that, don't you?' said Tac.

'Yes, I know. I will take the deal,' said the dragon.

Then from the end of the staff came a flash of light. The dragon was surrounded by a glow, a force field that would keep him safe.

'When the food gets here,' said Tac, 'you must not say thank you, any of you. It would look suspicious - you are meant to be slaves.'

Then the locks were turned back. 'Here's your food and water.' Four dragons walked in with trays piled high with meat, vegetables and fruit.

'These people are to have three square meals a day, or as the gods are my witnesses I'll have your heads,' said Tac. He looked at Elk and winked. 'I will have you for my woman. I promise we will be back to get you out of this rotten stinking hole,' he added softly. The dragon officer got up to join in the feast, but one of the guards threw a hard loaf at him, hitting him on the head.

'This is not for you.'

So the dragon went back to his corner.

Then the guards left. When their footsteps could no longer be heard in the corridor, Wildcat walked towards the dragon. A woman grabbed him by the wrist.

'Let me go,' he said and pulled, but he could not get away. Sunny shouted: 'Let my brother go or I will smash your face in.'

'You and whose army?' answered the woman.

Their aunty stood up and said: 'Me for starters.'

'But he is a dragon. We are here because of him,' the woman protested.

'Yes, but if it weren't for him Fox would be dead,' said Elk.

'So what difference does that make?'

'Because Fox is alive and has raised an army. They will come and save us all - it's guaranteed.'

The woman let Wildcat go. He walked up to the dragon and gave him a chicken. 'Thank you for my father's life.'

'Thank you for my life and the chicken,' replied the dragon. Wildcat walked off, then turned round and the dragon smiled.

Tac knocked on the door. 'Let me out.'

'Yes sir.'

As the guard opened the door, Tac said: 'Give them all bread.'

'But sir...' began the guard.

'Don't 'but sir' me. If any of them die you could end up the same way. I want my slaves to work and they won't do that dead, now will they?' snapped Tac.

'No, I don't suppose so, sir.'

Then Tac went back to the Great Hall and the king.

'So, my little man, do we have a deal?' said the king.

'Yes, of course, my lord. I have counted the slaves and I hope there will be the same number here when I next see them.'

'It is assured,' said the Dragon King. 'Tell the guard that if anything happens to the slaves the same thing will happen to him.'

As the rebels had hoped, the Dragon King underestimated the situation. He sent only a single section of dragon warriors and Tac was going to lead them straight into the trap, as he had assured the king he was the best tracker in the whole of the territory. So the army set off on the six mile march to the land of the treedwellers being led by Tac to their untimely death.

The rebels had already planned the whole thing. They were all ready in place, waiting impatiently for the attack. The sweat was running down Wolf's face.

'My hands are wet and sticky,' said Fox.

They had taken up a position just outside the boundary of the treedwellers' land, hoping the treedwellers would play their part in the plan. If they didn't, the rebels were going to be in one hell of a lot of trouble. It would be like lambs to the slaughter. And then that would be the end of any chance of a rebellion. In fact, it would be the end of the rebels, full stop, something that Fox did not relish very much and nor would the others either. Still, it was too late to turn back now. It was time to stand up and be counted - a case of do or die.

Fox felt rather guilty about using the poor unsuspecting creatures in this way but in his heart he knew that the dragons would conquer the treedwellers eventually along with everyone else in the lands that surrounded the dragons' lair unless something drastic was done. At least now they stood a fighting chance and would not be killed in their beds like the people of Scrapford. Fox's mind was then brought back to reality by the sound of marching feet and the clashing of armour as the dragons swung their shields to the time of their steps.

Then Wolf said: 'Look - a column of dust - that can only mean one thing: dragons heading this way, straight down the main track.'

The dragons were halfway down the track by now. The woods were still very quiet, not a living thing moved. Suddenly the column came to a halt. The trees above them began to shake. The dragons looked up and at least a hundred treedwellers fell from the branches on top of the dragons.

'Look, it's raining treedwellers and the dragons are getting soaking wet,' said Wolf.

Now the battle had begun. Six treedwellers standing in front of a dragon were sprayed with flames, sending them running for cover. A treedweller stuck a trident into the dragon's stomach, making it explode with a loud bang.

Then Fox stood up and shouted: 'For the honour of Castlewood, let's get them!' The rebels left their cover and joined in the fray.

Bull stood with his hands in front of him. Wolf ran towards him, placing his foot in Bull's hands and Bull lifted him into the air, sending him flying towards two dragons. He landed on top of them, smashing their heads together and knocking them to the ground. He picked himself up, quickly took out his sword and stabbed them before they had time to recover.

Now Wolf was in the thick of the battle, punching, kicking and slashing at the dragons.

Fox stood and took out his bow and arrows and started to fire, taking two or three of the dragons out.

Bull rushed in, swinging his battleaxe, slicing dragons who were unfortunate enough to come into range. Then one dragon blocked his blow and another smashed his hand, making him drop his battleaxe. For a moment he stood there defenceless. He had to get to his weapon, so he put his head down and shouted 'Charge!', ran towards the dragon standing by his battleaxe and hit him full in the stomach. As he did so a burning arrow whizzed past his head and ignited the gases that were escaping from the dragon's stomach. There was a bang and a blast of flames shot past his face singeing his hair. Bits of burning dragon flesh landed on the back of his shirt and set it alight. Bull started to jump about.

Fox saw Bull was in trouble so he picked up a blanket, rushed over and smothered the flames.

'Stay down, I think the fire's out.' As Fox finished speaking a dragon punched him in the jaw, knocking him to the ground and stamping on his head. Bull swung round, kicked the creature in the stomach and punched him in the face. Then, screaming with anger, he grabbed the dragon by the arm and swung him against a tree. The creature slumped to the bottom of the tree trunk. Bull reached for his trusty battleaxe and despatched it with one blow.

Wolf was smashing dragons over the head with a mace - you could hear the skulls cracking.

Then out from the undergrowth charged Black Knight on his horse, lance in hand. He impaled the dragon in front of him in the chest, pulled his lance free and turned. He charged again, this time catching a dragon in the shoulder. His horse moved backwards, ready to charge again and finish the creature off. As he raced towards his victim with his lance aimed for the heart, another dragon jumped out and put his shield in Black Knight's way. His lance shattered. Before he could do anything else he was hit in the left shoulder by a mace, then grabbed on the right, pulled off his horse and sent crashing to the ground. Two dragons then started to strike him. He managed to get his shield up over his head where one of them was battering him. The other was hitting him in the stomach with a mace. As that part of his armour was vulnerable, only being made of chainmail, he was in a lot of discomfort. He looked up and saw the marks left by the mace, as it repeatedly hit home.

Suddenly he heard someone roar 'No!' Black Knight couldn't see who shouted or what was going on. All he could see was his shield taking a battering. Then he heard a thud and a scream of pain. The mace stopped hitting his stomach and a heavy weight fell on his legs. Next the battering on his shield stopped. He could hear a fight going on nearby but he didn't lower his guard for a second. Instead he peered out from under his shield just as a dragon's head fell by his side. He sat up and pushed the body off his legs.

There standing beside him was Bull with a big smile on his face and blood dripping from both sides of his double-bladed battleaxe.

'There, that's the one I owe you,' he said. 'A life for a life.' Years before Black Knight had saved Bull's life.

'Thanks a lot,' said Black Knight.

Bull ran off towards Oak. His sword had been knocked out of his hand and he was defending himself with a sledgehammer. A dragon rushed towards him and he swung round, catching the creature on the jaw and smashing it in two. As he turned round another attacked from the front. Oak brought the hammer down, embedding it in the top of the dragon's head and killing it outright. Another caught it in the stomach. Bull ran in behind and finished off the two wounded dragons.

Opium and Ibex were working as a team. As the dragons ran towards Opium, Ibex hit them in the stomach with a log, Opium then punched them in the face and finally Ibex ran them through with his sword. After they had pulled this trick two or three times the dragons got wise to it. As Ibex went to hit the dragon it grabbed the log, swung him round and then let go, sending Ibex flying into the undergrowth. Unfortunately for the dragon it made the mistake of watching Ibex, and Opium came up from behind and stabbed him in the back. He fell to his knees and Opium drop-kicked him, then he fell face first into the dirt.

The battle was in full swing now: they were fighting for their very existence. At first the treedwellers had taken heavy losses but by this time they had turned the tables on the dragons. Now it was the dragons' turn to take a hiding for a change, with the rebels' help of course.

The rebels had to hope and pray that they defeated the dragons before the treedwellers realised that the rebels were there. Fox was firing arrows at the dragons in rapid succession. Bull was about to hit a dragon with his axe when an arrow from Fox's bow hit the creature in the stomach and it exploded in flames. Bull threw himself to the ground to avoid them.

'Sorry, Bull, pure accident - promise,' said Fox.

'Yes, I'm sure,' replied Bull.

Hawk had been knocked over and lay on the ground winded. Ibex was out of action. He had been struck with a pike and it had sliced an artery: the blood was pumping out fast. 'I'm going to have to sit the rest of this one out,' said Ibex.

By now there were bodies all around - in the trees, on the track, in the undergrowth, in fact everywhere you looked.

Wolf was suddenly grabbed by two dragons. A third started to punch him in the face, then went to work on his stomach. As more and more blows struck home, Wolf could feel his legs giving way. He fell to the ground and they started to kick him. He shouted: 'Fox, help me!' and as he did so he got kicked in the mouth. Fox turned round and saw one of the dragons stick a pike in Wolf's chest. A pained expression came over his face. 'Help me, Fox,' he cried again. The dragons stood there laughing as Wolf fell backwards. Fox was furious, watching them laugh at his little brother. He saw red, plucked an arrow from his quiver and shot one of the dragons in the neck. It made a gurgling noise, then dropped to the ground, dead. Never before had Fox taken such pleasure in killing anything. As the arrow went thud into the dragon's flesh, Fox could almost feel the pain and it made him feel good.

There were two left. He wanted to be close enough to see the pain so he dropped his bow and ran towards the pair of dragons who had just helped kill his brother. They were standing by an overhanging branch. Fox jumped up and swung towards them, kicking them in the face and knocking them backwards. Fox let go of the branch and landed in front of them. One got to his feet and Fox handed him a sword.

'Let's see how you do one to one.'

Then the sword fight began. Backwards and forwards it raged, striking and blocking, thrusting and parrying. It seemed to go on for ages. Then with one almighty blow Fox disarmed the dragon, sending his sword spinning from his hand. He grabbed the creature by the throat, looked him straight in the eyes and, gritting his teeth, stuck the blade in.

'Let's see you laugh at this,' he said and took great delight in twisting the blade around and watching the creature squirm in pain.

'That's for my brother.'

Then Fox felt a sharp searing pain and found he couldn't breathe properly. A blade had gone straight through his ribcage and his lung had collapsed. He fell forwards and came to rest slumped up against a tree. He could no longer defend himself. His head was against the trunk and his arms were wrapped around it as he tried desperately to breathe.

Bull had seen Fox taken down. He put his head down and charged towards the dragon who was just going to finish Fox off. He hit the dragon in the side, the horns on his helmet piercing him. Bull kept pushing the creature until they hit a tree. Bull pulled his head backwards but his helmet was firmly embedded in the creature's side, though he was still very much alive and kicking.

Bull had to do something and fast. So he unbuckled his helmet and pulled backwards very fast. He reached out and picked up Fox's sword and slashed the creature across the throat, killing it instantly.

By now the dragon raiding party was greatly depleted in numbers. They had started with between forty and fifty; now a mere ten or fifteen were still standing. Oak was still lowering the numbers, fighting with his sledgehammer and staff, then suddenly he was hit in the head from behind by a chain and mace and fell to the ground unconscious. The dragons were now going down one after the other until there were only two left.

This remnant hastily beat a retreat back to the king.

Tac had been fighting treedwellers to make it look good and not blow his cover with the dragons, but he had just zapped them with his staff, knocking them out with no other ill effects. Now he stood up to survey the scene of carnage. The tracks were covered in blood and there were bodies everywhere with arms and legs missing, men with chest wounds, stomach wounds, the dead and dying surrounded him everywhere he looked.

The treedwellers had fought well. They were not afraid of death and they had made the dragons pay dearly for their mistake of entering the woods.

Tac announced: 'I must leave now to fulfil the rest of the plan.'

'Oh no, you don't,' said Hawk. 'You must sort out the wounded - my brothers Oak and Ibex among others need your help. Then there are the treedwellers - you can appear and disappear at will, so catching up with them will be no problem for you. We can't afford to lose a single man.' Then Hawk slumped against a tree for support.

'You took a blow to the head, did you not?' said Tac.

'Yes,' replied Hawk.

'Then let me sort it out for you.' He placed his hands on her head and started to hum while he moved his fingers around.

'There, isn't that better?' asked Tac.

'Yes, much, thanks,' said Hawk.

'Good. Now I must get on with sorting out the others.'

First he went over to Oak. By now he was sitting with his head in his hands, blood trickling down the back of his neck.

'I see you were hit by a mace of some sort,' said Tac.

'How do you know that?' asked Oak.

'Because you have the imprint left in your head.' Tac placed his hands on the wound. He muttered something and waved his staff over the cut. Then came a puff of smoke and the injury was gone.

'Are you married to Fox's sister and do you have a child?' asked Tac.

'Yes, I do. Are they still alive?' Oak pleaded for information.

'Yes. I saw all the slaves. It was part of my bargain with the king. She is alive and well. Your son was ill but I cured him. I told Elk help was on its way and she told me to give you a message. She said: 'I love you and come and get us soon. We miss you."

'Thank you. This means a great deal to me. It makes me more determined to fight on and is something to live for,' said Oak.

Fox was lying face down in the dirt and leaf litter. Tac went over to him.

'Well?' asked Hawk.

'Well, I can sort it out. He has a very strong life force, never known one stronger,' said Tac.

'He is certainly a very stubborn man. He won't die before he's good and ready, which won't be until he has defeated the Dragon King and rescued his children,' said Hawk.

So Tac waved his staff and muttered his magical incantations once again. A puff of smoke and a flash of light appeared.

'There, it's done,' he said.

'There's not a mark on Fox,' said Hawk. 'You're a little marvel. Now work your wonders on Wolf.'

Fox and Hawk walked over to where Wolf was lying. They both knelt down by his side. Tac came over and took a look at Wolf.

'I can do nothing for him but relieve his pain,' he said.

'Then do it,' screamed Hawk.

Wolf stretched his arms up and grabbed Fox and Hawk by the shoulders.

'I'm sorry, little brother, I should never have got you involved,' said Fox.

'He has lost the will to live,' said Tac. 'I think it's because he lost his woman and he feels there's no-one to fight for any more.'

'And how do you know this?' snapped Hawk.

'I can feel it.'

'Then make him feel wanted, because he is,' said Hawk.

'I can't - he won't believe me. He wants to die but he doesn't know it,' said Tac. 'I will sort Ibex out.'

By now Ibex's whole body was covered in blood. Tac soon stopped the bleeding and healed the wound.

'You can't die - we need you,' Fox said to Wolf. 'It's the truth. I can't lose another brother, not two brothers in as many days.'

'If I had not thrown my lot in with you I would have been killed at Scrapford along with old Grey Bear and all the others,' Wolf replied. 'I know I'm dying. These are my last words. I'm sorry I hit you and shouted at you. You were right to do what you did and I was out of line. I'm glad I'm with you and my family. Now it's my turn. I love you all and of course I will see you on the next great battlefield.' Wolf breathed his last and then was no more.

Hawk jumped to her feet. 'It's your fault, you stupid little man. If you had seen to Wolf first, he would still be alive.' Then she burst into tears and started to punch and kick Tac.

'It would have made no difference. His time had come. I cannot cheat Death of what is rightfully his,' he said, between blows.

Hawk pulled her dagger out and lunged at Tac.

'Oak - quickly - your staff!' shouted Fox, and Oak sent it sailing through the air. Fox caught it and struck the knife from Hawk's hand. Then he brought the staff up under her chin, knocking her out cold.

'What did you do that for?' asked Bull.

'Have you ever seen Hawk lose her temper?' said Fox.

'No,' Bull replied.

'She would have killed him with something else, even though I took the dagger away. This will give her time to cool down and by the time she comes round Tac will be gone. He is a rebel and a very important one - the whole plan rests on him,' said Fox. 'Now let's get on and sort out the treedwellers.'

Out of the hundred or so treedwellers who had fought, twenty-five were dead and about thirty were badly wounded. But, true to form, Tac healed them all.

'Right, can you do some more magic for me?' asked Fox.

'I can but try,' Tac replied.

'Can you make Wolf's body stay exactly like it is now so we can bury him properly later?' said Fox.

'Of course, no problem,' Tac responded, and it was done.

'Now I must take my leave of you and catch up with the two remaining dragons before they make it to the castle.'

'Wait, you can't go back without a scratch. The king will get wise to our little game.' Bull took hold of Tac by the arms and Fox said 'Sorry about this' and punched Tac in the face, making his nose bleed. Next Fox punched him in the eye, blacking it. Finally he took out his dagger and put a small cut on Tac's cheek so blood would run down his face.

'There you are. By the time you get back to the castle it will look like you've been in a hell of a fight,' said Fox.

With that Tac disappeared.

'So why didn't you let Hawk have him, if you knew you would have to do that?' asked Bull.

'Well, Hawk would have killed him. I was placing punches where they would make a mess, not do the most harm,' Fox answered. 'We must bury Wolf and the treedwellers. Make sure you mark Wolf's grave, so if any of us survive we can come back and get him,' said Fox.

'That's nice - if any of us survive,' said Bull.

'Well, I'll tell you what - one way or the other this is my last war. I'm getting too old for this game. I ache all over. My body can't take the beatings any more - I think it's telling me it has had enough,' said Fox.

So Bull went and got Black Knight and Opium and started to dig graves for the treedwellers and Wolf. They picked up all the dead treedwellers and buried them in a mass grave. As it was their land they would not need to be moved. They then put a plaque up over the grave telling of their brave fight against the dragons and how all the treedwellers were heroes.

Then they placed Wolf in his temporary resting place.

'Throw some water over Hawk to wake her up. She would not want him covered without being able to say good bye.' So Bull did.

Hawk jumped up swinging her fists around and shouting 'I'll kill the little sod.'

'Calm down, Hawk, this is not the time for that,' said Fox.

'We are just going to cover Wolf,' Bull told her.

It all went quiet as they moved round the graveside and stood there praying over his body. Fox and Hawk had tears in their eyes: another member of their family dead and still they did not know if they would ever see the children again or their sister Elk. So all the rebels picked up a handful of dirt and filed past the grave. Black Knight walked past the grave, threw the dirt in and said: 'See you on the next great battlefield, my friend.' Then Ibex: 'Goodbye - you fought well.' Oak said: 'We will win - you will not have died in vain, I promise.' Next it was Hawk's turn. 'I'll miss you. Goodbye. I love you.' Finally, Bull said: 'I'm not much good with words but, wherever you are, be happy.'

All this time the treedwellers had been looking on in amazement. They could not understand what all the fuss was about. One of them came up to Fox and tugged at his trouser leg. 'Why all the sadness over one man?' asked the creature.

'You can speak!' said Fox in amazement.

'Of course I can,' said the treedweller.

'He was my brother,' Fox told him.

'There are at least ten of mine in that grave over there,' said the treedweller.

'We were close and I got him involved in this mess,' answered Fox. 'Now we must go.'

So they left the woods and headed for Waterdown. Their hearts were heavy and their spirits low at the loss of Wolf.

As they walked along, Hawk suddenly said: 'Why Wolf? Why did it have to be him?'

'You might as well say, why Old Grey Bear,' replied Fox. 'He was killed trying to stay out of trouble. At least Wolf died fighting and was not slaughtered like a beast. It's no good your taking on like this. You will see a lot more deaths maybe including mine or Bull's. Any of us could be next. Wolf knew the risk he was taking. I feel worse than you. I got him involved in this mess. Anyone who is not prepared to pay the ultimate price must leave now - and that includes you, my little sister. I can't promise you won't have to pay the price. I loved Wolf too but you can't hold Tac responsible for his death. It was meant to be. Nothing I say or Tac has done can change that.'

After that there was no more conversation between the two or from the other rebels. It had been their first loss in battle and everybody wondered who would be next.

Then, as the sun was setting, they saw Waterdown. It looked like a beautiful jewel, with the gold of the sun reflected in the blue of the water surrounding it. The tall slim buildings looked very inviting. By now the drawbridge had been pulled back for the night, so Hawk rang the bell as hard as she could.

A sentry shouted: 'Who are you and what do you want?'

'It's me - Hawk - and I want to come in to my home village.' The sentry shouted: 'Cat, your troublesome wife is back.'

Cat replied: 'Then get that drawbridge across.'

'But she's got a raiding party with her,' said the sentry.

'Hawk, is that you, sweetheart?' called Cat.

'Don't you sweetheart me. Just get that bridge over here.'

'Yes, that's her, no-one else talks to me like that. Who have you got with you?'

'It's me - Fox - and friends.'

So Cat ordered the drawbridge across and the rebels rode over it into the safety of the village.

'Where have you been?' asked Cat as he flung his arms round Hawk, giving her a welcome home cuddle.

She turned round to see the other rebels collapsed in a heap in the middle of the square.

'Well, Fox, haven't you got something to say to my people?' Hawk asked.

'No, it's your village. You know how to get action from them better than me,' said Fox.

'Cat, can you get all the villagers together in the main square,' said Hawk, 'so I can talk to them.'

When all the people were there, Hawk started a speech.

'We are looking for warriors to fight the dragons. They will come here. We have already arranged it. So if there is anyone in the village who does not want to fight, then they had better leave.'

Then from the crowd came a voice: 'Why should we leave? If you are not here, then the dragons will leave us in peace.'

'No, they won't,' said Hawk. 'My brother had the same idea and instead of fighting with us he stayed at home. The dragons wiped out the whole village - women, children, everything and everyone. We are not safe. If it does not happen now, it will come eventually. The Dragon King wants to rule over everyone and the only way he can do that is by eliminating all opposition, which means you, my friend. He has already destroyed two villages. Maybe this one is next. And you are not going to stop it by sticking your head in the sand. I can assure you one day it will come. So why not fight on our terms and not his?' Hawk paused. 'So do we fight or lie down, let him walk all over us and take whatever he wants?'

Then the crowd roared 'No! We stand and fight!'

'Right, Cat, we'd better fortify the village. Women and children - pack up and move out. You can come back the day after tomorrow. It will be over one way or the other, by then.'

'You must take Colt and leave,' Hawk said to her mother.

'I can't,' said her mother.

'Look, we have lost enough members of this family.'

'What do you mean?' said her mother.

'Were you not listening? Bear's whole village was wiped out, including him. Wolf has been killed. Elk, her son Mole and all Fox's children are rotting in the Dragon King's dungeon. Now please do as I ask.'

So Hawk's mother wandered off to pack up her belongings and get Colt ready to leave.

At last the women and children were assembled in the main square, where they were joined by the men who were too old to fight or did not wish to join in. So Cat said: 'Right, off you go and don't forget, whatever happens, don't come back until the day after tomorrow.'

The carts pulled out of the village. Hawk and the rebels stood and watched as the column moved away. Colt shouted to his uncle Fox: 'Take care of my mum and dad, and bring them back to me.'

'I will, boy, I promise,' said Fox.

Then the column reached a great field and a cloud of dust rose into the air obstructing their view. After that the column just seemed to disappear into the woods.

Hawk said: 'I hope that's not the last time I see that sight. Well, it's no good waiting around - let's get on with some work.'

'Oh God, do we have to - I'm knackered. After an hour and a half of marching and a battle, I don't think any of us feel like doing anything, let alone digging,' said Bull.

'Oh, stop moaning, you bunch of wimps, and get on with the work at hand,' said Hawk.

'You cheeky bitch,' said Fox, but they all got up and crossed the drawbridge to get on with the work that had to be done.

'Right, let's put firing pits by the drawbridge.'

Just as they were going to break earth, a rumbling was heard and suddenly a head appeared from under the ground. Bull was just about to hit the poor creature over the head when Fox shouted: 'Don't! It's a burrower. They are harmless and not only that he could save you a lot of work.'

'Hello,' the creature said. 'What are you doing?'

'We are building defences,' Fox replied.

'Against what?' the burrower asked.

'The dragons are on their way. They destroyed Castlewood amongst other things, and we are going to defeat them,' said Fox.

'Oh, my God, I think my people might be responsible,' said the creature.

'How's that, then?' demanded Fox.

'Well, you know when we find something underground we trade it for whatever we want. When we were passing under your village we found a big deposit of cadadite and told the king. We didn't think it would cause this much trouble. You know we are peaceloving people. We thought he might ask us to get it for him. We were hoping for a good trade. We could have taken the stone and the village would not have been affected at all,' the burrower concluded.

'So that's why he attacked,' said Fox. 'It's all right, I don't think it's your fault. As you said, you could have got it, no trouble.'

'Is there anything I can do to make amends for what has happened?' asked the burrower.

'Yes, you could dig these firing pits for us,' said Bull.

'Consider it done.'

Within a couple of minutes the first was done, and after ten minutes all the firing pits were dug.

'Is that it?' the burrower asked.

'How are you with water?' asked Fox.

'Not bad - why?' said the creature.

'Well, I want a tunnel from the lake to the firing pits so that if the dragons get in we can flood the pits and kill the sods,' said Fox.

In no time at all, it seemed, the thing was done. Then the burrower announced: 'I must go now. Here, take this. If ever you need my people, just blow it. I promise on my honour that my people will come to your assistance - count on it.' Then he went.

'Well, Bull, that saved you a lot of work, did it not?' said Fox.

They camouflaged the pits and then went back across the drawbridge to make further preparations for the battle to come.

'I hope they do not damage Waterdown too much - it's a lovely place. Bull, you and Black Knight and Opium get the barrels of oil and pour them round the perimeter of the village.' The three moved off.

'Now what?' asked Ibex.

'Now we sit and wait,' said Fox.

Then the sentry shouted: 'There's someone at the drawbridge, my leader.'

'Call them across - everybody be on your guard,' said Cat.

So the sentry shouted: 'If you've come in peace, come across and identify yourself.'

'I am the leader of the treedwellers and I seek Fox, leader of the rebels.'

'He's in there, through the gate.'

Then, to everybody's amazement, in walked the treedweller.

'What in hell's name are you doing here?' asked Hawk.

'We heard about Castlewood from the burrowers and as you have already got us involved we thought - what the hell - why not go the whole hog?' said the treedweller. 'You seemed like honourable people and not troublemakers at all. You proved that the second time we met. You tried your utmost not to hurt any of my people, and besides that we would have done the same in your situation.'

'I'm very sorry about getting you involved, but we couldn't ask because we didn't know you could speak our language. We knew you were good fighters, especially when you felt threatened by strangers wandering through your land without permission. And from the painful experience of being beaten up by your warriors plus the fact that we knew if we set up the ambush on the other side of your wood the dragons would be too arrogant to walk round. It was the ideal situation - too good a chance to miss - and all I can say is sorry again. Honestly, it was the only way to beat them,' concluded Fox.

'Well, it doesn't matter. It's in the past and thanks to your wizard friend I lost less than I expected to. He is very handy to have around. We want to join you and defeat the dragons. We know that they will attack us when it suits them. So we will fight till the end with you. By the way, my name is Hawthorne.'

'Well, welcome to the finest band of dragon-slaying rebels in the whole land,' said Fox.

Hawthorne marched back across the drawbridge to collect his men and the treedwellers marched over in columns. As they entered the gatehouse, Cat shouted: 'Three cheers for the treedwellers!' and everybody cheered loudly.

Now they had seven rebels, Cat, thirty men from Waterdown and forty treedwellers.

'Have we got time to kill, by any chance?' asked Hawthorne.

'Yes, as it happens we have,' Fox replied.

'Then I shall tell you why my people always attack creatures who trespass in our wood. About fifty years ago it was completely different. We were trusting. People even camped in the woods. But that was soon to change. It was early one morning and everybody in the settlement was asleep when a band of slavers fell upon us and took nearly all the tribe. They just left the old people, some women, the cripples and the children. We never saw our fathers or older brothers again. Rumour has it that they all died in some stinking mine. Since that day the woods have been off limits to anyone except treedwellers, and that's the way it's likely to stay, I'm afraid,' said Hawthorne.

'So we had better get ready.' Cat took ten men of Waterdown and ten treedwellers to the firing pits. As they were leaving, Hawk shouted: 'Take some food and water - it could be a long wait.'

They crossed the drawbridge and got into the firing pits. They sat down and made themselves comfortable.

'So, chief, what the hell are we going to do when we get overrun - we will be caught like rats in a trap,' said one of the Waterdown men.

'It's not us who will be caught in a trap - quite the opposite. See those reed mats at the back of the firing pits?' said Cat.

'Yes, so what? You don't think they are going to protect us, do you?'

'No, they won't, but behind them is a tunnel leading under the lake. We go down, followed by the dragons, then we punch holes in the roof letting the water in. It will kill the dragons in the tunnels and flood the firing pits,' said Cat.

'So, just out of interest, what's to stop us drowning in the tunnels along with the dragons?' said the man.

'The burrowers dug them on a slant so the water will only run one way. What's my name and what am I?' he asked.

'Your name is Cat and you are my leader,' the man replied.

'So I wouldn't steer you wrong, would I?' said Cat.

'No, I suppose not,' said the man.

Time slipped by very slowly, so the fighters had something to eat and relaxed. Patch walked over to Fox.

'Hello, boy, it won't be long before we are in action again. Let's hope we don't lose too many men this time.'

Patch and the others settled down to wait.

Chapter 7

Tac caught up with the two remaining dragons and returned to the castle with them. The gates were opened.

'The king wants to see you,' said the guard.

So Tac and the two soldiers marched into the great hall.

'Well,' bellowed the king, 'have you eliminated the rebels?'

'No, my lord, we were ambushed by the treedwellers, then the rebels jumped in afterwards and beat our force. We were taken by complete surprise.'

'Well, tracker, what have you to say?'

'I know where they are going,' said Tac. 'I heard them talking. They thought I was dead. They said they were going to Waterdown. There are only eight of them. The people of that village won't help them. It's a fishing village.'

'So how many of my warriors will you need this time?' said the king.

'Only two sections. They should find little if any resistance at all, my lord,' said Tac.

'Don't I recognise you from somewhere?' said the king.

'No, I don't think so, my lord,' answered Tac. 'I would have remembered such a brave warrior if I had met you before.'

The king's chest puffed out with pride. 'Of course not, how silly of me. Right, you go with two of my sections of foot soldiers and finish off this rebel scum Fox once and for all.'

'This time we will avoid the land of the treedwellers,' Tac said. 'We don't need any more trouble with them. We will go across country. It will also be quicker.'

Tac started to worry. 'I hope they are ready,' he thought to himself. 'I can't slow this lot down. They are eager to restore their pride and kick someone's behind to make them pay for the humiliation they feel they have suffered. Fox, we're coming, whether you are ready or not - and let's hope you are or else you're in trouble.'

Fox and his band were ready and waiting.

From the sentry came a shout. 'A column of dust coming this way, and at quite a fast pace.'

'Right, action stations,' said Fox. 'You men in the firing pits - try to split the column. But don't leave it too late before you escape down the tunnels. Hawk, Bull and Black Knight - draw them onto the first island.'

The drawbridge from the island to the village was raised. Hawk, Bull and Black Knight took up their position on the first drawbridge and faced a terrifying sight - eighty dragons bearing down on them all baying for blood, unfortunately theirs. As the dragons got closer the rebels began to shake.

Hawk said: 'For god's sake, Cat, give the order to fire.'

As the enemy got to about two hundred yards Cat shouted 'Fire!' then from the firing pits came a shower of arrows. The first line of dragons dropped. The men in the pits fired again but the dragons kept bearing down on them. Again and again they fired. Hawk, Bull and Black Knight stood and watched.

Fox shouted 'Run, run for your lives if you treasure them!' They ran to the island followed by about fifty dragons.

The people from the village shouted 'Run faster - they're gaining on you!' They got to the island and jumped into a boat which was waiting. Hawk shouted 'Row you two for all you are worth!' Bull and Black Knight pulled on the oars as hard as they could. Just as they left the shore the dragons reached the water's edge and were going so fast that one of the dragons got pushed in. There was a bubbling then sizzling and he went bang and exploded. Bits of dragon rose to the surface and floated on the water.

The dragon officer then shouted 'Fire!' and the dragons launched their spears. As the rebels ducked, two spears struck the back of the boat and one landed in between the seats and pierced the bottom.

Hawk shouted 'Pull, pull, we're taking on water!'

The dragons laughed but the laughing didn't last long. As they turned round, the drawbridge was being raised - they were stuck. The other dragons were fighting the men in the pits and had not noticed.

'I hope Cat's all right,' said Hawk.

'I think so,' Bull replied. 'The dragons haven't overrun the position yet and they're still dropping like flies. Besides that, cats have nine lives.'

They finally reached the shore and went into the village through a side gate. The archers on the village walls took aim and fired onto the island. As the arrows hit their targets the dragons were running backwards and forwards. They were in total panic, not knowing what to do. Then Fox spotted four dragons putting the drawbridge back.

'That means they must have overrun Cat's position - I hope he's all right.'

Back in the pits there was much confusion. The dragons had got through by jumping onto the camouflage over the top of the pits which was only made of thin twigs. About twenty had broken through.

Cat shouted 'To the tunnels!' and the rebels dived into the escape tunnels followed by the dragons.

'Run for your lives!'

Some of the defenders were not so lucky and were caught by the legs and then torn apart.

'We must be over halfway across,' said Cat. 'You hold them off while I dig through to the lake.'

'How?' said one of the defenders.

'Fire your bows.'

'But we can't see anything.'

'You can't miss in this tunnel, you dozy sod,' shouted Cat. 'Just fire - you will hear when you hit something. Just keep firing.'

'Yes, my leader,' said the man.

'Why have they stopped?' asked one of the dragons.

'I don't know,' said the sargeant. 'Just get them.'

'Hurry, Cat, they're getting closer.'

'I'm going as fast as I can.' Just as Cat finished talking, water began to run down his arm. 'It's going - get behind me,' ordered Cat. As he stepped back the water gushed into the tunnel.

'I can hear water, sargeant,' said a dragon.

'Of course you can - there's a lake above us, you numbskull.'

'No, I hear running water and the sound echoes which means it's down here, my sargeant.'

'Right then, run.'

But it was too late. As the water washed down the tunnel it swept the dragons away. Then as the water engulfed their bodies and pushed them further down the tunnels, the rebels could hear them going bang as they exploded. The water then rushed into the firing pits killing the dragons that were still fighting there.

Cat said: 'Come on, let's get out of there while the going's good.'

They scrambled up the ladder and into the lake, bobbing about in the water. Men in boats had heard the dragons exploding and were looking for the rebels who had survived.

Out of the twenty one men who went into the pits only eleven now lived, and they were in the water.

'Hey, you lot in the boats, we are here!'

Four boats came over and picked the men up.

'Right, row for the shore. Let's get back into this battle.'

By now the dragons had got the drawbridge back in place and had regrouped. From the thirty that had tackled the firing pits only seven were left. None of the twenty that had overrun the firing pits had survived. They had all been killed by the water. They had also taken heavy losses on the island. Now they numbered thirty seven.

The drawbridge was down once again. The dragons charged across and into the village. As they came through the main gate the rebels set about the dragons. Bull lit the oil.

'That's not going to help you rebels, we don't mind fire. You don't know your enemies very well, do you?' said the dragon officer.

'It's not for your sake, you fat dipstick. It's for our escape - which you can't do. You're stuck here and when the arrows start to fly you'll see another reason,' said Fox.

By now the fighting was well under way, with the noise of the clashing of swords and shields filling the air. There were dragons wounded and dying, treedwellers impaled on dragons' pikes, men from Waterdown lying on the ground bleeding from wounds.

One poor man was on the ground while a dragon was chewing on his arm. The man could hear his own bones being crushed as the dragon bit down. His arteries were cut and blood sprayed all over him. He could see his own flesh jammed in between the creature's teeth and the sight made him feel sick but there was nothing he could do about it. Then Bull came up behind the creature. He put one hand on its bottom jaw and one on the top and prised the jaws apart, then continued pulling until they snapped, killing the creature outright.

Tac said: 'I will go for help. It's the only way you're going to get off this island. They have removed the drawbridge again and there are none of our men over that side to put it back this time.' So Tac jumped into the water and the officer shouted 'Good luck!'

By now the flames from the oil had grown high enough to give the rebels a chance to escape safely. So Fox gave the order 'to disengage' and the rebels moved back, away from the dragons. Cat said, 'Gather up the wounded.' So the men picked them up, put cloths over their faces and threw them through the flames and into the water where they were picked up by the waiting boats.

'Now run,' said Fox, and all the rebels ran for the wall of flames. Just at that moment the dragons launched their spears, hitting Fox's allies in the back. As the rebels made good their escape there were treedwellers falling into what was supposed to be their cover, their bodies being burned by the fire.

The men from Waterdown were also caught out by the spears and shared the same fate as the treedwellers. Fox and Bull rushed forward and tried to pull their bodies from the flames but the heat was so intense they had to move back. So they put some rags over their heads and tried again. This time the wind changed direction and blew the flames over the two of them. Their hair was singed and their clothes started to smoulder.

'It's no use - we are going to go up in flames as well, even if we do get them out. There's not a lot left, anyway. Fox, come away,' said Bull.

'No, I can't leave them.' Fox started to go forward again. Bull grabbed hold of his shirt and pulled him back.

'I won't let you waste your life on somebody you can't possibly save. We need you - the living and your children,' said Bull. But Fox seemed to be mesmerised by the flames and kept walking forward. Now he was not even attempting to save anyone, just moving closer and closer to the fire. Bull shouted at him but got no response.

'I'm sorry to have to do this, Fox, but it's the only way.' Then Bull smacked Fox round the face so hard that Fox lost his balance and fell to the floor.

'I'm sorry, Fox,' said Bull again.

Fox came to his senses. 'That's all right, thanks,' he replied.

As they stood there, Black Knight came through so fast that he went straight into the water. As his head broke the surface, a spear hit him in the back. He went under and did not come up. Fox dived into the lake and managed to pull him to the surface.

'Bull, help! He is wearing full armour. I don't know how long I can hang on to him.'

Bull picked up an empty oil barrel and threw it in. 'Hang on to him, Fox, I'm coming.' Then he threw two more into the water, dived in after them and pushed them towards Fox and Black Knight.

'It's all right, Fox, I've got him. You can let go,' said Bull.

'Get that boat over here and be quick about it,' said Fox. Bull and Fox pushed Black Knight into the boat.

'You stay with Black Knight. I'll swim back to shore and see if anyone needs help there,' said Bull.

Just as he reached the bank Hawk sprang out from the flames. 'Are you okay?' asked Bull.

'Yes, fine. Have you seen Cat?'

'He just left on one of the boats with the wounded,' Bull replied.

'He's not...' but before Hawk got the chance to finish her sentence, Bull said, 'No, he is not wounded. He went along to help.'

'Oh, thank god he's all right,' said Hawk.

'Is there anyone left in there?' asked Bull.

'I don't know,' Hawk replied.

Just then a man stumbled through the flames. He had a dragon's pike stuck in his shoulder. He fell face down in the dirt. Hawk pulled the pike out and they rolled him over. He was still breathing. He started to twitch and moan.

'Quick, Bull, move him - his feet are burning.'

Bull lifted the man and placed his feet in the lake. You could hear his feet hiss as they hit the water.

'Ah, that's better,' said the man. 'Thanks.'

'I'm going to go through to see if anyone's still alive,' said Bull.

'No, don't,' said Hawk, but it was too late, he was gone. Hawk heard shouting. 'Get off them, you great fat green blob.' Then she heard a punch landing and to her surprise a dragon landed in front of her. She heard Bull say 'Hold tight' and he appeared with three wounded warriors. He had a Waterdown man on his back and a treedweller under each arm. As he jumped through the flames, the dragon went to get up. Bull kicked him and stood on his neck. 'You stay where you are.' Hawk took out her sword and stabbed the creature in the stomach.

'Get one of those boats over here,' she shouted. They loaded the injured into the boat. 'Was there anybody left in there alive?' Hawk asked.

'No, I'm afraid not. Let's get to the bank and finish this off once and for all.'

As the boat reached the shore, Bull and Hawk jumped out and pulled the craft onto dry land. Fox was sitting holding Black Knight up and Opium was on the other side.

'Where's Tac, for god's sake?' asked Fox.

'I'm here,' said Tac.

'Come over here. Can you save him?'

'No, I can't. He has lost too much blood and his life force is too weak,' answered Tac.

'Well, it looks like my turn to go,' said Black Knight. 'We have fought together many times, Fox my dear friend. You and your brothers mean the same to me as Opium does. And your sisters were like the sisters I never had. I will always be grateful to your mother and father for treating Opium and me like family. My brother, you know I love you even though we don't always see eye to eye.' Black Knight looked up at Fox. 'I'm sorry I let you down just when you needed me most.'

'You could never let me down. You have saved my life many times and, if I could, I would give my life in return for yours,' said Fox.

Hawk said: 'Goodbye, Black Knight, have a good journey.'

Then Bull said: 'Thanks for my life.'

'Goodbye, old friend,' said Ibex.

'I'm sorry I couldn't help you,' said Tac.

Oak just said: 'Another member of my family is dying. I can't think of anything to say.'

'You said it better than anyone could. You called me family. That means a lot,' said Black Knight. 'I want to be placed on my horse and be in death as I was in life, a nomadic wanderer. Well, my friends, I will see you on the next great battlefield.'

The others walked away leaving Opium holding Black Knight in his arms. 'Don't go, little brother,' said Opium.

'I have no choice.' With that Black Knight closed his eyes and died.

Cat had already lined up the archers, ready to fire into the village. 'Fire!' he shouted.

The air was filled with arrows. They rained down on the village and the trapped dragons. After hearing several explosions the rebels knew their plan had worked. As the arrows hit the dragons the gases escaped from their stomachs and as there was fire all around the village they just blew up.

'That should have halved their numbers,' said Cat, 'as they have nowhere to go. Put the bridge back - let's finish them off.'

'Then we can have something to eat,' said Bull.

'Is that all he thinks about?' asked Hawk.

'Yes - now charge.'

The rebels ran across the drawbridge yelling: 'Kill them! Let's finish them!' Then the dragons rushed from the other direction. They met halfway across when the rebels ran straight into them.

Fox took out his sword and swung it as he rushed past the first line of dragons, catching one in the chest and dealing him a fatal blow. Bull brought his battleaxe down onto a dragon's head. He pulled it out, then swung round taking a dragon's arm off at the elbow. The creature just stood there in shock, green blood spurting out. Then it fell to the ground gripping its arm and shaking and whimpering. Bull just walked off.

Cat was in the middle of a fight with three of the beasts. He sliced one across the leg. It went down onto its knees and Cat hacked its head clean off. Just then another swung a chain and mace at Cat. He saw it coming out of the corner of his eye and got his shield up to block the blow. The chain and mace caught on the side of his shield. Cat pulled, throwing the dragon off balance. It came crashing down on top of him, knocking his sword out of his hand. The worst thing was that the third dragon was just about to cut Cat in half with a battleaxe. Then there was a scream 'No, don't!' and Hawk launched herself into the air and landed on the dragon's back. She started to chop at its neck with her tomahawk. It seemed to have no effect until she moved round to the front of his neck and chopped him in the windpipe. Then he dropped his battleaxe and fell to the ground.

'Thanks, sweetheart, I owe you,' said Cat.

'Yes, you do,' Hawk replied.

The dragon couldn't believe it. 'Have a conversation as if this was a teaparty,' he said.

Cat reached down to his waist, pulled out his dagger and plunged it deep into the dragon's stomach, making sure it was the right hand side. The dragon slumped forward, letting all its weight fall into Cat.

'Hawk, get him off,' yelled Cat.

She pulled the creature off her husband. 'This is going to cost you a lot of pampering,' she said.

Ibex had just despatched a dragon when a rock hit his hand and made him drop his sword. As he turned round he saw a dragon charging towards him with a pike in both hands. 'I hope this works,' he said to himself. He grabbed the pike and pulled the dragon forward. Then he stuck his feet on its chest, took the creature's weight and flung it over. It landed on its back. Unfortunately the dragon still had the pike in his hands while Ibex was unarmed. Oak shouted across and threw a sword. Ibex caught it by the hilt and drove it into the creature's throat. 'Thanks, Oak,' he said.

A massive battle was rampaging all around them. Oak smashed a dragon round the side of the head, knocking him off the bridge and into the water. He watched with great delight as it hissed and boiled up, then it just exploded as the gases built up. Cold water has a heating effect and as the water puts out the pilot lights there is no way to release the build-up of pressure.

It was hard work pushing the dragons back to the island. Fox shouted: 'Not one single dragon must be allowed to reach the other side or Tac will be finished. I didn't expect so many of them to have survived,' he added, half to himself.

The dragons began to push the rebels backwards. So the man picked up some buckets, filled them with water and threw them at the dragons, making them retreat rather quickly. When they had been moved back far enough, the buckets were discarded. The hand to hand fighting continued.

In front of Fox was a man from Waterdown until a giant chain and mace swung in his direction and smashed him in the side of the head, knocking him into the lake. Fox dived in and pulled him back towards the bridge.

'Bull, pull him out, he's still alive.' So Bull took hold of the man under the arms and pulled him out. 'Tac, come and sort this one out,' he shouted.

'I can't, the dragons are watching me,' said Tac.

'It doesn't matter,' said Fox. 'None of them are leaving this island alive.'

'I'm not sure about this,' said Tac.

'I don't care whether you're sure or not,' said Bull. 'Just get on with it.'

Just then a dragon grabbed hold of Bull and another started to punch him. Fox was still in the water. Bull headbutted the dragon and at the same time Fox pushed his leg from under him, sending the creature toppling into the lake. The bubbles started to rise.

'Duck, Fox, he's going to explode!' Bull shouted.

So Fox dived under the water, just in time. The dragon went bang.

Fox swam under the bridge, came up behind the second dragon and stuck a knife in the creature's ankle. It released Bull. He snatched Tac's staff from his hand and thrust it into the dragon's head. It screamed in pain and fell backwards into the water, then exploded. Tac's staff disappeared. Fox said 'I'll get it,' and dived back under the water. A couple of minutes later he surfaced. 'I can't find it.'

'I'm so sorry,' said Bull.

'Don't worry, watch this,' said Tac. 'Staff, staff, do your trick; come back here and make it quick.' The staff came spinning up out of the water straight into Tac's hand.

'That's amazing,' said Bull.

When the battle had started there had been two sections of dragon warriors totalling about eighty. Now the creatures' numbers were so depleted that only fifteen were left standing and they were being reduced with every onslaught. Fox was slicing and stabbing one after the other. Ibex smashed a dragon over the head with a chair sending it crashing through a hut door. Ibex took out his dagger and pounced on the dragon in a frenzied attack, stabbing it again and again. Fox ran up behind him. 'He's dead. That's enough. Get off him. Calm down.' Ibex just kept on stabbing the by now very dead dragon, so Fox picked up a bucket of water and threw it over him. Ibex's hand stilled and he looked down at the body. 'Oh, my god, I got a bit carried away, didn't I?'

'Just slightly,' said Fox.

Then Opium was grabbed from behind by two dragons. He struggled, kicking and punching at the dragons, but all to no avail - he was held in a vice-like grip.

Then one of the dragons said: 'Let's see what rebels have inside them. You hold him and we'll take a look.' Then it took its razor-sharp pike and sliced deep across Opium's chest, cutting straight through his breastplate and shirt and opening up his chest wide. The blood poured out. Opium let out a scream of pain.

Patch leapt onto the dragon holding Opium and started to rip at the creature in a mad frenzy of biting and tearing. Then the dragon had to let go when the dog ripped a big chunk of muscle out of his arm. Opium fell to the ground. The dragon kicked Opium in the ribs and hit him over the head with the handle of the axe, knocking him out. Then the dragon turned his attention to Patch, kicking him and punching him, making him whimper. After the dog was down it picked him up by the back legs and swung him round, then let go, sending the dog flying out over the lake. Then splash, the dog had a long swim back.

By now Opium was coming round. The dragons took hold of his curly hair and pulled him up to his knees. 'So this is a big brave rebel.' Then they slapped him round the side of the face with such force that they knocked one of his teeth out.

'If you think I'm going to beg for my life, you are very much mistaken.' He spat blood over the dragon and shouted: 'You're just scum and you will never, never defeat the rebels. If you kill all of us there will be someone else to take our place.'

'Oh, is that so?' The creatures kicked him in the face and when he went down they started to kick him all over the body and head.

'Beg for mercy, you scum.'

'Never, never, I won't beg. I'll see you in hell first,' and he lunged forward with a dagger, catching one of the dragons in the stomach.

Then Fox and Bull spotted Opium, his face completely covered in blood. But they were too far away to stop what was going to happen next.

Again the dragons took hold of his hair. Opium looked towards Fox and shouted: 'I'll see you on the next great battlefield. Goodbye, my friend, and make my death worth something. Beat the sadistic sods.'

Then, before Fox or Bull could move, one of the dragons brought down his axe and chopped Opium's head from his shoulders.

Bull and Fox ran towards the dragons. Two other dragons stood in their way. Bull just charged straight through them, knocking them into the water. 'Get out of my way!' He just kept going as the creatures exploded. 'You rotten gits.' Then he chopped off the head of the dragon that had just killed Opium. Fox grabbed the second dragon and started to punch the creature. He hit it in the face with the hilt of his sword and then went on to beat it with his shield and stamp on it. Finally he drew his sword and slashed the creature's throat open so wide that its head nearly came off.

Oak pushed two more dragons into the lake and took great pleasure in listening to them going bang. Hawk was holding her own. The treedwellers were all over the dragons. The fact that the dragons were twice their size didn't make any difference to them.

Then it was all over - for the time being. The rebels had won their second victory. Two of the dragons and Tac ran off, the only survivors of the invading force. Waterdown was a total mess: buildings with holes, doors and windows smashed, fires burning, dragons dead and dying all over the place. There were fourteen dead Waterdown men and ten of the treedwellers were out for good. The whole village was littered with dead and dying men and dragons.

'Bull, finish the dragons off,' said Fox.

'My pleasure. Oak, give me a hand.'

'No problem.'

So Bull took his battleaxe and chopped their heads off and that was the end of them.

'So let's get the dead cleared away, build a bonfire and burn the dragons.'

It was like a giant firework party. As the bodies began to burn they all went bang and blew up into hundreds of pieces.

The dead men of Waterdown were loaded onto rafts. It was their right, the way of the fisher folk, to have a burial at sea, so to speak. So the rafts were cut adrift and when they were far enough out the archers lit their arrows and waited for the command. Cat shouted 'Fire!' and the burning arrows thudded into the oil-soaked rafts, setting them alight. The sun had started to go down and the burning rafts lit up the evening sky. It was a sad but strangely beautiful sight - the rafts drifting further and further away as the flames consumed more and more of the wood. They slowly began to sink and as they went down there was a hissing and a bubbling, then they were gone.

After that it was time to bury the dead treedwellers. Hawthorne said 'We will take them home to their own land and meet you back here in the morning.'

'Take a cart, it will save you a walk,' said Cat.

'We can't - we don't know how to control the beasts that pull them,' said Hawthorne.

'I will send two of my men with you,' said Cat.

'Thank you very much,' Hawthorne replied.

So the treedwellers all jumped onto the cart and set off for their beloved woods with two men from Waterdown driving for them.

When they had left, the rebels that remained began to pick up the pieces of the village. They started by patching up windows, putting doors back on their hinges and dousing fires. Once they had cleared up as much as they could, they had to face the part that none of them relished. It was of course to say goodbye to their fallen friends and comrades in arms. It was Black Knight's wish to be placed on his horse and to be in death as he had been in life - a nomadic wanderer travelling all over this bright and beautiful land. So Bull placed Black Knight upon his faithful black steed with tears in his eyes and said goodbye. Then the other rebels gathered round his horse to say their last farewells and after that Bull slapped the horse on the rump and it galloped off into the misty darkness.

Fox shouted: 'We will see you on the next great battlefield, my friend,' and they watched until the horse disappeared from view.

Then Fox said: 'Oak, you and Bull dig a grave for Opium and make it deep so the houndcats don't dig him up. We will come back for him soon. Did you get Tac to cast the same spell on him as he did on Wolf?' Fox asked Hawk.

'Yes, he did,' she answered.

'The grave is done,' said Oak, after a while. 'Shall we put him in it now?'

'Yes, let's get it done,' Fox replied.

So they placed their friend in the ground. By this time, it was all too much for Hawk. No matter how hard she was, she had grown up with all the rebels who had died and of course one was her brother. And then there were the men of Waterdown she came into contact with every day. Some were even related to her husband Cat. Now she burst into tears, but Cat was there to comfort her.

They all knew that after this second defeat the Dragon King would not rest until he had destroyed the rebels or died trying.

Fox suddenly said: 'I hope Tac gets away with his ploy. He's definitely pushing his luck with the Dragon King. He has got to get suspicious, especially since one of the dragons might have seen him treating the Waterdown men. And he is also one of only three survivors. It's got to look a bit fishy, don't you think?'

'Well, maybe not. Tac can take care of himself, I hope,' said Bull.

'I do hope so,' said Hawk.

'Well, the next part of the plan is to ride back to the land of the hillanders,' said Fox.

'But how, without getting too close to the dragons?'

'We will cut across the great swamp,' said Fox.

'But what about all the bogs and quicksands, and the creatures that live there? I'm not too sure about this one, Fox,' said Bull.

'Look, trust me, I know what I'm doing,' Fox told him.

'Yea, but I'm not so sure about that. I don't like the great swamp,' said Bull.

'Why, what's wrong with the great swamp?' asked Ibex.

'You mean you don't know?' said Bull. Ibex shook his head. 'Apart from the fact that it's an evil, smelly bogie place, I also had a bad experience there. It was about five years ago. I had come to see Fox and to recover from a war wound. It was pretty bad. Anyway, I stray from the story. Fox and nearly the whole village were going after a herd of wild horses and I said 'I'll come with you.' So we set off after these horses. We caught up with the herd about two miles from the great swamp. Then one of the men shouted: 'We must turn the herd, otherwise they will end up at the bottom of a bog or quick sand.' So, like the fool I am, I volunteered to head them off.

'We managed to get in front of the herd but, just as we were going to turn the horses, out of the swamp jumped this mudlink. It spat its venom over my horse, killing it instantly. I went down like a ton of bricks and the horse was on my legs. The mudlink was not interested in me, but to add insult to injury a houndcat jumped out of nowhere and as you know he would have eaten me if he could. Well, I managed to pull myself clear from under the horse and found I had left my battleaxe behind at Fox's house. So I picked up a stick and started to back up, then I tripped on a tree root and fell back into a bog.

'They say things happen in threes and that day they did, as to top it all the houndcat just kept coming forward. I was definitely on his menu. I thought 'This is it - breakfast for a scruffy houndcat.' Then to my relief I heard horses hooves and the sound of arrows in flight. Then thud, thud, as the arrows hit their target and the creature dropped to the ground, dead.

'Just then I heard more hooves coming my way. I couldn't see a damn thing because of the hole I was in. I heard the mudlink kick up a fuss then heard it spit again and by the sound it made it hit a shield. I heard a voice and it said 'Go on, clear off, come back for your meal later.' Then a voice I knew said 'Thanks, Black, where's the rider of the horse?'

'The man said 'Over there, I think. That's where I shot the houndcat.' Suddenly a rope came over, then another. The voice I didn't know said 'Why two ropes?'

'You will see when we pull him out. Let's put it like this - if he were a fish, you would not throw him back,' said Fox. 'Right, pull.' Both horses moved forward and I was released from my sticky trap. As I pulled myself onto the bank there was a nomad sitting astride a jet black stallion in full armour complete with lance and shield and all in black, shining and bright.

'Hullo, Bull, taking a bath were we? Next time, try water,' said Fox.

'Oh, very funny.' I was not amused at his remarks one little bit.

'This is my old friend the Black Knight, prince of the southern deserts,' said Fox. 'You, my cousin, owe him your life.'

'I am very grateful - thank you. I hope one day I can repay the service,' I told him.

'No doubt one day, my friend, you may find a way,' said Black Knight. 'Well, goodbye, my good friend Fox.'

'Fox said: 'Goodbye and give my regards to your brother.'

'I will,' he said as he rode off. That was the first time I met the Black Knight and it was the unluckiest day of my life when I nearly got myself killed three times. Our next meeting was also our last.'

'Look, Bull, don't you trust me? When have I ever steered you wrong?' asked Fox.

'Never. But I can't go back - it's bad luck for me, that place. I'd rather die with my battleaxe in my hand than in one of those horrible bogs. Or, worse still, at the hands of one of those disgusting mudlinks or being eaten by a houndcat,' said Bull.

'Look,' said Fox, 'when you were in trouble at home, who came and sorted it out for you?'

'You did,' Bull answered.

'Nothing is going to happen to you in the great swamp, I promise you on my honour,' said Fox.

'How in hell's name can you swear that on your honour?' said Bull.

'Well, that's easy. One, we are not going to be galloping through the swamp and I know the place like the back of my hand. You forget we used to play there as children. Two, the mudlinks are not there - they are either hibernating or have gone south for the warmer weather. And three, houndcats won't attack a large number of armed riders. Does that satisfy you?' asked Fox.

'Yes, I suppose so,' Bull replied.

'Now, let's get some sleep. The treedwellers will be back soon.'

So they took some well-earned rest only to be woken a couple of hours later, in the early morning, by the clatter of cartwheels as the others returned from their unpleasant task.

They didn't stop for breakfast. Cat shouted 'Let's move out,' so they all pulled out, the fifteen treedwellers on the cart and the rest on horseback. Patch for some reason was excited, jumping and barking round Fox's horse. 'All right, boy, calm down,' said Fox.

After about four miles, Fox looked behind him. Bull, who hadn't got much sleep, was nodding off in the saddle.

'Hawk, give Bull a nudge. It's not too far to the great swamp and I don't want him falling off his horse into something nasty.'

So Hawk poked Bull with a sword and he jumped.

'What, was I asleep?'

'Yes,' Hawk replied.

Then Cat suggested they should pick up the pace because they still had a long way to go, at least another twenty miles.

They pushed the horses hard and eventually came to the edge of the great swamp.

'Now, listen to me,' said Fox. 'You must stay on the tracks. If you wander off I will not be held responsible. Is that clear?'

'What about the cart?' said Hawk. 'We won't get that through there, will we?'

'No, unhitch the horses and load the gear onto them. The treedwellers can double up with the rest of us. Well, Bull's right about this place - it is creepy.'

The mist was hugging the ground very closely; you could hardly see your hand in front of your face, let alone make out the small tracks they had to follow. The paths seemed to twist and wind for ever as they followed Fox. Bull's horse stumbled off the side of the track but luckily enough it regained its footing and pulled itself back onto the path.

'Now stay awake, will you, Bull,' said Fox.

'I'll try,' Bull replied.

Then they came to a clearing. 'We must be nearly at the end,' said Hawk.

'No, we are only halfway through,' Fox said.

'Look, there's a fruit tree over there. I'm going to get some,' said Bull. He started to walk towards the tree.

'Don't step off the path,' shouted Fox.

'Why, I'm starving. Look, it's only a couple of steps away.'

'If you take those steps you won't want to eat again,' said Fox.

'You're on a wind up,' said Bull.

'Right, watch this.' Fox picked up a log and threw it into the bog. With a gulp and a bubble the log just disappeared beneath the surface of the ground. 'That's why I told you not to leave the path. Now will you take some notice of me, for god's sake, if you want to stay alive. Please don't be fooled into leaving the path again. It's the swamp's way of getting you. It's all a trick. Now we'll stop here for a while and move on when the horses are rested.'

Meanwhile Tac had returned to the Dragon King with yet more bad news. This time the king was not so forgiving.

'So,' he said, looking closely at Tac, 'I do know you, don't I?'

'No, you don't,' Tac replied.

'You are the keeper of the unicorns - I knew we had met. I had your family put to death, didn't I?' said the Dragon King.

'Yes, that's right. I wanted my revenge and I got it,' said Tac.

'Well, unfortunately I know how to take your powers away from you. Your wife was tricked into giving me that knowledge by me telling her I would save her children and you. That was just before I ran her through with my own sword,' said the king.

'I don't believe you,' answered Tac.

'All right, I will tell you how, then we will put it to the test.' The king ordered his guard to get a hairdresser. Tac's face dropped in amazement.

'So when the hairdresser cuts your hair and beard are you then going to have your powers?' laughed the king.

'All right, so you know,' said Tac.

'You have betrayed me,' the king said, 'so now you will get your just reward.'

Then the hairdresser came into the hall.

'Cut it all off,' ordered the king.

So the hairdresser did as he was commanded. By the time he had finished Tac was nearly bald with tiny cuts on his head and on his face from the razor. He looked a right sight.

Two guards grabbed him from behind and a third started to punch Tac in the stomach. He doubled up in pain. The king lifted his head up by his ear and said: 'Have you anything to say, traitor?'

'Yes, plenty. I'm not a traitor because to be one you must start off being loyal to the person or thing you betray, and I was never that to you. I will never tell where the rebels are. That is a promise on the graves of my wife and children.'

'We will see,' said the king. The guard went to work on Tac again, hitting him in the face. He punched harder and harder, making the blood pour from Tac's face like a waterfall. The floor where he stood was one giant puddle of blood.

'Well, keeper of the unicorns, are you ready to talk now?' said the king.

'Never. I don't care what you do to me. My life means nothing, nor has it for many years since you took my family away along with my beautiful unicorns. So you will get nothing from me, no matter what you do.'

'Well, as you won't tell me what I want to know, and you have no powers any more, we will see how you stand up to the dragons' line.'

So in came a section of dragons. They walked past Tac and made two lines with a space down the middle. Then a rope was tied round Tac's neck. As he was pulled across the floor he coughed and spluttered as he tried to stop the rope from cutting off his air supply. Then he came to the first of the dragons who kicked and stamped on him. As he went up the line he was hit with clubs and pikes and punched. Just as he thought it couldn't get any worse the rope he was attached to was slung up over one of the beams.

'Are you ready to talk?' said the Dragon King.

'No, I'm not,' Tac answered.

So the rope was pulled tight and Tac was lifted from the ground. The king took out a sword and said: 'This is the sword that took your wife and children's lives.' The Dragon King cut a big wound in Tac's chest. The blood gushed out all over the king.

'Let me down. I'll tell you where you can find the rebels,' gasped Tac.

'Ha ha, I knew you would come round to my way of thinking, you scum. Now, healer, heal thyself.'

Tac could do nothing without his powers. The only thing he could do was to die slowly and painfully.

The king had no intention of making Tac's death easy or quick. He turned to the sargeant at arms and said: 'Send one hundred of my best foot soldiers and a detachment of flying dragons and take this miserable traitorous creature with you. Before you start the final battle to eliminate these pitiful rebels who think they can defeat the force of the Dragon King, give them back their spy. Tell them it's a gift from me to them.'

'Yes, my lord, it's as good as done,' said the sargeant at arms.

'One more thing: if you can't defeat this pitiful rebellion then you had better not return, any of you. I want you to order your warriors to fight to the last till either every one of you is dead or every one of them. I don't want any of my soldiers returning here saying they've lost again. So go and make me proud and victorious,' concluded the Dragon King.

So the dragons formed ranks and were just going to move out when the king shouted: 'Take a cart for the rebels' bodies so I can see them when you return.'

So they hitched up a cart and threw Tac on the back of it, then marched off towards the hillanders' territory.

The ride was long and painful for Tac. They had tied his arms to the back of the cart so he could not even attempt to stop the bleeding from his chest wound. He also felt every bump in the very uneven track which was no more than a footpath. The dragons seemed to enjoy watching him in pain. The driver seemed to go out of his way to find every pothole he could. So Tac decided to do some taunting of his own.

'You know you're not coming back, don't you?' he said. 'Fox and his rebels will eat you for breakfast. I expect they will be very hungry by now. And if you don't win - and you won't - you can never return home to the castle. You will be outcasts with no honour and nowhere to go.'

A guard walked up beside the cart and hit Tac on the head. 'Shut that nonsense up,' he said, but Tac didn't hear as he was out cold.

The rebel army was now made up of five of the original rebels, fifteen men from Waterdown, fifteen treedwellers and, last but not least, Cat.

'Right,' said Fox, 'the horses have rested enough. We still have a hard route march ahead. It's twelve miles to the hills and we have to make twelve in the same time it's going to take the dragons to do nine.'

'Yes, but we have horses - they don't,' said Hawk.

'That's right,' agreed Bull.

'But we can't push the horses too hard for two reasons,' said Fox. 'One, we happen to be in the middle of a swamp which stretches all the way from here to the hillanders' territory. We have to be there before the dragons because Ibex has to find his men and convince them to fight with us. If they don't you may as well cut your own throat now. Besides that, even with the hillanders' help, we must be in position for the plan to work at all. Furthermore, fifteen of the horses are carrying two people.'

'Yes, and no doubt they will have flying dragons with them - they can move a lot quicker than the foot soldiers,' said Oak.

'Yes, but without the support of the foot soldiers we could defeat the flying dragons, no problem, and they know that. They are never sent too far ahead of the main column,' said Fox.

'So less of the chat and let's get moving,' said Cat.

'One more thing,' said Fox. 'If any horses go lame, the riders will have to catch up the best way they can. Ibex must get there in time. We can't afford to stop and wait for anyone, whoever it may be.'

So the rebels set off as fast as they could given the conditions they were up against. The mist had still not lifted or thinned. They still could not see too far in front of them.

Ibex then said: 'To hell with it!' and prepared to gallop off. 'If I don't make it, tell my people it was my last request for them to fight to the last.' Then he disappeared into the mist, followed very closely by Fox.

Ibex and Fox finally came to the edge of the swamp.

'There are my wonderful hills,' Ibex said.

'Are you sure your people will fight with us?' asked Fox.

'Fox, of course - am I not their leader? They will follow me to the ends of the earth if I asked, and anyway they will have to fight the dragons because when the dragons run out of cadadite from under Castlewood they will come for our mines. So it might as well be now rather than later, while we have a force where all the fighters are tried and trusted and we have the dragons at a disadvantage.'

'It sounds sensible to me but it's not me you have to convince of that fact, is it?' said Fox. 'They might think it's none of their business and they might feel it's safer to sit this one out. Why should they put their lives on the line for us?'

'Because it's not for us, as you put it. They will die at the hands of the dragons - it's a foregone conclusion.' As Ibex finished talking the others turned up. 'Don't worry, I promise I will win them over,' he said.

'Let's hope you're right or we are in big trouble.'

They came to the edge of the hillanders' territory.

'You wait here,' said Ibex. 'I will go and talk to my people.'

'Well, make it quick - the dragons can't be far behind us,' said Bull.

'Please bring plenty of men with you,' said Oak. 'We are going to need everyone you can muster.'

'I have one hundred good fighting men. I shall return with as many as I can persuade to come with me.'

'Yes, but for god's sake make it quick,' said Fox. 'We can't afford to get ambushed out here in the open with only thirty-seven men - it would be a massacre.'

Ibex then disappeared from view.

'I hope he doesn't take too long,' said Hawk. 'I don't feel very safe sitting here in the open and undermanned.'

Ibex reached the village and asked his people to gather around.

'I have something to ask you,' he said. 'I want you to come with me to fight the dragons. They are at this very moment heading towards our lands.'

'But why are they coming here? We have done nothing to them,' said one of the villagers.

'Down in the valley there is a band of rebels. They have already fought two battles with the dragons and won. They have lost loved ones and, if we don't help, all thirty-seven of those warriors will certainly be killed. They also had done nothing to the Dragon King but their villages were destroyed and their families were taken as slaves. Fox's brother's village was completely destroyed, all the women and children were slaughtered like cattle.'

'So what's that got to do with us?' said one of the women.

'Well, it all started because cadadite was found under Castlewood,' Ibex explained. 'What do you think will happen when it runs out?'

'I still don't see what it has to do with us,' said one man.

'Are you really that dense? Everybody knows we make a living from mining these great hills of ours and we come across cadadite. Then the dragons move in, take over our land, destroy us or worse still turn us into slaves to work our own mines and get nothing for our trouble. So how would you like to watch as they kill our women and children in front of your eyes? It's going to happen, maybe not today or tomorrow but, take my word for it, one day it will happen.' Ibex took a deep breath. 'So, do we fight or do I go back to my friend Fox and tell him I have a village full of cowards? Whatever you decide, I am going, for the honour of the village and for my own peace of mind. I could not live knowing I let my friend die on his own, and I would rather die than live in a village that has no honour, because that village will die. People will stop trading with us. The inhabitants may live but the name of the village will mean nothing in the history books after someone has written about the rebels and the great battle and how other villages gave their all in the struggle for freedom. The treedwellers, Waterdown folk, Scrapford, Castlewood, Fox has lost two of his brothers, his children, two of his lifelong friends, all have laid down their lives in the struggle. And what will the hillanders go down as in the history books? I will tell you. As the only village surrounding the dragons' lair to throw in the towel before the battle even started, then was overrun a couple of months later and put up no fight.

'I'm leaving now and if you don't throw in your lot with the rebels and I don't die, you will have to find yourselves a new leader. And who would be willing to lead a village with no pride?'

So Ibex picked up his weapons, mounted his horse and headed for the valley to meet the other rebels. He knew in his heart that his people would fight. They could not bear the thought that they would be considered cowards and, as Ibex had said, a village with no honour could not be trusted which meant no-one would trade with them.

Then, as he rode down the track which led to the valley floor, he heard many hooves coming up behind him. He turned round and smiled at his men.

'You knew damn well we would come,' said one of the men. 'You shamed us into it.'

'No, I told the truth as I saw it. You know it's true. And I know my people. You could not live with the shame of being called cowards and you could not fight everybody who labelled you with that reputation, so you would rather die. Am I not right?' asked Ibex.

'Yes, my leader, you are right. We could not live that way,' said the man.

So they all went down to meet the rebels together.

It was half an hour later when Cat said: 'I can hear someone coming. I can hear rocks falling. It can't be the dragons, can it?'

'It must be Ibex,' said Hawk.

It was indeed Ibex, with eighty men.

'Great one, Ibex. It looks like we will have enough to hold them off, even beat them again,' said Bull.

'Thank you, I told you I would not fail you, or at least my people wouldn't.'

'How did you get them to follow you, my old friend?' asked Fox.

'Between you and me, I went straight for the jugular. I must admit I shamed them into it. I don't know if they would have come anyway but I just did not give them a chance to say no without losing their honour.'

'I don't suppose you brought anything to eat and drink?' said Bull.

'As it happens...' said Ibex.

'You didn't?' said Bull.

'Yes, we did. There's beef, fowl and lamb in the saddlebags.'

'Oh, good man,' said Bull. 'So let's get to it. I hate to fight on an empty stomach.'

So they all sat down to eat while they had a chance to, before the dragons turned up for their revenge. When they had finished their meal they sat chatting and laughing for a while, because before long they would have nothing to laugh about. And maybe there would be some who would never laugh again.

'Right, if I've done my sums right, I work out that in the first battle they lost roughly one section,' said Fox. 'In the next they lost two sections. That means, in all, about one hundred and twenty warriors. So the Dragon King now has two hundred and eighty men.'

'Do we have to face two hundred and eighty of the things?' said one of the hillanders.

'No, of course not. He has to hold half of his force back to protect the castle,' said Fox.

'How do you know?' asked Bull.

'Because he does not know how many we are,' Fox replied.

'What if he has tortured Tac?' asked Ibex.

'Even if he has, Tac can't tell him what he doesn't know. Don't underestimate the Dragon King - he is not stupid. He would not send all his dragons. It would leave the door open for us if we defeated his army and he is not absolutely sure we couldn't do that. So I reckon about one hundred and forty dragons have been despatched.'

A man's hand went up at the back. 'Just out of interest, how many men did you lose in those two battles?' he asked.

'As it happens, fifty-two. Do you want me to list them? Three rebels, thirty-five treedwellers, fourteen men from Waterdown. That's nearly three to one in our favour. And what's more, this time we have the swamp to help with the odds,' said Fox.

'We have one hundred and twenty-two warriors,' said Ibex. 'More than a match for one hundred and forty dragons.'

'I do hope so, because look what I can see overhead,' said Hawk.

They looked up and there they were, the flying dragons.

'According to my darling cousin, the column can't be far behind,' said Bull.

'Now then, Bull, sarcasm does not become you,' said Fox. 'The main column is just over there, take my word for it.'

Then to the rebels' surprise a dragon warrior marched through the mist waving a white flag and carrying something on his back.

'Here is a present from my king to you, the rebels,' announced the dragon in a loud voice.

'Well, let's not waste any more time. Let's see what you've brought for us.'

So the dragon tipped up the sack and out fell a bloodstained body.

'Who the hell is that supposed to be?' said Hawk.

'I don't know, as yet,' said Fox.

The person spoke. 'It's me, Tac.'

The dragon just stood there grinning as Fox shouted at Bull: 'Pick him up.' So he did and took him away out of sight of the dragon who was practically laughing.

Oak shouted at the creature. 'You evil green lump of slime!'

'Clean him up, Hawk,' Cat said. So she took a bottle of water and some rags and cleaned the blood from his face.

'Where's Fox?' Tac asked.

'I'm right here, my friend.'

'The Dragon King remembered me and the guards saw me helping you,' Tac told him. 'He wanted me to tell him where you were. I could not just tell him - he would have known it was a trap. I didn't tell all the time they were kicking and punching me. I waited for them to string me up then when he cut my chest open I screamed for mercy and told him what he wanted to hear. It's too late for me now, I'm dying, but I didn't let you down. They're here, are they not, and I did not let on what you were planning for them, I swear.'

'We know you played your part well. We would never have got this far if it had not been for you. You're a very brave man to go back in there. Your family would be proud of you. Is that not right, Bull?' asked Fox.

'Very proud,' Bull agreed. 'And I must say you have more courage than me, that's for sure - the bravest one of all of us.'

'Well, my rebellious friends, I will see you on the next great battlefield,' said Tac, and passed away in Fox's arms.

The dragon roared with laughter. 'This will be your last battlefield, so you won't have to wait long before you join your pitiful little friend who squealed like a pig when my king stuck him with his sword. That is just what he is, a stuck pig,' said the dragon, still laughing.

This was too much for Hawk to stand. She took out her knife and plunged it deep into the dragon's chest, so deep in fact that the creature's blood trickled down the knife and onto her fingers.

'Then laugh about that if you can,' she said, smiling at him.

But the creature could do nothing except stand and stare in amazement. Then he fell backwards, landing with a thump on the ground.

Lightning suddenly filled the sky and thunder crashed all around. Dark clouds moved quickly in and then the rain fell, battering the armour of the rebels. It came down so hard it became quite painful.

Bull said in disgust: 'We've got to fight in this.'

'No, I'm sure the dragons will wait till the weather's just right for you,' said Oak. 'Of course we've got to fight, you dipstick.'

'How would you like a knuckle sandwich?' said Bull.

'Will you two stop bitching, for god's sake,' Hawk screamed at the pair of them.

'I don't believe it,' said Cat. 'Look, those clouds look just like unicorns running across the great plains.'

'It looks like Tac's found his beloved herd of unicorns,' said Hawk.

For a long moment the rebels gazed up at the scudding clouds. Then they braced themselves for the dragons' attack.

Chapter 8

A loud roar came from the dragons' ranks and then the air was filled with flying dragons. They stayed in such tight formation that they blacked out the sun. It was as if someone had taken the sun away. It was as dark as that for a time, then the sun started to break through as the creatures dived onto the rebels, scratching and tugging at them.

Hawk was grabbed by the arm and the attacking dragon started to drag her up. She screamed and pulled backwards and managed to catch hold of a tree branch. She hung on for dear life. Now she was being stretched. She could feel the dragon's claws digging into her wrist as the creature pulled and tugged, trying to break her grip on the tree. She could feel her muscles tearing. As the pain became unbearable she looked down and saw Cat.

'For god's sake, do something!' she cried. As quick as a flash, Cat launched a battleaxe from his hand and took the creature's wing completely off. It fell to the ground. Cat rushed to the bottom of the tree and caught Hawk as she fell.

'Thanks, darling,' she said.

'For what?' said Cat.

'For being there when I need you, as always.'

The flying dragon was on the ground. Bull stamped on its neck to hold it down while he struck it a fatal blow.

Then all hell broke loose as the dragons threw everything they had at the rebels. Flying dragons came in again for the attack and the archers fired again and again. By now there were two types of rain because it was also raining bits of dragon. Everybody was now soaking wet and covered in green spots from where dragons had exploded overhead.

The foot soldiers advanced with their pikes down, making an impenetrable fence, then the row behind launched their spears into the air. They landed on the front rank of the rebels and they fell to the ground. Amongst the dead was the hillander Ropeman. His skill and balance had not saved him. In this situation the front line of dragons simply moved forward, mowing down anyone who stood their ground.

Fox looked up to see men being ripped to pieces by flying dragons. He watched as a hillander was held by one while another took hold of his arm and flew in the opposite direction, ripping the man's arm out of its socket. The man screamed in agony. The dragons knew he could no longer fight - he was no threat anymore - so they just dropped him on the men below.

The rain was still coming down hard as well as bits of bodies, blood and discarded weapons. It was a difficult choice between putting your shield over your head to stop something hitting you from above or putting it in front of you to avoid being struck by a dragon's pike.

Bull looked to his left and saw a dragon strike at a hillander. The warrior blocked the strike and ran the creature through. Then a body fell from the sky, smashing the man on the back of the neck. The hillander fell to the ground, his face in the mud. As he was dazed he couldn't push the body off. Bull watched as the man began to blow bubbles as his face was pushed into the mixture of blood, rain and mud. Bull went to help but before he could get there a dragon stabbed the hillander with a sword.

There were treedwellers impaled on pikes, dead and dying all round. Hawk was hit in the arm by a spear. 'That's it,' said Fox, 'this situation is getting intolerable. Time to put the next part of the plan into action.' So Fox shouted 'Withdraw!' The fighting stopped and the rebels started to back up, keeping their eyes firmly fixed on the dragons as they moved towards the swamp. Quite a few of the rebels tripped over the dead as they went.

Withdrawing was not going to be an easy task. As most of the warriors had full armour on and it had been raining for about half an hour, the battlefield was soaking wet, a disgusting mixture of water and blood. It was like trying to run on a block of toffee. Every step they took made their feet sink deeper and deeper. It was extremely hard work and it made their legs ache. As they ran they had to pull hard and all that could be heard was the sound of squelching feet. It got harder and harder to walk as the mud stuck to the bottom of their boots. It was as if their boots were made of lead. Then to their horror the dragons' line advanced faster. The rebels forgot all about the mud and panicked. The rebel lines scattered and they all started to run, slipping and sliding all over the place.

Quite a few of the rebels ended up on their backs in the mud. One man tripped over a body and slid along the ground. As he did so water sprayed up on from the side of him. Ibex was standing talking to Fox. The man's body turned sideways; he could not shout a warning because he could not see anything. He just kept going and swept Ibex's feet from under him, sending Ibex into the air. He came back to earth with a thud.

'Are you all right?' asked Fox. Ibex didn't reply but lay there winded, so Fox waited for a minute to give him a chance to get his breath back. Then he and Bull pulled Ibex to his feet.

'Come on, Ibex, we haven't got time for you to lie around,' said Fox.

'Ha ha, very funny,' said Ibex.

Then one of the hillanders said: 'So this is how we keep our pride - by making fools of ourselves for the dragons' amusement.'

'No, because we will have the last laugh, I promise you,' said Fox.

The dragons were cheering. 'They are running like scared little rabbits. Look at them falling around like drunken fools. Now they are on the run, let's give chase and go Fox hunting. We can take a tail home for our king. Now let's put this rebellious scum out of its misery once and for all.'

'Right, Ibex,' said Fox, 'since most of the men are yours, you take them and set up our little surprise party. I'll take Bull, Cat and a handful of treedwellers with me and we'll lead them to the place we discussed.'

'I'm glad it's you running and not me,' said Ibex.

'I only hope we make it. Hawk, since you're wounded, you go with Ibex. No buts, you will do as you're told for once in your life. You're losing too much blood - you would never make it with us.'

Hawk looked at Cat. 'He is right. Now go,' said Cat.

Ibex and his party slipped off towards the hills. Ibex looked back at Fox. 'Don't worry, I know what to do. I will be there. I won't let you down, I promise.'

'I know you won't,' Fox replied. Then he shouted: 'Right, lads, if you value your lives, then run!'

The small party of rebels ran towards the swamp and, as they had hoped, the dragons took the bait and followed them into the ambush.

'Now we've got you! It's the bog and quicksand or us! Attack!'

The dragons charged forward and Fox shouted: 'No surrender!' Cat threw a tomahawk at a dragon. It hit him in the chest and the creature dropped to the ground. Bull swung his battleaxe round, cutting a dragon's arm off. Fox moved forward, cutting and slashing at the dragons. The treedwellers were stabbing at them with their tridents.

'Pull back!' shouted the dragon officer. The dragons disengaged and moved back about twenty feet. 'Now listen,' said the officer. 'You might as well surrender. Those cowardly hillanders have cleared off and left you to it. Why all die here?'

'Because we would rather die standing up like true warriors than be taken to your castle to be humiliated and killed like dogs,' said Fox. 'And, besides that, who said we are going to die here? Take a look behind you.'

'Do you really think I'm going to fall for the oldest trick in the book?' said the officer.

'Please yourself,' replied Fox.

Then from behind two of his men fell to the ground. The officer turned round and saw that his men were dead. The trap was sprung: Ibex and the others were attacking in force.

'Now you're surrounded,' laughed Fox. 'Let's get them!'

So they attacked from both sides. Fox charged through the dragons' ranks towards the officer. As he went, Bull came up behind him, protecting his back, cutting down dragons as he went.

'What's the matter with you, Fox? Have you got a death wish?' said Bull.

'No, I just want to teach this cocky officer a lesson. Give me a boost.'

'You have lost it if you think I'm going to launch you in amongst that lot,' said Bull.

'Look, I'm going to get him. This battle will be over quicker and with less hard work if I kill him. It will demoralize the dragons and with any luck they will fold and give in,' said Fox.

So Bull cupped his hands together and bent his knees. Fox ran up and put his foot into Bull's hands, then with all his strength Bull pushed Fox upwards. He sailed through the air, over the heads of the dragons. 'This is great - the only way to travel.' Then he saw the officer in question and managed to direct himself towards him. He took out his dagger and as he landed on the dragon's back he plunged the dagger deep into the back of the creature's neck. It fell to the ground with Fox still on its back. Fox looked up to see himself surrounded by hordes of angry dragons.

'Oops, just dropped in for a chat.' The dragons stood and glared at him. 'Not funny? That's the trouble with you dragons - no sense of humour,' said Fox. He stood up and as he drew his sword two dragons attacked with pikes. One lunged at his stomach. He knocked it down, then swiped it round the face. It backed off. Then the second dragon came in for the fight.

Fox shouted: 'Bull, for god's sake throw me my shield.'

'I told you so.'

'Forget told you so and throw it now,' Fox called with panic in his voice. So Bull threw it as hard as he could. As it came down it bounced off the head of the dragon that was attacking Fox. The creature fell to the ground, unconscious.

'Great shot, Bull.' Fox made sure it didn't get up again by slashing its throat.

More dragons attacked, smashing on Fox's shield. Suddenly everything came to a stop as a horn was blown. Ibex shouted: 'Rebels, form ranks by me!' Fox took the opportunity to escape. He put his shield on his back; in front of him was a dragon holding his pike in both hands. Fox thought to himself 'I can use him as a springboard.' He ran up and jumped onto the pike, pulled on the dragon's head and sprang into the air. He passed over the dragons' lines, headed towards the rebels and crash-landed at the feet of Bull and Ibex.

'I know you worship me, Fox, but there's no need to throw yourself at my feet like that,' said Bull.

'Ha ha, just help me up,' Fox replied.

'Bull pulled Fox to his feet. 'Did you get him?'

'Of course,' Fox replied.

'Then what took you so long to get here?' asked Bull.

Ibex shouted: 'Archers, concentrate on the flying dragons. Keep them off our men's backs.'

The archers opened fire and the flying dragons began falling like autumn leaves. Unfortunately some of the dragons were falling on or around the rebels. Bull shouted at Oak: 'Look out!' He looked up as a dragon fell directly above him and got his shield up in time. The creature crashed onto the shield and Oak's legs buckled under the weight, landing in a crumpled heap on the ground. He got up from that and shouted 'Thanks, Bull.'

By now there were nearly as many flying dragons on the ground as there were in the air. Most had not been killed outright. They were snapping at the rebels' heels and legs. They still had enough energy and pigheadedness to bite the rebels, cutting them and making them jump. Several of the rebels had deep bite wounds.

Fox shouted: 'Ibex, get a squad of men together.'

'What for?'

'Because this is a ridiculous situation - even when we've shot them down they're wounding our men. We need to run every one of them through as they come down, just in case,' said Fox.

So a squad of men ran in between the warriors killing the flying dragons as they came down.

Then the rebels charged at the foot soldiers, pushing them back and breaking their lines, scattering the soldiers. Presently, the sargeant at arms shouted the order to reform ranks. Then he ordered pikes down and there was again an impenetrable fence in front of the dragons.

One of the flying dragons swooped down, picked up Patch and flew upwards again. Luckily enough a Waterdown man shot the dragon down and Ibex was in the right place at the right time to catch Patch.

The flying dragons had by now all been shot down, so the rebels turned their attention to the foot soldiers. The plan was to drive the dragons into the swamp.

'Archers, take aim, fire!' Forty bowmen opened fire on the foot soldiers, arrows filled the space between the archers and the dragons and then the front rank fell down. The archers fired again and the next line went down. Now just the back line was left.

'Please don't kill us,' the dragons pleaded.

'I'm sorry but we can't trust you. You've already broken your word by taking Castlewood. You promised no trouble but went back on your word,' said Fox.

'You can't expect any mercy. What mercy did you show to the people of Castlewood and Scrapford?' said Hawk.

The dragons started to back up, then splash they fell into the swamp. Some of them exploded and the others were shot dead.

After the battle was done with the rebels began to count the cost of the encounter. They had lost twenty hillanders, three men from Waterdown and seven treedwellers, and of course Tac.

'That leaves eighty-six warriors against one hundred and forty dragons,' said Fox.

'We are outnumbered,' said a hillander.

'We were outnumbered in the battle we have just won,' said Fox. 'We have just killed two sections of the Dragon King's best warriors. That means what's left are the older ones and maybe the lame and sick. Anyone who can't handle it should leave now. I think you should take Hawk home, Cat, she doesn't look fit enough to carry on.'

'I'm seeing this through - I've come this far,' said Hawk. 'It's the final battle tomorrow and I'm going to be there, come hell or high water. Not you or anyone else will stop me, I want to be there to see the look on your children's faces when we win and release them from that hell hole. I will cut the first warrior who tries to stop me.'

'You know Hawk as well as I do, Fox. Once she makes up her mind there's no changing it,' said Cat.

'Has anyone here got some magic herbs about their person, then at least we can close the wound,' said Fox.

'The medicine man at the village has,' said Ibex.

'That's no good - at the rate the blood's coming out, she won't make it as far as your village.' Fox called Cat to one side. 'She's your wife - knock her out and I'll sew her up.'

So Cat walked over to Hawk and shouted her name. She turned round and he punched her in the jaw, knocking her out. As she keeled over, Ibex caught her from behind.

'Sorry, darling, it had to be done,' said Cat. 'Come on, Fox, hurry up and sew her up.'

'All right, I'm coming. You stay around just in case she wakes up, then you can hit her again.' Fox ripped up some rags. 'Oak, you give me a hand. You mop up the blood and I'll stitch.'

So Fox began to sew his sister up. It took a lot of stitches to close the gaping wound which had sliced through the muscle. By the time Fox had finished he had put in twenty stitches and the rag was completely red.

'Right, let's get her on a horse. Cat, you'd better ride with her and for goodness' sake don't let her fall or you will open the wound again,' said Fox.

'Let's go to my village,' said Ibex. So they headed for the foothills. They were giant sand stones that you could climb, but unless you knew the secret path there was no way you could get horses up there, let alone an army. Then if you managed to find the path at all, which could take all day, you would discover it was guarded. If you managed to take the guard out without alerting the whole village, then there were all sorts of traps set off by ropes and sticks causing landslides and giant logs to fall on you. You could also run into giant planks of wood with spikes in them that sprang up and killed you outright. If you managed to get past all that you would have to face nearly two hundred angry villagers. If you survived all that, you were either very lucky or a great warrior.

Ibex took them to a rock and said: 'Come on, go through.'

'We can't - it's solid rock,' said Bull.

'In this case, don't trust your eyes, trust my word - go through.'

So Fox thought 'what the hell' and just went straight through the rock, then shouted: 'Come on, you lot!' So they all went through.

Ibex said: 'You must follow me carefully now, to avoid the traps.' So they all stayed in single file.

'We are being watched,' said Bull.

'They've been up there watching us throughout the whole battle,' said Fox.

'Ibex, how did you get your magic rock?' asked Hawk.

'Well, the mudlinks had cornered a wizard and were just going to make a meal of him when a hunting party I was in came across him and chased the creatures off. He was so grateful that he cast a spell and lo and behold the magic rock.'

'But mudlinks don't as a rule attack humans for food,' said Fox.

'No, but that was a very lean year, as the animals stayed away for some reason, god only knows why,' said Ibex.

As they finally came to the top of the pass, the hillanders started to cheer. The rebels took a bow. 'Thank you,' they said.

'Right, get these brave warriors something to eat and drink and tend to their wounds,' said Ibex.

'Yes, my leader,' said the villagers.

The fires were already burning nicely, so the fighters sat down to warm themselves. It was still drizzling but the rebels were shielded from the rain by the overhang of the cliffs. They were also just too tired and hungry to worry about the weather.

Then the food was served, so they ate and drank while they grew warm.

A hillander asked his leader: 'Why does Fox call you Ibex, and how come you know each other, when as a rule the villages don't have anything to do with each other?'

'Well, Chief Hillmond of the hillanders did seem a bit of a mouthful, as we were both chiefs in our own right. Ibex seemed to fit the bill, as Fox said, when he saw me jumping about on the rocks, he thought I looked just like an alpine Ibex, with the tiny beard I had then. We both received our titles by inheritance, from our fathers, who were still very much alive and kicking, then. So we formed a band of fighters, helping wherever we were needed, mainly fighting the Dragon King and warlords just like him.'

Then a Waterdown man said: 'But I thought Fox had an elder brother.'

'Yes, that's right, but my brother married the daughter of the Scrapford leader and, as he had no sons, my brother became their leader when her father died. So I was next in line.'

'So you have crossed swords with the dragons before?' said a treedweller.

'Yes, many times,' said Oak. 'There used to be a lot more villages, before the Dragon King came to the land. He was hungry for power, if he wanted something he just took it and laid waste to whatever he could not use. That's why we must stop him for good this time, before all the people surrounding the dragons' castle are put to the sword or made into slaves.'

'So how many of you were there originally?' asked Hawk.

'Well, there was me, Wolf, Oak, Opium, Black Knight, Ibex and Old Grey Bear. Then there was cousin Snake and of course your husband and many others whose villages and people are no longer there, in other words extinct. Opium and Black Knight were brothers, as you already know: they belonged to a nomadic tribe called the Knights of the Desert. They were the bravest fighters I have ever known,' said Fox.

'So why did you all join together to fight?' asked Bull.

'That's an easy question to answer,' said Ibex. 'Fox was my best friend. His family had saved my life after a hunting party I was with was ambushed by a dragon raiding party. Just as I was ready to meet my maker Fox's father and his men saved me. In those days the dragons always killed their victims, so there was no evidence against them. They were not so powerful, and they did not like the idea of anyone taking revenge upon them.

'I was taken back to Castlewood, then Fox's father sent a runner to my village, to tell my father what had happened to me.'

'Why didn't they just take you back?' asked Bull.

'Because if a raiding party had turned up in the territory of the hillanders, they would have been attacked and, as we had been getting trouble from raiders, there could have been injuries or even deaths. The runner came back: my father and most of his men were not in the village, so he had left a message for my father to come and collect me. It was quite a few days before my people came, so Fox and I got to know each other very well and became the best of friends. We have stayed that way ever since,' Ibex concluded.

'What about the others?' asked a hillander.

'Well, Oak was from a tribe called the woodcraftmen, thanks to their skill at crafting wood into almost anything you wanted. They were also wiped out by the dragons, god only knows why, and Fox's father took him in. Black Knight and Opium's tribe was completely wiped out for the few sacks of cadadite they were transporting.

'So you see, we all basically joined forces for the same reason: hatred of the Dragon King and other would-be tin-pot rulers who thought they had the right to take anything they wanted,' Ibex concluded.

'So how did you stop the dragons last time?' asked Hawk.

It was Oak's turn to answer. 'All the villages that were left pulled together, and we beat them by sheer numbers. In the end the Dragon King had no choice but to surrender, which he did.'

'So why in hell's name did you not kill him while you had the chance, there and then?' asked Hawk.

'Well, after we had defeated him, he said he would leave this land never to return. He left, and we locked the castle up for what we considered to be for evermore. No-one went there and we lived in peace for about twenty years. Then the Dragon King sent his flying dragons to take the castle back,' said Fox.

'So why did you not throw him out when he set foot in there?' asked Bull.

'Well, he said he was sick of wandering with nowhere to call home,' said Oak. 'And he said he had changed: he and his people just wanted to settle down in peace. He had learned his lesson in those many years and was sorry for all the trouble he had caused. So the villages agreed to let him stop. Of course Fox made a fuss, but he let it go because he was out-voted.'

'So basically it's your own fault, this trouble you've got into,' said a hillander.

'You lot make me sick,' said Fox. 'You were not going to help this time. If it came to a fight, we were the ones that would suffer. I didn't want the dragons to stop here, but it was people like you who let them stay. They were not prepared to fight to clear him and his murderous band of cut-throats out, just like you are now. I wanted my revenge, but was not allowed, and because people are so forgiving and trusting I lost my village, two brothers, my children, friends and maybe tomorrow my life, so don't you take a self-righteous attitude with me, you little prat, or you will meet your maker here and now.'

'Oh yeah!' The man drew his sword and brought it down towards Fox.

'Look out!' Bull shouted.

Fox brought his sword up and blocked the blow, then jumped to his feet to defend himself. The clashing of swords filled the village.

Ibex shouted: 'Stop - save it for the battlefield!' and the hillander stopped in his tracks. Fox was going to strike when Ibex blocked his blow. The hillanders jumped up and drew their swords, the rebels drew theirs. The atmosphere in the camp became very tense as Fox and Ibex stood facing each other, swords locked together, both straining for the upper hand.

'I command you to stop,' said Ibex.

'No-one commands me to do anything,' Fox replied.

'In my territory I command who or what I want, or else,' said Ibex.

'Or else what?' asked Fox.

'Or else I will kill you myself.'

'If you think you can, then try,' said Fox.

'Look, Fox, I will have to try, to save face. Even if I lose, you and the other rebels won't leave this camp alive. I don't want you fighting with my people: he would not stand a chance against you. If you kill that young man, my people will not fight for you. He is a well liked man, though he is untried - green. It would be murder, like killing a child, and as it stands you are an outsider to them,' said Ibex.

Fox turned, looked at the other rebels, then to the villagers and noticed the swords drawn. He turned back to the young man.

'You'd better hope you or I die on the battlefield tomorrow. For your sake it had better be me - no-one draws a sword on me without someone spilling blood.'

Ibex said: 'I think it's time we turned in. We have a lot to do tomorrow, and let's hope we win.'

Now the situation had calmed down, the swords were dropped and everyone wandered off. Ibex went over to the young man who had insulted Fox and said: 'I think you had better apologise. If you value your life, I would be very humble. I have never seen him so angry before. If he said he is going to kill you, he will.'

'Thanks for standing up for me,' the man said.

'I was not standing up for you. If he had killed you, which is a foregone conclusion, the people would not have fought, that's why you're still alive.'

'You reckon,' said the man.

'I know it for a fact, and unless you're prepared to kill or be killed, don't ever draw your sword on anyone ever again,' said Ibex.

'Ha,' the young man laughed.

'Don't you dare laugh at something so important as a man's life,' said Ibex. 'Let me ask you something. Do you think you could defeat me in combat? Answer honestly.'

'No, my leader,' the young man replied.

'Well, Fox could: he and his village have just finished a tournament. Fox was the winner against men twenty years younger, and the men of Castlewood, as you well know, are famous for their bravery and skill on the battlefield. So you would be no problem for him. Do you understand what you have let yourself in for?' demanded Ibex.

'Yes, my leader, and I am sorry.'

'It's not me you need to convince of that fact, it's Fox,' said Ibex.

The young man hung his head and walked slowly towards Fox. He stood in front of him and coughed discreetly.

Fox looked up. 'What do you want?' he snapped.

'I'm deeply sorry for insulting your honour and being stupid enough to draw my sword on you. If you wish, I will meet you after tomorrow's battle to give you satisfaction.'

'What is your name?' asked Fox.

'My name is Reed.'

'Well, let me tell you something, Reed. I don't suppose I will be seeing you after the battle, anyway.'

'Do you mean you don't think I'm good enough to fight in this battle?'

'No, that's not what I mean, never mind,' said Fox. Then he got up and headed towards a sentry who was sitting by the edge of the cliffs.

'Good evening, how are things?' asked Fox.

'Not so bad, a bit cold and sleepy, other than that I'm fine.'

'How about letting me take over your shift - I can't sleep.'

'I can't. My leader would have my guts for his bow string,' the sentry replied.

'I'm your leader's friend and I promise I will clear it with him. You won't get into any trouble, you have my word on that,' said Fox.

'Okay, if that's what you want,' said the sentry. He stood up and walked away, and Fox watched as he disappeared into the darkness.

Fox sat down by the fire and gazed at the flames as they flickered and danced in the breeze. He wondered what he had done to deserve this heartache. Then his concentration was broken by the sound of falling rocks. He jumped to his feet, sword in hand, and looked out towards the mountain range and the hills that surrounded him. Peering into the darkness, he spotted a rabbit scrambling up the rocks and knocking debris down as it leapt from ledge to ledge.

'It's only a rabbit going home - I wish I could,' said Fox. 'I'm getting jumpy in my old age.'

He settled back down by the fire, his gaze returned to the flames and his mind wandered back to the events of the last few days. He had not had time to mourn the passing of his two brothers and his life-long friends. Now their faces flicked through his mind and tears came into his eyes. Maybe if he had not survived the massacre at Castlewood, his fellow rebels would still be alive. Fox's attention turned to the funeral fires that burned in the valley below, lighting up the splendour of the hills. Then he heard the sound of paws pattering on the ground behind him and he felt Patch licking him on the back of the neck. The dog had come to find his master.

'Hello, boy, how's you? We've lost a lot of loved ones these past few days. You know tomorrow will be our last battle. We are both getting too old for this game now. I have had this feeling for some time that neither of us is going to see the sun go down again. Still, we've had a good innings, haven't we? I'd rather go now in battle than die of old age in my bed, bit by bit, slowly. That would never do for creatures like us. Born to fight. The battlefield is the only place where we feel truly alive, so it is the only place we should be in when death comes for us, don't you agree, boy?'

Fox looked at his dog and noticed the animal was looking old and worn out.

'Good god, what must I look like? I haven't washed in days or shaved or even brushed my teeth. On the other hand, why the hell am I worried about what I look like? All those deaths in the past few days, and here is Fox worrying about whether he smells or not.'

Then Fox heard more footsteps behind him and this time they were too loud to be an animal.

'What are you doing here, Fox?' asked Hawk.

'I'm doing sentry duty,' he replied.

'Yes, I can see that. But why aren't you asleep like the others?'

'I will have all eternity to sleep after we have defeated the dragons tomorrow. Both Patch and I will join the others on the battlefield of death then,' said Fox.

'Please don't talk like that. You're going to be fine. You're just tired - all you need is a good night's sleep,' said Hawk.

'No, Oak was right when he said I should have died at Castlewood. At least you would still have had two brothers, and many warriors would be standing with their families and not resting in the cold earth this night.'

'Oak talks out of the back of his head. It would have come to this anyway. Don't you think we would not have found out who was responsible, and taken our revenge on the perpetrator of that evil deed? The warriors would still have given their lives, whether you had died or not. You're punishing yourself for something that's none of your doing. It's not as if you went out looking for a fight to prove how brave and fearless you are. It was thrust upon you, so stop beating yourself up.'

'I suppose you're right,' said Fox. By now Hawk was standing behind her brother, her arms round his neck. Fox tapped her hands. 'You'd better get some sleep - you will need it.'

'Why don't you take some of your own advice? Good night, Fox,' said Hawk.

She wandered off back towards the village; Fox called after her and she stopped and turned round.

'You know I love you, little sister, always have and always will, no matter what happens tomorrow.'

'Yes, I know, and I feel the same.' Hawk went on her way and Fox watched her walk back to the settlement, where the fires were burning brightly.

The light from the fires reflected off the hills, in turn lighting up the whole village as if it were still daylight. Fox could see the settlement quite clearly. The houses were built into the rocks, sealed against the weather by wood. Fox looked at the buildings: tree trunks were sunk into the top and bottom of the caves. The gaps had been plugged with a tar-like substance which Fox assumed was collected from the Great Swamp. From the top of the rocks he noticed lots of pipes, chimneys perhaps; there seemed to be an awful lot of them for one dwelling.

He looked round the settlement and noticed the horses were also stabled in a cutting in the rocks, and their gate went from bottom to top. There was no way they could bolt unless someone left the gate open. A channel had been cut in the rock, to bring a continuous supply of clean water to the horses. Any dirt or mess was simply washed away.

Then there was the main stream that supplied clean drinking water for the villagers. It ran through the middle of the settlement. As the light of the fires shone on it, it seemed to sparkle and leap. It ran the full length of the village, then gurgled down a hole in the rocks and disappeared from Fox's sight. So he stood up, took a piece of burning wood from the fire and walked to the edge of the rocks to where the stream seemed to vanish. He looked over very cautiously: it was a long drop to the bottom. The stream came out about three feet below the surface from an underground tunnel worn through the rocks over many hundreds of years. He watched with fascination as the water cascaded down hundreds of feet to join the Great Swamp below, on the valley floor. As it hit the stagnant water, the surface seemed to jump with joy at its arrival, as if it was pleased to see it. Clean water splashed into pools worn from the solid rock, making a lifeline for the animals around the Great Swamp. Without it, there would be nothing to drink, as the swamp water was deadly to every animal except the mudlinks.

Fox watched for a little while, then returned to the fire. His gaze once again fell on the buildings: there were so many families in the village, but not so many houses. Fox saw a hillander walking back from the stables, so he shouted: 'Can you spare me a minute?'

The man came over. 'Yes, Fox, what can I do for you?'

'Well, I'm puzzled. You have lots of people in the village, but not many huts. Where do you put everybody?'

'The buildings may look few, but looks can be very deceiving. We build the entrances small because of lack of wood. It's very hard bringing heavy building materials up two hundred feet. It all has to be pulled up on ropes, that's once we've got it here, cut and transported. Then getting up to the top can take nearly two weeks. Most of the wood is used for tunnel props, which we must have or else we would not be able to make a living. The caves are massive inside, very warm and cosy in winter and cool in summer.'

'So you all live together?' asked Fox.

'No, far from it. The families have separate accommodation made possible by weaving walls of reeds which we harvest in autumn. Two reasons for this: one, the reeds are dry and two, there aren't any mudlinks around then. We can't afford to lose horses; as you know, horse is their meat. It's hard work harvesting the reeds, so we turn it into a celebration. The women and children help cut the reeds and load the horses. The most amazing part of it is standing above the pass and watching the horses walking up on their own, long lines of them - at least fifty.'

'On their own?' Fox asked the man.

'Yes, of course. They have nowhere to go but up - it's too narrow to turn round - so they just wander up slowly. When they get to the top, they're unloaded and led back down. And that's how we accommodate all our villagers, my friend,' concluded the man.

The hills surrounded the village and seemed to cuddle it and keep it safe, like a father looking after his child, watching and protecting his offspring. By now Fox was beginning to get a bit sleepy. So he said: 'Patch, watch,' and pointed at the emptiness beneath them. 'Wake me if anything comes, but I think the king of dragons is waiting for us to come to him this time.'

So Fox fell asleep, knowing full well that Patch would not. He just sat close to his master, watching the horizon, waiting for something to move, but Fox was right and no-one came near at all.

When the sun came up, the dog nudged Fox to wake him. He jumped to his feet. 'Who? What? Where? Oh, it's morning. Good boy.'

Fox went down to one of the many waterfalls, took all his clothes off, as no-one was around, and had a refreshing shower. Patch jumped about frantically in the water, leaping up at his master's legs.

'Be careful. Look, you've marked me - your claws are hard.' The dog stopped and stared at his master guiltily, his ears down. He was such a pitiful sight Fox had to call him over and tell him it was all right. He patted him, and the dog automatically responded by wagging his tail.

'It doesn't take much to make you happy, does it?'

When he had finished, he went back to the fire he had been sitting by all night, took his shaving kit out from his saddlebags and had a shave. When he had finished he sat back and looked at the dog.

'Amazing how much better you feel after a wash and a shave. Now I feel like a new man.'

He then walked to the edge of the rocks to take one last look at the view. You could see everything spread out in front of you. It was like looking at a map. Below him was the great swamp, to the left were the ruins of Scrapford, then to the left of them was their objective, the Dragon King's castle. Three miles behind the castle were the remains of Castlewood. He could also see the woods of the treedwellers and finally his sister's beautiful village of Waterdown, all set in a sea of lush green grass.

Then he heard Hawk shouting: 'Come on, up and at it, you lot. It's breakfast time.' All the rebels got up and started to get something to eat, then suddenly the village was wide awake. People were rushing about, everywhere Fox looked men and women were readying horses, cleaning swords, checking weapons. The village was charged with a feeling of excitement, fear and readiness. Fox wandered down to eat with the others.

'Good morning, Fox. You look neat and tidy - you make the rest of us look like a bunch of tramps,' said Bull.

'Well, if I'm going to die today, I want to be remembered as clean shaven and smelling pretty,' replied Fox. 'And, while I have your attention, I would like to say a few words to Ibex and his people.'

Now the whole village stopped to listen. 'Thank you for your warm hospitality, and your help in our hour of need. To my men who have already fought with me, I am honoured to have known such brave, fearless fighters. To my family who have stood by me, I love you all and hope I may return the debt in full one day.'

'It's we who have repaid the debt to you over the last few days - you owe us nothing,' said Bull. He walked over to Fox, picked him up by the waist and proceeded to give him a hug. Unfortunately Bull did not know his own strength, and Fox found it increasingly hard to breathe.

'Bull, let go. You're squeezing the life out of me - I can feel my back breaking.' In fact Fox could hear his back clicking.

Bull released his grip. 'I'm sorry, Fox, I didn't mean to hurt you. I just get carried away sometimes.'

Fox got his breath back and went to clean his armour. By the time he had finished it sparkled like a jewel. The other rebels finished eating and they too had a wash and shave.

'We don't want Fox to show us up,' said Bull.

'No matter how much you scrub, you'll never come up clean, you ugly old so-and-so,' Fox laughed and turned away.

'You cheeky sod,' said Bull and threw a horse brush at Fox.

'Missed me,' he laughed again. He walked up the hill and got his saddle then returned to where his horse was stabled and took him out. First he cleaned the animal's hooves, flicking bits of mud and stones out with a spoon, as it was the only thing to hand. Then he gave the horse a good brushing ready for the journey to come. He placed the saddle on the horse's back, checked the bridle, then sat down to wait.

Fox hated waiting. It was the worst thing about the whole situation. It gave him time to think, which made him nervous. Things started tumbling through his mind. What if he died before he even got through the gate? And, if he did, would he see his whole family wiped out in front of his eyes? Could they win? It would be a lot easier just to charge in, both fists flying. Then you have no time to think of the consequences - you just do it automatically. Then he heard a voice.

'What's the matter, Fox - nervous?' said Hawk.

'What? No, no - just daydreaming.' He sat and watched the others getting ready for what was to come.

Everybody was now in the corral getting their mounts ready for battle, so Fox took his horse out and tethered him to one of the bars of the corral. There were warriors here cleaning armour and weapons and brushing down horses. The village was buzzing with activity. Ibex came into the middle of the village.

'Come on, you lot, move yourselves. The time has come to face our last battle, one way or the other. So come on, pull your finger out and let's get to it.' Ibex turned to Fox. 'You really started something with this smartening yourself up business, now everybody's at it.'

'Well, if you've got to go, why not go in style,' said Fox.

'Come on, you lot, we have a date with destiny,' said Hawk.

So the rebels mounted their horses for the final confrontation. Then Ibex handed a banner to the man named Reed. 'You can carry our colours into battle,' he said.

'So it's to end in death. The Dragon King must die,' said Fox.

Now they rode off on the nine mile ride to their possible death. But this battle they could not afford to lose, because defeat would be the end of everything they held dear.

Down through the pass, out from the secret rock and then they looked up and saw the hillanders waving and cheering, shouting: 'Good bye, good luck and come back safely.'

Then past the great swamp to the great plain which stretched to the Dragon King's back garden, so to speak. Here Fox signalled for the others to stop.

'Now's your last chance. If there is anybody who wants to turn back, they had better do it now. There will be no shame attached,' said Fox.

A shout went up. 'No way! We are with you till the end and victory!'

Fox looked along the line. This sight would stay in his memory for ever. How smart the men looked, and how proud they made him feel.

So they started off across the great plain, and it wasn't long before the castle came into sight. Fox said: 'Bull, go and cut down a big tree to make a battering ram. You never know, we might need it to get in.' So Bull took six men ahead of the column to do the job.

By now the rebels' hearts were racing with excitement and fear, as the castle and the dragons got closer and closer. The time was getting near for the final battle.

Bull came back. 'It's done. The tree-trunk is in the cart and ready for use, if needs be.'

They were now right on the doorstep of the castle. The party stopped.

'Now, my fine warriors, it's time to say your last words or prayers,' said Ibex.

So the rebels bowed their heads and prayed for a successful campaign.

'All finished?' asked Ibex.

They all replied 'Yes.'

'Let's get it done then.'

So the rebels set off again, walking slowly towards the gatehouse. Then Fox dismounted, went up to the door of the gatehouse and knocked on it with the hilt of his sword.

'Open up!' he shouted. 'I want to see your king, or is he afraid to come out and face me?'

The guard shouted back: 'My king fears nobody, let alone an insignificant fool like you!'

'So if he fears nobody, let's see this fearless king of yours,' said Fox.

'I will find out if he wants to see you,' said the guard.

Suddenly the Dragon King appeared on the battlements.

'So, Fox, we meet again. What took you so long getting here and, more to the point, what do you want in my kingdom?'

'You know exactly what I'm here for, and if I don't get my family back you and your green scum are going to pay the ultimate price, that's a promise.'

'I'm not prepared to succumb to your silly little whims. The slaves are mine and will stay mine - you and your little band of rebels are nothing to be concerned about,' said the Dragon King.

'Then one of us is not going to see the sun come up tomorrow,' said Fox.

'Then I will say goodnight now,' said the king. As he left the battlements, he waved his arm and said 'Crush the scum.'

The last battle was about to begin.

Chapter 9

Fox stood shouting 'Come back, you coward.' He was still shouting when the dragons started to tip the rocks. Hawk shouted 'Fox, look out, above you.'

'Oh, my good god.' Fox managed to get his shield above his head just before the rocks pounded down on him. Crash, bang, with each rock that hit Fox felt himself getting closer to the ground. Then Bull shouted 'Now, run for your life.' So Fox got to his feet and ran towards the others.

By now the rocks were raining down on the other rebels, smashing onto breast plates and shields, taking the riders off their mounts, leaving the men lying helpless on their backs. Many of the men were winded, gasping for breath. The rebels who were out of range rushed in and dragged their helpless comrades out of the way of the missiles that were still raining down on them.

For one man, help came too late. He was lying beside the moat and, as two hillanders grabbed his feet to pull him out of the way, a giant boulder hit his head, splattering it like a ripe melon. The two men who were dragging him did not realise that the man had been hit until they turned round and asked 'Are you all right?' Then one of them said 'I'm going to be sick.' The other just stood there in shock, watching the blood slowly pumping out of what was left of the mangled neck and the body twitching involuntarily.

Ibex saw the man and shouted 'Don't just stand there, move!' He took no notice. Fox said to Ibex 'He's in shock. We will have to go get him.' So the two of them ran towards the man. Ibex slapped him round the face.

'Come on, snap out of it.' He got no reaction at all.

Fox shouted 'Look out!' then basic instinct took over and both Fox and Ibex dived to the ground.

'What is it?' shouted Ibex, lying on the blood-soaked grass.

Then thud, the man they had been trying to save fell to his knees. Ibex looked up, the man was bolt upright, a dragon lance through his chest, his mouth wide open, and gurgling on his own blood. A moment later he fell forward, ramming the lance straight through his back, taking vital organs with it.

Ibex shouted to the archers 'Give us covering fire, keep the dragons' heads down.'

The archers fired, the sky was filled with arrows heading towards the castle. At that moment Fox and Ibex got up and ran faster than they ever had before.

'We made it,' said Ibex and called the warriors together. 'Hillanders, come with me - we are going to scale the walls. Archers, we will need plenty of covering fire and make sure you aim well above the battlements. I don't want you killing our own men. Fox, the rest is yours.'

'Thank you. Bull, you find eleven strong men and get to work with the battering ram. The rest of you be ready to charge the gates.'

So the archers opened fire and the hillanders moved into position. Bull took the battering ram to the entrance and started to smash it against the portcullis. Bang, crash, it went. The portcullis shook and Bull shouted 'One, two, charge!' The battering ram hit again and again, but because it was flexible a lot of the force simply evaporated. After about twenty attempts Bull looked at the portcullis.

'This is no good, we've hardly scratched it.' He took out his battleaxe and started to hack at it with that.

Ibex meanwhile was ordering his men 'Attack, lads, over the top.' As his men neared the top of the battlements, the archers stopped firing. The dragons appeared again and started smashing the hillanders over the head with rocks. The men fell to the ground, breaking arms and legs on impact. Some unlucky ones fell into the moat. Ibex could hear their screams as they were eaten alive.

Fox shouted to Bull as he saw the dragons tipping hot oil through a hole above the portcullis. Bull and the others moved back. 'That's handy - has anyone got a light?'

Just then two flying dragons swooped down and picked Ibex up. Fox shouted 'Archers, when they get above the battlements, shoot the dragons.' So they took aim and fired. The dragons fell in front of Bull, and Ibex fell onto the battlements. Bull and the others picked up the dragons. Bull laughed 'I was looking for a light.' He grasped the creature round the stomach and squeezed with all his might. The dragon blew out a huge stream of flame, igniting the oil that had soaked the portcullis. Bull then threw the creature into the moat, closely followed by the other one. Bull took great delight in listening to the dragons squeal as they were eaten alive. 'That's poetic justice, if ever I saw it.' The last dragon to go in was flapping about and somehow began to take off, but the creatures in the moat were not willing to let their meal go. They were like eels, with row upon row of razor-sharp teeth, about six feet long and dark green, to match the slime they lived in. One of them had the dragon by the foot and two others grabbed it by the wings. Once that happened it was all over for the dragon. In minutes, it was gone.

Fox turned to Oak and asked 'Any planks around here?'

'I don't know. There is a woodpile behind us. I'll see what I can find.'

A few minutes later Oak came back. 'Got one.'

'Is it solid enough to take my weight and take the strain of you and Bull jumping on it?' asked Fox.

'Yes, I think so, but there's only one way to find out.'

'Put it over the battering ram. Bull, you and Oak spring me up to the battlements. Ibex is up there alone,' said Fox.

'Okay, but if you don't make it, don't blame me,' Bull replied.

So Bull and Oak stood on two other men's shoulders, put their arms around each other, then jumped together. They hit the plank, sending Fox flying into the air and up over the battlements. Bull shouted 'Happy landings,' then turned to Oak and said 'Look, Fox is going up in the world.'

'I suppose you think that's funny,' said Oak.

'As it happens, yes I do,' Bull laughed.

Fox landed safely behind Ibex, who instantly turned to strike him.

'It's me - I'm on your side,' shouted Fox.'

'Oh, jolly decent of you to join me,' said Ibex.

Fox leaned over the battlements. 'Well done, lads, I made it,' he called.

Then Ibex saw a dragon running along the ramparts towards him. 'Here comes trouble,' he said.

'I know what you mean,' said Fox.

Coming from the opposite direction, another dragon was charging straight at him. It was blowing flames, so Fox put up his shield to protect his face. The creature kept coming forward but luckily enough for Fox it had to stop blowing flames because they were rebounding off Fox's shield and hitting the dragon. Fox thrust forward with his sword, catching the dragon off balance. He seized the advantage and ran at the dragon, hitting it on the left shoulder, knocking it off the ramparts and sending it crashing onto the courtyard below. It landed on two fellow dragons who were holding their pikes straight up in the air. The pikes went straight through its body. The two dragons it had landed on did not get up.

'Three for one, not a bad start,' said Fox.

Ibex was still trying to get rid of his opponent. The dragon lunged forward with his pike. Ibex jammed the weapon on the floor with his foot and sliced the dragon across the chest. Then he swung his leg around, kicking the dragon in the side, knocking it over the battlements and sending it hurtling to the cobbled courtyard below. He hit with an almighty thud spraying blood and innards all over the ground.

'One apiece,' said Fox.

'Yes, but look.'

Fox turned round and saw a crowd of dragons coming up the steps that led to the ramparts. He knelt down, took his bow off his back and fired at the dragons. The one on the top stair keeled over, leaving the others to clamber over him. Ibex tapped Fox on the arm. 'Look.'

One of his men was trying to get over the top. As he pulled himself over a dragon rammed a lance straight through his chest. The man clung on, so the dragon took out a sword and chopped his fingers off. The man screamed and fell backwards. The man directly beneath him watched helplessly as his friend hurtled past him and crashed onto the ground. He couldn't help wondering if he would share the same fate.

Ibex said 'Get him, Fox.' Fox took aim and hit the creature in the neck. It slumped forward and the man climbing the wall grabbed onto the dragon's horn and pulled himself up.

'The green lump's still alive,' the man shouted.

'You go and help him.' said Fox. 'I will try to hold them off.'

So Ibex ran along the ramparts. The two of them took the dragon by the feet and tipped him over the side. Then they ran to help the others who were scaling the walls by attacking the dragons.

Fox was firing off arrows in rapid succession. The dragons kept coming, even though Fox had shot six and watched them go over the side.

'Bull, it's getting very hot up here, and I'm running out of arrows,' he called. 'We haven't got enough men up here - a lot of the hillanders aren't getting over the top. Do something about that portcullis. We need some warriors up here quick. Get the doors open.'

'Right, pick up the battering ram and charge,' said Bull.

Smash, crack, it went as they hit the portcullis. It gave way and broke up, sending hundreds of burning embers showering down on Bull and the others. They danced about, trying to flick the pieces off themselves. Oak and the other rebels ran up and threw buckets of water over them in an attempt to put the embers out.

'Thanks, now I'm dripping wet,' said Bull.

'There's gratitude for you. Put him out and he still moans,' said Hawk.

'It's done, Fox, now for the doors,' Bull called up.

'Hurry up.'

Then the pounding started and the doors shook. By now Fox had one arrow left; he fired it and a dragon fell. Fox ran towards Ibex, who was now standing at the other end of the wall.

'You take a couple of men and open the doors. It's going to take Bull ages. We will hold them off up here for as long as we can.'

'OK,' said Ibex. He ran down the spiral staircase leading to the courtyard. Halfway down he stopped and said, 'Shush. Listen, dragons.' Coming up in front of him was a torch holder. The dragons were just round the next corner, so Ibex swung on the torch holder and, as the dragons came round the corner, they were greeted by Ibex's feet kicking them in the face. They tumbled back down, then the rebels jumped on them and slit their throats before they had a chance to recover from their dazed state.

Back on the battlements Fox and the remaining four men were surrounded by dozens of dragons on every side. One man was picked up by two of the creatures and hurled over the wall. He landed on one of the many sharpened stakes stuck in the moat. At first he gripped the end of the stake, which was protruding from his stomach, then he slowly realised how futile it was to try to hang on to his life, so he slowly released his grip on the stake and gently slipped into the green slime. As his body reached the surface, the liquid bubbled and jumped as the mad feeding frenzy began. Within seconds his body was no more than bones.

Fox shouted to Bull 'For all that's holy, get those doors open. We are running out of luck and men. It does not look like Ibex made it.'

'I'm coming. Come on, you bunch of weaklings. One, two, three - charge! Put some muscle into it.' Bang, the battering ram hit with such force that the ramparts shook, but still the doors held fast. Bull and the others were just going to charge again when a voice said 'Bull, don't charge yet. I will slip the bolt back. When I say 'now', you run at the doors and don't stop.' It was Ibex.

Bull shouted 'Hawk, you lot mount up and be ready to charge.'

'Yes, but what about Fox and the others? They need help now,' said Hawk.

'Get the archers to fire at the battlements,' Bull told her.

The archers fired upwards and again the air was filled with arrows. 'Fox, duck!' shouted Hawk. As he did, the dragons surrounding them fell to the ground thud, thud. The sound of dragons hitting the courtyard below could be heard all around.

'Nice one, Hawk,' said Fox.

Then Ibex slipped the mighty bolt back and shouted 'Now, Bull!' The others ran at the doors. They swung open with such force that when they hit the walls they splintered. Ibex turned round and saw that running towards him were six or seven dragons. He simply stepped out of Bull's way, and the twelve men and battering ram ran straight into the column of dragons, knocking them flat on their backs. Bull and the others dropped the battering ram on top of them.

'Here, you have it. We don't need it any more.'

Then they took out their weapons and finished the creatures off. Bull chopped one's head off, then looked up at the battlements and saw that a dragon was punching Fox while two others held him captive. It was just taking a swing at Fox with a sword when Bull launched his battleaxe, sending it spinning through the air and hitting the dragon in the back.

Now the dragons sent reinforcements to try to shut the gates. But it was too late: the rebels were thundering across the bridge and through the gateway, and nothing could stop them now. Hawk and the others jumped off their horses straight onto the dragons. Hawk stabbed one. Oak rode in, leant to one side and smashed a dragon with his hammer, crushing its skull. Cat jumped off his horse holding a piece of wire and garrotted one of the dragons, nearly taking its head completely off.

By now the foot soldiers that were on the battlements had been called down to reinforce the gate, and they had been replaced by flying dragons. As the archers came in, they were ordered to concentrate their fire on the flying dragons. Fox had followed the foot soldiers down, as lots of hillanders had now made it to the top.

Fox shouted 'Bull, Hawk, Oak and Cat: take the treedwellers and get our people out of the dungeons. I will stay here with the others and hold them off.'

So Hawk and the rest of the group went off to do their part.

The fighting was fast and furious. Fox set Patch to work snapping the biting at the dragons. The archers were kept busy shooting down flying dragons and keeping them away from the other rebels. They had done a good job, as there weren't many of the creatures left.

Ibex turned round to see one of his men stuck to a door by a dragon's pike, and more of his men were being cut to bits, but he knew he had to turn away and get on with the matter in hand, which was winning the battle.

Otherwise, he could never go home, because there was a distinct possibility he would have no homeland to go back to.

In spite of some grievous losses, the rebels had begun to turn the tide of battle in their favour.

Suddenly Fox spotted the Dragon King and made a mad dash for him before anyone else realised he was there.

Fox stood in his path. 'So it looks like it has come down to you and me,' he said.

'Then prepare to join your brothers on the great battlefield.'

The battle began. The king swung his mighty battleaxe and Fox ducked. In response, he thrust his sword towards the king which the dragon blocked with his shield. Then the king hit Fox's shield with such force that he virtually cut it in two and nearly sliced Fox's chest. His breastplate had a dent in it where the axe had hit.

'Now I have you,' said the Dragon King.

'You think so?'

'Yes, I do,' the king replied.

Fox put up what was left of his shield to defend himself. The axe hit again, finishing the shield off. Now the dragon blew flames at Fox and he had nothing to stop the flames from burning him. Fox put his arms up in front of his face in a vain attempt to protect himself, but it was hopeless. The flames hit him full in the face. Fox dropped his sword and staggered backwards, tripping over what was left of his shield and landing flat on his back.

Fox had made a big mistake: he had underestimated the Dragon King. Unfortunately he had forgotten about the flames, which had just disabled him and perhaps cost him his life.

'Now it's me who will despatch you,' said the king, and laughed.

Fox scrambled to his feet, but could not see much. He clung to the battlements for stability. The dragon smashed him with his shield, knocking Fox head over heels. Then the king sat on Fox's chest and put his axe to his face. The king was enjoying every moment of his victory over Fox, just sitting smiling down at him, as the sweat ran down Fox's face.

'I see you're going to squash me to death. Different, I suppose,' said Fox.

The king did not answer. Instead, he pulled the blade of his axe down Fox's face, making a wide gash. As the blood started to run, he laughed loudly, as if someone had just told him a side-splitting joke. Then he stood up to finish Fox off. He raised his battleaxe above his head, and began to bring it down. Just then Fox scrambled for his sword, grasping it in his right hand. As he was trying to get it into his left hand, the dragon king knocked the sword. It flipped and Fox caught the blade point down in his left hand.

Again the king stood upright to deliver the final blow, which would snuff out Fox's life for good. Again he brought the axe down, but this time the story was different. Fox brought the hilt of the sword up towards the dragon's stomach, then pushed the little fox's head on the handle and the blade sprang out of the hilt. Fox lunged forward and pushed the hilt and his fist into the king's stomach.

When Fox withdrew the blade it was covered in green blood. The dragon placed his hand over the gaping hole. He looked down at his hands as the green blood oozed from between his fingers and trickled down his hands, dripping onto the ground. Then the blood just poured out: he could no longer stop it. The king stood and looked at Fox in amazement.

'You beat me - you won. How?'

'Call it sheer luck or skill, but one thing's for sure, we had right and justice on our side,' said Fox.

The Dragon King started to stagger backwards, then he fell off the battlements and landed on a giant stake which was stuck in the ground and was used for tying prisoners to. It went straight through his body. He burst into flames and exploded into tiny pieces.

The dragons that were in the courtyard fighting the rebels had seen what had occurred on the battlements.

Fox shouted down to them. 'Your king is dead. Give up. Why die for nothing? We will treat you fairly if you lay down your arms and stop fighting now. There are not many of you left, so don't make us destroy you all. You cannot win and, if you force us, we will win by killing you all.'

Fox stood and looked over the carnage that surrounded him. There were dead and dying everywhere he looked. The walls were soaked in blood, there were men and women with arms and legs missing, and the dead bodies of dragons lay all around.

So the dragons stopped fighting and waited for their orders.

'Ibex, get them to drop their weapons in a pile in the centre of the courtyard, then place them in the stables until we can figure out what to do with them all.'

The dragons filed past the steadily growing pile and dropped battleaxes, shields, pikes and chains and maces. The castle was filled with the sounds of metal clanging on the ground. Two hillanders started to thump a dragon.

'You two, leave him alone,' Fox shouted.

'Why should we?' they asked.

'Because I gave my word,' said Fox.

'When have they ever kept their word?' the men said.

'That's nothing to do with it. I gave my word, in turn yours. That's what makes us different from them. Ibex, they're your men - stop them, or I'll stop them for good.'

Ibex and two men went over. Ibex put his sword to one man's throat. 'How dare you dishonour me and the village in front of all these other creatures?' More hillanders took the two men's swords away and started to beat the men in question.

'You have disgraced our village. You and your families could be banished for this,' said Ibex.

'Please, don't banish us and our families, anything but that,' the men pleaded, on their knees.

'Right, as it was done in the heat of the moment, your punishment will be that you have to look after the dragons' every need until we leave,' said Ibex.

'Thank you, chief.'

'Now go, and if anything happens to them you will pay with your lives.'

'Well, my friends, we have victory. Right once again prevails over wrong, good over evil. Now's the time to look forward to returning home, rebuilding and living in peace.'

Once the last of the dragons were herded into the stables, the creatures sat down. One dragon asked: 'Are you going to kill us?' His guard answered: 'Fox gave his word you would not be hurt, and we are men of our words. Well, most of us are.' The two men who had struck the dragon hung their heads in shame.

'Honour means everything to us. Without honour we are nothing. Look what happened to the two hillanders who punched one of your people. Ibex could have had their lives for breaking his and their word.'

Just then Fox heard a whimpering. It was Patch, and he had been badly hurt. Fox walked over to the dog, looked at his wounds and tried to make the animal feel more comfortable. While Fox knelt by him with his hands resting on him, a blue glow surrounded Patch, as he began to draw energy from his master's life force. The energy flowed so quickly between the two of them that Patch was up on his feet in no time at all. It didn't heal the dog's wounds, but gave him the strength and the will to survive.

'That's amazing. Look, he's standing and he is happy,' said Oak.

'I told you how it was, but I don't think you ever believed me, did you?' said Fox.

The hillander called Reed then came up and said: 'Well, Fox, we're both here, so do we meet on the field of honour later, or not?'

'Well,' Fox began to say, as he came down the stairs. Then a big oak door swung open, banging against the wall. It was Hawk and the others coming out from the passage that led from the dungeons that had held the children and the other prisoners. As they came through, from the corner of his eye Fox saw a dragon on the battlements. It was one of the officers. He launched a lance that headed straight for Hawk and the children.

Fox shouted 'Move!' He ran towards them and jumped, knocking Hawk and the children back down the stairs.

The lance hit Fox square in the chest, nailing him to the door. Hawk came back up the stairs shouting at her brother.

'You stupid fool, you could have killed me and the children.' Then she looked and saw Fox stuck to the door.

His feet were not touching the ground, and his whole body was twitching.

'Oh my god, the last thing he hears from me is an insult.' She burst into tears. Cat came up behind her; she turned to him and said 'He saves my life and I scream at him for it. What can I do to make amends?'

'Well, for starters, you can get me off this door. It's not a very dignified way to die,' said Fox.

The rebels gathered round to get him down from the door. Reed was the first to get to Fox. He smiled and said: 'It looks like we won't be meeting on the field of honour, my friend. This is going to hurt: brace yourself,' said Reed and pulled the lance out. Fox didn't murmur.

'He's in shock,' Reed said. 'Lay him down gently.'

Hawk was now fussing about. Patch howled and ran to his master and lay down across his legs.

'It's no good, boy, you can't help.' The dog just lay on his master crying.

As Hawk looked up to see where the lance had come from, she saw their cousin walking along the battlements behind the officer. Looking down at Fox dying on the floor, Bull went beserk and suddenly grabbed the dragon by the throat and punched him in the face. Then, before the creature had time to defend itself, Bull dealt it a fatal blow by headbutting it in the jaw, practically taking its jaw off its face. Then, while the dragon was still stunned, Bull picked the creature up and with a mighty roar lifted it above his head. This was no mean feat as the dragon was twice Bull's weight. You could see his muscles straining under the pressure. Bull then launched it from the battlements, sending it crashing onto a horse rail. You could hear its back breaking as it hit. There was no point checking; it was a foregone conclusion that it was dead. No-one could survive that sort of impact.

Bull started to run along the battlements, heading towards the stairs. Then he saw a pile of hay and thought 'Why waste time?' and jumped down. As he passed the dragon he had thrown off the battlements he spat on it and kicked its lifeless body. 'You scum.'

By now the others had taken Fox's breastplate off to assess the amount of damage done.

'It's bad,' Reed said.

Bull ran over and pushed everybody out of the way. He took one look at Fox and tried to push Fox's insides back in. Fox was screaming in pain.

'Bull, stop it, you're hurting me. It's no good - I'm finished.'

Bull put his head in his giant hands and sobbed. Then from the corner of his eye he saw the dragon who was to have been executed on the orders of his king. He jumped to his feet, knocked the dragon to the floor and started to punch him. Then he took out his dagger.

The children shouted 'Stop him, father. This is the dragon that saved your life at Castlewood. If he had not listened to Aunty Elk you would have been dead then, and for his good deed he was sentenced to death.'

'Bull, stop, I gave my word. They have deprived me of life; will you deprive me of my honour and my final resting place on the great battlefield?' said Fox.

Bull stopped in his tracks. By now he had a mixture of the dragon's blood and Fox's all over his face.

'Hawk, take Bull away, clean him up and cool him down.' Fox looked at the dragon. 'What is your name?'

'Yoshfell. In my language it means 'one of feelings'.'

'When your kind are split up and sent to different villages, I want you to go with my children. They seem to be fond of you. Do you know, I never did know your king's name.'

'His name was Axemod, meaning Death.'

'Surprise, surprise,' said Fox.

Bull and Hawk returned.

'I need to talk to you. Bull, listen carefully. You must cut off my tail, as you will probably be the only one of the rebels still left who will carry on fighting. Wear it on your waistband each time you go into battle. You must not forget to wear it, or your luck will run out. Do you understand?' said Fox.

'Yes, I understand and I will remember,' said Bull.

Hawk pulled Fox forward and Bull took out his knife and cut off Fox's ponytail. Then he walked over to the horses, took out a needle and thread from one of the saddlebags, and started to bind Fox's hair together good and tight. Then he sat there clutching the ponytail in his hands.

Hawk knelt down beside Fox. 'You made it this far - you can't die now.'

'I told you I did not think I would make it. But as always you did not believe a word I said. There's no hope for me. Tac was the only one who could have saved me and he's dead and gone.'

Just then Tac's staff appeared from nowhere. Hawk picked it up. 'Tac sent this to help you. Hold on to it and concentrate.'

Fox took the staff in his left hand, then said 'I must live long enough to say my last words to everybody. I have so much I want to say and so little time to do it in. Where are my children?'

'We are here.' The children gathered round their father. Wildcat said 'You came for us.'

'Of course I did. Did you doubt that I would, for a moment?' said Fox.

'We thought you were dead. You can't leave us again. We love you so much.' Sky and Jage started to cry. 'Please, Dad, don't go. Who will look after us?'

'I can't stay. My insides are all cut up. Death has come for me and I must go. Look, you are my sons and I love you more than life itself, that's why I came for you. One of you will be leader of Castlewood one day. Be brave, and remember don't look for trouble. Plenty will come your way simply because of who you are, but never run away or hide from it - you cannot escape your destiny. Your honour is your most prized possession. Without honour a man is nothing in this land.'

By now Fox's daughters were holding their father tightly. Badger said: 'I love you. Please don't go.'

'I have no choice in this matter, but I will promise you this. I will always be there to protect and love you as I have in life,' said Fox. 'Sunny, you must care for and protect your brothers until they are old enough to look after themselves, and love them as I have loved you.'

'I do love you, Dad, even though it seems that I didn't a lot of the time,' said Sunny.

'I know you do, sweetheart,' said Fox.

'Jage, I want you to have my horse. He is over there, tied up by the stables. Take my sword too and be careful with the hilt blade.'

'Thank you, Dad, I will take very good care of them both,' said Jage.

'Wildcat, I want you to go to a house two miles from Castlewood. There you will find a man who has a bitch with a litter of puppies. Tell him Fox sent you for the pick of the litter. That dog will live as long as you, so take very good care of him. Don't forget - plenty of physical contact,' said Fox.

'I won't forget, I promise, Dad. I won't let you down. I will make you proud of me,' said Wildcat.

'I'm already proud of all of you,' Fox told them. 'Sky, you can have my bow and arrow. It's straight and true: you try to be the same. That bow has saved lots of lives over the years; use it well and it will save yours, one day.'

'I will do my best not to let you down, Dad. That's a promise,' said Sky.

'I have only ever asked you to do your best, and you always have. I love you all very much: don't ever forget that. Badger, you take my armour, get it repaired and when you wear it no harm will come to you, that I promise.'

'Yes, Dad.'

'Sunny, I want you to have the house, the land, and a long and happy life.'

'Thank you, Dad.'

'Now, my children, kiss your father goodbye for the last time and then leave me to talk with the others.'

The children gave their father a kiss goodbye and clung on to him tightly. So the other rebels pulled the children away screaming and kicking. Their Aunty Elk said 'Calm down, children, you're hurting him.' The children released their grip on Fox, and walked with Elk over to the stables where they sat down on bales of straw, sobbing. Elk did her best to comfort them.

Fox turned to Hawk and said 'Promise me two things.'

'Name it and it will be done, you have my word.'

'Firstly, look after my children and teach them well: one of my boys will be leader of Castlewood one day. The second task is to place all the rebels that have died over the last week in one grave, so we may rest together for evermore. I'm going to die very soon and not long after that Patch will pass away. Place him on my chest before you fill the grave in, please,' said Fox.

'It will be done, I promise,' Hawk told him.

Ibex stepped forward. 'Well, my friend, we spent a lot of our lives fighting together,' said Fox. 'Nothing has ever split us up before, but this is a journey I can't make with you by my side. It's time for me to go and I'm glad I got mine while surrounded by my lifelong friends and trusted family members. It was great fighting this final battle with you, Ibex. I'd rather go like this - it's better than dying in bed reminiscing about how strong and active I used to be. I will see you on the next great battlefield.'

When Fox finished speaking Ibex had tears in his eyes. 'I will never fight again. Now my left arm is dead and I have no taste for it any more.' He took Fox by the forearm and said 'Goodbye, my old friend.' He went and sat with Fox's children.

Elk and Oak walked over. She knelt down. 'Fox, I knew in my heart you weren't dead. Thank you for sending Tac: my son owes you his life and so do I, many times over. If I could, I would gladly take your place. Thank you for coming. I love you and will never forget you or let your memory die. I will make you a solemn promise to tell your children all about you and the other rebels. You will live in the minds of generations to come. Goodbye, my dear brother.' Elk kissed her brother's forehead, cuddled him and then returned to where the children were seated.

Oak looked down at Fox and broke down in tears. 'Please forgive me for casting doubt on your honour. I was so devastated by the news. I felt so helpless because I was not there for Elk when she really needed me. I thought I had lost the family I had spent my whole life looking for. If you do not restore my honour to me I will be a broken man for ever. I suppose it's just what I deserve for letting my temper get the better of me. You have been good to me over the years and have refused me nothing. You made me feel like a true brother, and here you are dying and I'm asking you for something else. I'm so ashamed of myself.'

Fox looked at his adopted brother who was down on his knees with his forehead on Fox's hand, trembling.

'I have fought with my other two brothers many times in the past. Sometimes I have been wrong and at fault. You have nothing to apologise for, but if you feel it is necessary and it means that much to you, then with all my heart I forgive you a thousand times over. You fought well, my brother. You proved your valour and honour many times over in the last week. You have no reason to reproach yourself, and let no one say otherwise. Without your bravery we would not have made it this far. See you on the next great battlefield,' said Fox.

'Thank you, Fox,' Oak replied.

Bull walked back to Fox and gathered him up into his giant arms. 'Well, my dear cousin, I'm glad to have known you and been here at the end. But why, if you felt this was your last battle, did you ride out? We could have fought without you,' said Bull.

'Because you can't hide from fate. It was the only course left to me. If I had stayed at home, no matter what anyone else said, I could not have lived with myself or looked my children in the eyes, and felt good about myself. Now go - we will meet again.' Bull went to join the others.

Hawk took Fox by the hand. He turned and smiled at his sister and said in a low voice: 'You know I love you. Take care of yourself and stay away from spears.' Then he coughed and a trickle of blood ran from the side of his mouth. His hand became limp, releasing the staff, which rolled across the courtyard.

Hawk held her brother's body close. 'Don't go - I've got so much to tell you. Now I shall never get the chance.' She burst into tears and held her brother's body tightly. She would not let go. Instead, she just kept rocking backwards and forwards, speaking to him. Cat came up and put his hands on her shoulders. 'Let him go - he is dead. It's over.' Cat took Hawk over to Elk and the others, then he returned to Fox's body.

'Well, my friend, I didn't speak in front of the others. What I've got to say is between you and me. I will miss you - we've been through a lot since the first battle. Goodbye till we meet on the next great battlefield.'

When Fox passed away the dog started to cry. Wildcat came over to Patch. 'It's all right, please don't cry. I can't stand to hear you in pain.' The dog looked up, then there was silence as its head fell into Wildcat's lap. The tears ran down Wildcat's face as he realised the dog had died. Dad was right. He moved the dog onto his father's body, sat next to him and put his father's arm round him, desperate for his dad to give him a last cuddle. But he got no response. He whispered 'I love you very much.'

He looked around and saw that Bull had a massive gash across his chest: Wildcat could almost see Bull's ribcage. His uncles Oak and Cat had come out of the battle unscathed. Ibex however had not been so lucky. He had a deep gouge running the full length of his face. The blood was everywhere: his chest was covered in it.

Ibex said: 'I must go now and take my people back to our village.'

'No, you're not going now. You can't travel like that,' said Hawk.

'I must go,' Ibex told her.

'Look, do as you're told or I will give you a cut on the other side to match. It won't take long. Now sit down and I will stitch the wound. Besides, your men have just fought a long and tiring engagement. This will give them some breathing space, and time to get their strength back.'

Hawk had nagged Ibex into doing what she wanted. 'All right,' he said, and sat down.

It took Hawk about half an hour to close the wound. When Ibex at last stood up his men were lying on the ground, some asleep and others tending to their injuries.

'Come on, you lot. Load the dead and wounded onto the carts.' Ibex looked towards Hawk. 'I have lost a lot of good friends and men on this evil battlefield. I can't say I will be sorry to leave, and I never want to see this place again.'

'I will do my best to make sure your wish comes true. Goodbye and thank you all for your help,' said Hawk.

Reed walked over to Fox's children and said 'If ever you need anything, or I can help in any way, just ask. I owed your father a debt of honour. I wronged him and never got a chance to make things right between us, so now the debt is passed on to you. My life is yours to command until honour is satisfied.'

'Thank you,' the children said.

Ibex left followed by thirty men.

'Bull, come here - it's your turn,' said Hawk.

'No way,' Bull shouted.

Hawk walked over to Cat and the others. 'He must have the wound closed. I'll distract him and you knock him out.' So Hawk shouted 'What's the matter with you, showing yourself up in front of the children, you big baby.'

Bull started to say 'Shut up' but he didn't get the chance to finish his sentence, because Cat hit him over the head, knocking him out.

Hawk sewed up Bull's gaping wound. It took twenty-five stitches to close it. Bull eventually came round. 'You sneaky little so-and-so!'

'Now, now, Bull, language,' Cat laughed.

Just then Hawthorne, leader of the treedwellers, came over.

'Goodbye. I'm sorry about your brother. He was a brave and just man. I must take my leave of you now.'

He left, and only six of them lived to tell of their bravery.

Five men from Waterdown were left. They turned to Cat and said 'We are going home now. See you there.'

'Yes, okay boys - see you later,' Cat replied.

Cat looked at Hawk. 'There are going to be a lot of fatherless children in our village.'

'Many villages will be in the same situation after today,' Hawk responded. 'Are you feeling fit enough to collect Opium, Wolf and Tac's bodies?' Hawk asked her cousin.

'Yes, of course I am,' snapped Bull. He then prepared to set off with a wagon drawn by two horses to fulfil Fox's last wishes.

'Oh, Bull, can you take the dead treedwellers?' Hawk asked.

'Yes, all right, help me load them onto the cart,' said Bull. So they put them on the cart and Bull left. As he went up the track he passed the men from Waterdown and the treedwellers. 'I've got your dead. Do you want a lift?'

Hawthorne said 'Thank you.' They climbed on.

'What about you lot from Waterdown - want to get in? I'm going your way,' said Bull.

'Great one - thanks.'

The wagon rumbled off toward the land of the treedwellers. It was an extremely uncomfortable and bumpy ride, due to the roughness of the track which was filled with ruts and potholes. The wagon went up and down and from side to side. It was like being at sea during a storm. Bull felt quite seasick.

All the occupants of the cart had been in the battle, but not one of them wanted to discuss their feelings or express an opinion on how the battle had gone. They were deep in thought, all suffering the mixed emotions of guilt, remorse and helplessness over the deaths of friends and loved ones. Bull felt this way more than the others as he had lost three cousins and friends he had known for many years, and most of all Fox. He had always been there for Bull and it seemed to Bull that whenever Fox needed him he was never around. If I had been there at the right time, he thought, Fox would still be alive.

Presently the silence was broken by a man from Waterdown saying 'Can you slow down? I'm feeling sick and getting battered about and collecting more injuries from this cart than I did from the battle.' His friends told him to shut up.

'Look here, you're lucky to be alive, and I have a long way to go. Unlike you, I can't go home until I have fulfilled my mission, which is to pick up three bodies. I gave you a lift out of the kindness of my heart, so if you don't like it, get off and walk.' Bull told him.

'I'd like to see you make me,' the man said.

Bull pulled hard on the reins, bringing the horses to an abrupt stop. He jumped off the front of the cart and walked round to the back. 'I've had enough of you.' He grabbed the man in question by the scruff of his shirt and pulled him over the side of the cart.

'Oh, dear, you're really scaring me,' the man said sarcastically.

'I'm so glad,' Bull said. Then he punched the man in the stomach so hard you could hear his breath being forced out of his body. He doubled over and Bull brought his knee up, hitting the man in the face, knocking him off his feet and leaving him flat on his back. Bull jumped back onto the wagon and shouted 'Giddy up.' The horses began to pull away.

The man on the ground shouted 'Are you going to let him get away with that? I'm one of your own people.'

'Tough - you should have shut up when we told you. You asked for everything you got,' shouted the men from the cart.

'Stop the cart - what am I going to do?'

'Walk - it might teach you to be more grateful in future,' the men in the cart laughed as the wagon rolled away throwing dust over the man sitting on the ground.

'Look,' Bull shouted, 'you're home.' Hawthorne popped his head up.

'Ah, my beautiful trees. Home sweet home.'

They pulled up close to where Wolf was buried. The treedwellers and Waterdown men unloaded the dead from the cart while Bull went and dug up Wolf's body. He placed it gently on the cart.

Now he set off for Waterdown to collect Opium's body. It wasn't long before the wagon was standing in front of the village. The men from Waterdown jumped down. Bull said 'I'm sorry about that little bit of trouble with your friend. It was either throw him off the cart or kill him.'

'That's all right, we understand. You didn't need his moaning. You're like us - you had more important things on your mind. We all lost good friends and for you it's worse because you lost so many family members. It was not your fault. About Fox: he was a good man and will be greatly missed. Thanks for the lift and see you around perhaps.' The men walked over the drawbridge.

Bull went over to the raised mound of earth and started to dig. He had just located Opium's body when he got the feeling someone was watching him. He turned round sharply, spade in hand, ready to strike, and found it was Fox's mother, Hen.

'Oh no, it's you. I'd hoped I wouldn't see you,' said Bull.

'That's not very nice. What are you, a grave robber now?' said Hen.

'No, aunty, I'm collecting Opium's body.' As Bull put the body onto the cart Hen noticed Fox's ponytail on Bull's belt.

'How come you've got my son's tail?'

'I haven't - it's a trophy from a battle,' said Bull.

Hen examined the hair hanging from Bull's belt. She looked underneath; sure enough, it was white, just like a fox's tail. 'You're lying - it is my son's hair. Do you think I don't know my own son's hair when I see it? No-one has hair like my Fox. Now, what's happened to him?' Hen demanded an explanation from Bull.

'Oh, can't this wait till you see Hawk?' Bull whined. Hen had made him feel like a naughty ten year old being told off for pinching apples. 'Please don't make me do this. I hate these situations. I can't handle them.'

'Tell me or else,' said his aunty. Bull didn't like the sound of 'or else'.

'All right. Fox is dead, but he did keep his promise to you - he sent Hawk back alive. That's how he died, saving her and the children.' Hen broke down in tears. 'It's not just Opium; Wolf's in the back and I have to go to the great swamp and collect a man called Tac. It was Fox's last wish that they should all be buried together - I must go now and finish what I have to do. Hawk's waiting for me.'

'I'm coming too. I want to see my sons for the last time, and be with my family, so don't bother to argue.' Hen got onto the back of the wagon and held her youngest son, Wolf, in her arms.

As they pulled away Colt ran up. 'Let me come, grandma.' He jumped into the back of the cart and they headed for the great swamp. Bull could hear his aunty sobbing behind him. He turned round and saw that she was clutching Wolf's body in her arms.

'Why my sons - why all of them?'

'Is Uncle Wolf hurt?' Colt asked his grandmother.

'No, he is dead,' Hen told him.

'I've never seen a dead man before,' the boy said as he peered over his shoulder.

Hen looked over at Opium. 'I've known him since he was a little boy. I suppose he was in reality a son of mine too. I mean I did take him and his brother in and I was the nearest thing they had to a mother. What about Black Knight and Oak?' asked Hen.

Bull looked at the old woman in the cart. She looked broken, as if her whole world had fallen apart. In one way it had.

'At least you still have your daughters and grandchildren. Oak survived, and Cat, Ibex and Elk, but Black Knight perished on the battlefield.' Hen sat there dumbfounded by the news, just staring into outer space, clutching Wolf's body and weeping.

There in front of them was the great swamp. Bull jumped down and dug up Tac's body and placed him on the wagon with the others.

'We must leave now; Hawk is waiting for me to return,' said Bull.

'Can we stop at Scrapford, so I may pray for my firstborn, old Grey Bear, and his family, please?' Hen pleaded.

'Okay, but not for long,' said Bull.

So they headed towards Scrapford. As they entered the gates, the village was deathly still: not a creature moved or made a sound. The village that once had thrived was now dead. Skeletons of huts, barns burnt and decaying, the ground uneven with mounds of earth. Everywhere you looked there were nothing but graves.

'The village of the dead,' Hen said sadly.

'Your son is over there with his family,' said Bull.

Hen walked over to the large grave and knelt down beside it. 'Oh, my son, I will miss you very much. A mother should never have to bury her sons; it should be the other way round.'

Bull left her to grieve in private. He sat on the wagon, wondering what it was all about and why these things have to happen. If nothing else, it keeps the human race in check, he thought, or, put another way, stops overcrowding. It seemed to Bull that man has a built-in destruct button, which is triggered when man's numbers become too large. Then it starts a battle for battle's sake, no other real reason. Bull looked backwards at his aunty kneeling at her son's graveside.

'Come on, we must go.'

She stood up slowly. 'Goodbye, my son,' she said, then walked towards the cart. Bull got down and helped her on.

'Get up,' Bull shouted and the horses headed off to the castle of the dragons.

Meanwhile back at the castle Hawk was sitting in total amazement at the carnage that surrounded her. There were dragons dead and dying, weapons everywhere, discarded after the surrender, wounded and dead men of Waterdown.

'Cat, you and Oak organise the dragons into burial details and clear these bodies away.'

Cat took a work party and told them 'Pick up your dead and throw them into the moat.'

'Aren't they entitled to a decent burial? We will not do it,' said one of the dragons.

'You will do exactly as you are told. You slaughtered our people and left them to the birds, so why should I have any sympathy for your dead? Now let me simplify the whole situation for you. After all you have done, you're lucky to be alive. If you don't do what you are told we will kill you. Is that clear enough for you?' Cat said.

'Yes,' the dragon said in a nervous voice.

The dragons began to throw their dead into the moat. The water bubbled as the creatures in the green slime thrashed about in a mad feeding frenzy. Each dragon was stripped to a carcass by the time the next body was thrown in.

One of the dragons they thought was dead was moaning; he wasn't quite dead. The dragon who had answered Cat back said 'We can't throw him in, he's not dead.'

'Can you heal him?' asked Cat.

'No.'

'Can anyone here?'

All the dragons shook their heads.

'You, my friend, are getting up my nose. Our promise was not to kill you so I challenge you to a fight,' said Cat.

'I accept your challenge, you puny human. Prepare to meet your maker,' the dragon replied.

Cat threw him a sword. 'Let it begin.' Their swords clashed. The dragon swiped at Cat's face but he ducked and brought his sword up, catching the creature across the jaw. It was not a fatal blow but he dropped his sword and put his hands to his face. Cat now dealt the final blow: he drop-kicked the dragon backwards into the moat.

It let out screams of agony. Cat had never heard such a horrific sound before. It was so ear-splitting that he had to cover his ears. The dragon splashed around, trying to get the creatures off, but to no avail. He should have known better. His kind had thrown many a captive into the moat for amusement, and none had ever survived the ordeal. As the dragon jumped about, the creatures tore pieces of flesh from its living body. He kept screaming until one of the creatures tore his throat out, then he sank beneath the surface for good. All that could be seen of him was a few bubbles and the thrashing of the creatures' tails.

'Now, any more of you want to disagree with me?' said Cat.

'No, no, not us,' the dragons said, not wanting to share their friend's fate. So they went back to work, feeding their evil pets on their dead comrades' bodies.

'Bit of a turn around,' laughed Cat.

Oak was supervising the loading of the bodies of the men from Waterdown. Two of the dragons threw one of the bodies into the cart.

'Steady on there, have some respect for the dead,' said Oak.

'Why should we - you have no respect for our dead,' said one of the dragons.

'One, because I said so and two, because if you don't, you can change work parties.'

Just then Cat shouted 'Any trouble?'

Oak turned to the dragon. 'Well, have I?'

'No, no, there's no trouble,' the dragon said.

'No, everything's all right, thanks,' said Oak.

Hawk shouted 'Oak, bring the wounded over here and we will tend to their wounds.'

All the injured sat around a giant fire which burned brightly, warming them. Hawk, Elk and Sunny began to patch them up.

'As soon as Bull returns we will take you back to Waterdown.'

They finished tending to the Waterdown men.

Elk said 'Are there any wounded dragons?'

'Yes,' Cat replied.

'Then bring them over here,' Elk told him.

'No way - let the slimes suffer,' Cat said indignantly.

'Tell him, Hawk, that Fox promised them they would be treated fairly, or have you forgotten Fox so quickly too?' snapped Elk.

'Of course I haven't. Cat, do it or as the gods are my witness, I will make your life a living hell on earth. This I swear on my honour,' said Hawk.

Cat knew she meant what she said, and reluctantly he brought the dragons over. They were soon patched up.

'All finished. We will take them back to the stables now,' Oak said.

Hawk found the horn that would summon the burrowers. She filled her chest with air and blew with all her might. Nothing happened. She was just about to try again when the ground was filled with vibrations. At first they were very weak, then they gradually became stronger and faster, gathering momentum, as the creatures came nearer to the surface. The ground rippled up in banks; it was quite shocking to see the earth running as if it were alive. Then suddenly two feet in front of Hawk a mass of black fur shot up. It shook itself, showering the rebels in dirt and bits of roots. Hawk spat the mud from her mouth, and wiped it from her eyes.

'Oh, I'm terribly sorry. You called for my help and I cover you in tunnel waste. I can't apologise enough,' said the leader of the burrowers. 'What can I do for you?'

'I want you to undermine the foundations of the castle and bring it down so we can wipe the place off the face of this land, and perhaps in time from our memories. And drain the moat, and kill those evil creatures that live in it,' Hawk added.

'I can do that for you,' said the leader.

Hawk shouted 'Get those horses out of there, and the wounded - and don't forget the dragons. This place is coming down, for good.'

Cat and Oak grabbed the horses by their reins, led them away from the castle and tied them to some trees well out of the way of the building. Hawk, Elk and the children helped move the wounded. Cat got the cart, with the dead men on it, out of the way. Then Fox's body was gently moved clear.

The burrowers' leader gave a long high-pitched squeal and five more of the creatures appeared from the tunnel. Hawk watched as the leader explained what had to be done. The creatures dived into the earth with ease, the same ease you or I would use to break the surface of water.

All six of the burrowers tunnelled away in different directions. The vibrations started again and this time it was six times more powerful. Hawk watched the earth moving in six different directions. Two went left and right of the castle; the mounds of the other four disappeared from view as they dived deeper underground in front of the castle, to prevent the ground under the moat collapsing prematurely and cutting off their escape route.

The rebels could feel the ground shaking very badly now, as the creatures scuttled about underground, undermining the foundations of the building. Hawk looked up and saw the mighty dragon's arms that surrounded the gate begin to shake. As she watched, they cracked away from the main part of the castle and fell forward. The first one came down on top of a cart as if it were trying to pick it up, with claws enclosing the cart, before the sheer weight of the masonry hitting the ground shattered it. It was followed by the other one, which smashed through the drawbridge sending tons of rubble splashing into the moat and splattering the rebels with the evil-looking green slime.

Then the towers started to topple and crumble, sending stone blocks crashing to the ground with such force that they left massive holes where they hit. The jaws that had formed the gateway slammed shut forever, as the rest of the masonry came smashing down on top of the set of jaws, crushing the teeth and finally cracking the skull totally in half.

Next the towers finally toppled to the ground, like felled trees. After that the whole structure simply collapsed in a heap of twisted metal, splintered wood and rubble. The burrowers then came back. On their way they drained the moat, leaving the horrible creatures in it high and dry, gasping for air as lumps of stone bounced around them, splatting them to nothing but a green mess.

Hawk could see nothing as the once mighty castle disappeared in a cloud of dust. She looked round and there in front of her were the burrowers.

'Is there anything else we can do for you?'

'You could dig a mass grave, to save us all that hard work.'

'What about there?' said the creature, pointing at the massive hole where the castle had stood.

Hawk walked over to the hole and peered in. It was about twenty feet deep and filled with rubble and wood. She noticed three doors; one had Fox's bloodstains on it and was holed where the spear had gone straight through his body and nailed him to it. There were broken tables and chairs there too. By now there were men down the hole.

'You bunch of scavengers,' she shouted, and turned away.

The men had found the Dragon King's treasure.

'No, Hawk, you can't begrudge them the spoils of war - they fought hard and well,' said Cat. 'You lot make sure you share it out, and save some for Bull and the widows of the hillanders who died - they will need it.'

'I don't want my brother and friends buried in that rubbish heap; I won't allow it,' said Hawk. 'Please dig another hole.'

'All right, as you wish,' said the creature.

So the burrowers went off and started to dig the grave. It was finished in no time at all. Hawk looked around the battle site - great mounds of earth surrounded it.

'It's done,' said the leader of the burrowers.

'What is your name?' asked Hawk.

'Didn't Fox tell you? Where is he, anyway?'

'He is over there, dead.'

He looked over and saw Fox's body propped up against a tree. 'I'm really sorry. I don't know what to say. My name is Backtomar.'

'Thank you for your help. We will finish off,' said Hawk.

'No, my people will stay and clear up. We will fill in all the holes and it will be as if nothing had ever stood here. I do feel somewhat responsible for this whole tragic situation.'

Cat and Oak collected timber from around the site, and built a bonfire to keep everyone warm. While they waited they threw on doors, bits of stair rails and smashed chairs and tables. The greatest satisfaction of all came when they put the Dragon King's throne on the fire and watched with glee as it burned down to nothing.

It had seemed as though they had been waiting for ever for Bull to return. Hawk looked down the track that ran behind where the castle had stood. In the distance, on the horizon, she saw a spot. It must be Bull, at long last. As he got nearer she shouted 'What took you so long?'

Bull didn't reply until he was close. 'You want to try digging up three bodies on your own, and I had people on board which slowed me up. Also, I had to take a diversion to Scrapford,' said Bull.

'Why?'

'Because your mother caught me at Waterdown and insisted that I take her along. How could I refuse her saying goodbye to her son. And not only that, I didn't have the fastest horses in the world.' As Bull finished speaking Hen and Colt got out of the cart.

'Where's Fox?' Hen asked.

'He's over there,' said Hawk. She led her mother to where Fox' body was lying. The old woman went over to her son's body and began to cuddle him.

Colt piped up: 'I see Uncle Fox kept his word.'

'Yes, my son, I'm fine. If nothing else your uncle was a man of his word,' said Hawk.

Cat walked over to Hen and said, 'Come on, mother, it's time to place Fox in his final resting place.

The old woman let her son's body go, reluctantly. Bull came over and helped Cat pick Fox up, and place him in the grave. Then they took Wolf off the wagon and placed him on one side of his brother.

'I'm not picking Opium up,' Hawk told him.

'Then you put Wolf's weapons with him,' said Cat.

She did so and then put Patch on Fox's chest.

Bull and Oak carefully picked up Opium's body and placed it on Fox's right side. Cat picked up Opium's head by placing his hands flat against the ears; then he moved very gingerly towards the grave in case he dropped it. Finally it was there. Then they placed Tac in the grave next to Wolf.

Hawk said 'Wait, here's Tac's staff. We must not leave this out. It could be dangerous in the wrong hands.' So the staff was placed in the grave, and just as the remaining rebels thought the ordeal was over Oak said: 'Quiet, I hear horses' hooves.'

Out of the darkness of the early evening came a black horse. As he trotted closer Cat looked shocked.

'It's Black Knight.'

'What a twist of fate. Let's put him in with the others,' said Hawk.

'But his last wish was to wander around the country,' said Bull.

'Yes, but who apart from those close to him would really know where he would like to end up,' said Hawk. 'It looks like his horse has decided that he should rest with his brother and lifelong friends forever more. Besides, if we don't bury him, he will become meat for the houndcats. That's no way for a warrior of Black Knight's standing to end up.'

'I suppose not,' the others agreed.

Bull approached the horse very slowly and it didn't move a muscle. It must have sensed that Bull meant him no harm. Bull took the reins in his hands and patted the horse's neck 'There's a good boy.' Cat and Oak came over and began to untie the ropes which bound Black Knight to his horse.

As Oak undid the last rope that had held the body securely on the horse, it began to topple over; before Cat had time to stand aside, Black Knight's body fell on him. Cat's knees buckled as the weight of Black Knight, still in full armour, crashed down on him and pinned him to the ground with his face in the dirt.

Cat didn't move; he just lay there motionless. Hawk screamed: 'Get him off Cat, he's killed him.' Bull let go of the horse and rushed round to help Cat, followed by Oak. They lifted Black Knight's body off Cat. He was dazed; Oak said 'No broken bones - he will be fine.' Hawk and Bull picked Cat up and dusted him down.

Oak took the saddle and bridle off the horse, which just stood by his master's body. Bull, Oak and Hawk picked Black Knight up. Even with three of them it was still a strain.

'He weighs a ton,' said Bull. 'Can't we take his armour off?'

'By the time we have undone all the straps and got him ready, we would have had enough time to carry him to the grave a dozen times over,' said Hawk.

As they struggled over to his final resting place, the horse followed, head down, sniffing the air. They finally put Black Knight into the ground, while the horse just stood and watched.

The mass grave was then covered. Hawk walked over to a pile of rubble and started to carry stones towards the grave.

'What in hell's name are you doing, woman?' Cat asked.

'Two of my brothers are in that hole, and one of them just took a lance for me. I'm not leaving them with nothing to mark their final resting place. If you don't want to help, then sod off home. The same goes for the rest of you,' Hawk snapped.

So the remaining rebels started lugging blocks of stone, which had once been part of the castle walls, over to the grave. By the time they had finished their task, it was more like a monument to the dead than a marker. Oak found a flat piece of rock and some chisels.

'Let me borrow your axe, Bull.' Without thinking, Bull handed it over.

Oak used the flat side of the heavy battleaxe as a hammer.

'Don't worry, I won't hurt it. There - finished,' he said at last.

'Let's have a look,' Hawk said. She took the slab of stone and began to read aloud. "Here lies the brothers Fox and Wolf, and Black Knight and Opium, the great magician Tac, and many other rebels who died fighting bravely for freedom and honour. They will be greatly missed by one and all.' That's great work, Oak,' Hawk said. She placed the plaque on the monument and stepped back with a satisfied look on her face. 'That will do nicely,' she thought. She looked at the others and at the burrowers who were levelling the site off so that there was not a trace of the castle and no holes or rubble anywhere.

'Let's eat,' Hawk said.

'That sounds good to me,' said Bull.

So they all sat down to eat. Hawk was looking at the empty space where the castle had once stood and she couldn't believe her own eyes. Grass began to appear, then there was a rumble and twigs began to come from the ground. Presently the earth cracked open and a full-grown tree popped up, then another and another. Each tree carried the coat of arms of a village involved in the struggle, including Scrapford.

'Look, Cat, here's our village.' As Hawk turned to look at Cat, she saw flowers growing from the grave. A unicorn's head appeared in the rocks, followed by a fox's head, Opium's coat of arms, Black Knight's head and last but not least a wolf's head.

The whole monument was now covered in pictures carved into the rocks, depicting the events in great detail. The rebels wandered around. 'Look, it tells the whole story of the battles.'

'Everything is perfect in every aspect, even when Tac was not around,' Hawk thought. As she saw her own character, it was like looking in a mirror. All the battle scenes were so lifelike, you could almost feel the pain of the men in the drawings. The blood from the warriors' wounds had a glistening look, giving the impression of movement. 'No-one will ever forget - the stones won't let them,' Hawk thought.

In front of the monument was a stone fireplace to keep visitors to the tomb warm; round the back was a trough of water to slake their thirst.

Hawk was transfixed by the details and mystery of it all when a voice she hadn't heard for many years entered her head.

'Mother, I'm here.' She swung round and found that it was not imagination. There in front of her stood her sister Many Voices. Her hair was matted and tangled, her face was covered in grime and her brown eyes were lifeless.

Hen stood up and held out her arms and they embraced. 'I thought you were dead,' her mother said.

'No, I have spent these many years in the dungeons of the castle. I wish I had taken notice of you,' said Many Voices. 'I was walking past the castle when a dragon shouted some insults at me. Instead of ignoring him and going on my way I stopped and traded insults. It turned out to be the king and you know the result.'

Hawk thought that she had not changed. She had got her name because no-one could shut her up - even when ill she found the energy to talk. Her mouth had got her into a lot of trouble.

Cat broke the silence by saying 'That was a complete waste of time and energy. We might as well have left it to Tac, and saved ourselves a lot of hard work.'

'It must be Tac's staff working its last bit of magic. He must approve.' As Hawk finished talking the words 'Until we meet again on the next great battlefield' appeared. The clouds above them turned dark and it started to rain, as if someone up there was crying for the rebels. 'Come on, let's go home,' Hawk said.

'No, I want to mourn my sons,' said Hen.

'You can't stay here on your own,' said Hawk.

'I will stay with Aunty and bring her back to Waterdown tomorrow,' Bull said.

'Can we stay with Father?' asked Sunny and Badger.

'Yes, I can't see why not, if it's all right with Bull and Mother,' said Hawk.

'Yes, that's fine,' Bull and Hen said together.

Cat mounted the wagon that was loaded with the dead. As he passed the grave he lowered his head and touched his forehead, a sign they made meaning 'may the gods protect and care for you'.

Fox's sons rode by all sitting on his horse. 'Goodbye, Father.' The tears began to run down their faces.

Next came the wounded on the other cart. It stopped in front of the grave and all the men touched their foreheads and bowed their heads, in respect for the dead.

Many Voices was going back to Castlewood with Elk. She came to the grave. 'I'm sorry I missed you again, my brothers. I would give anything to be able to say goodbye. Thanks for releasing me from that hell.' She touched her forehead and left.

Elk came past. 'Goodbye, my brothers. Thank you Tac for my son's life and thank you for sending him, Fox. I love you all and will never forget the sacrifice you made for me and mine.' She bowed her head, touched her forehead and caught up with Many Voices.

Oak came up, knelt down and lowered his gaze to the ground. 'Thank you, Fox, for my honour. I promise I will watch over your children. I will miss all my brothers who lie here, but you most of all.' He touched his forehead and left.

Now it was Hawk's turn. She dismounted from her horse and stood in front of the grave. She kissed the wolf's head on the grave and then hugged the fox's head. 'I promise to tend this grave and bring flowers and also to bring your children to see you, so you can watch them grow. I must go home to Waterdown now, but we will chat later.' She touched her forehead, jumped back onto her horse and left.

After everybody had gone, Bull took the embers from the bonfire, placed them in the fireplace on the monument and put twigs and then wood on it.

Soon it was burning brightly and Hen, our Nan, was seated in front of the fire, weeping and praying for her lost boys. She stayed that way. My sister and I cried for several hours until we drifted off to sleep. We had no need for blankets, the fire kept us warm, and somehow we felt safe and secure in the knowledge that nothing would happen to us. There was something supernatural in the air.

It was pitch black when we were woken by a banging sound. We were very frightened and looked to where the sound was coming from. It was Bull - he was repeatedly banging his head on the grave, chanting 'Why was I late again, I could have prevented his death' over and over again. We could see a trickle of blood running down his forehead, but still he kept banging and chanting. We shouted at him many times, but he did not seem to hear and didn't even acknowledge our presence, even when we stood directly in front of him. So we went and sat back down. Then there was a sudden gust of wind which nearly blew the fire out and chilled us to the bone. We looked at Bull and he seemed to be having a conversation with someone, but there was no-one around. Nan was still sitting in the same position as she had been when we went to sleep, all those hours ago. It was as if she was in some sort of trance. We went back to sleep, as Bull had stopped banging his head and seemed quite relaxed and calm now.

The morning came and we got up and had some bread for breakfast. Bull told us to get onto the cart, and he took us to Waterdown. The trip home was lovely; we passed Castlewood, Aunty Elk and Uncle Oak were going to rebuild it, with help.

Bull stayed for a couple of days, then went off to fight another battle. Before he went he told us why he had stopped banging his head that night. The wind that had made us so cold was our father's spirit; he came to comfort Bull and told him he should not hold himself responsible for his cousin's death, as our father didn't. We never saw Bull after that day. We assumed he was killed in one battle or another.

Castlewood was rebuilt and things did turn out the way Fox had wanted them. All the rebels rested in peace together. Till this very day Aunty Hawk and Uncle Cat have brought us up well, and Wild Cat became leader of Castlewood. Jage and Sky became nomadic fighters like our father once was. Uncle Oak is still alive and Aunty Elk too. Mole is a fully grown man and is now leader of Scrapford, which was rebuilt. Hen, our Nan, never got over the loss of her boys and died three months later, they say of a broken heart. The dragons that survived were split up and sent to different villages, and still live in peace.

My sister and I cried for days after our father's death. But, as promised by him, he came back to comfort and protect us, but that's another story. My sister and I visit the monument from time to time, and in the quiet of the long summer evenings you can almost hear the rebels talking to each other, together with the sound of horses and clashing of swords. It would be quite scary, if it wasn't for the fact that we knew all the rebels and know they wouldn't hurt us in any way. I did wear my father's armour into battle and, as Dad had told me, no harm came to me - not even a scratch.

We know this story is true because we are the daughters of *The Legendary Fighting Fox*.

Sunny and Badger.

THE END - until the next great battlefield or the next story.